Undertakers, Harlots, and Other Odd Bodies

By Mege Gardner

Copyright 2018 Mege Gardner

Front cover by Renee Barratt at The Cover Counts

Thank you for selecting this book. This book remains the copyrighted property of the author, and it may not be redistributed to others for commercial or non-commercial purposes. If you enjoyed this book, please encourage your friends to download or purchase their own copy from their favorite authorized retailer. Thank you for your support and for respecting the hard work of this author.

For my parents and their parents, who instilled in me a love of language and blarney, usually in that order. I am grateful for all our teachers, who lead us to love creating and researching oddities, some of my favorite things about being a person.

Acknowledgments

A quick note of particular thanks must be included for my intrepid editors and readers, who took the previews of this work more seriously than I had any right to expect. Some of you wanted to remain unlisted, so just know that I love you and your anonymous ways. Thanks to David Gardner and Kathy Kaiser, Este Gardner and Char Gardner for perfectly timed words of encouragement.

Thank you for your very thoughtful critiques Retired Covert English Teacher, G.T., Beth, Spiders, and my fellow Scribophile members.

Thanks for taking a sneak peek Pattycake, Allison, Crystal, Paula, Glenda, Lynn Bartell, Chris, Sheri, Rachel Poggi, Elizabeth M., Colm Horan, and Mason Stockstill.

Thank you, Bill and kids, all of you, for patiently dealing with my novel years and feeding yourselves when necessary.

Thanks to Carol Love and Owen Gardner for your dedication to art, great books, and humor, and all the things that makes marvelous siblings a pain to emulate.

Thank you Eileen Denney Marsh for the tremendous proofread and for letting no hyphenation or stray Anglicization get past you.

Author's Note

This book is full of lies. It's important to point out a couple of things about those lies; the surprising ones are true and some of the history you think you know is based on other lies.

If this book appears in the history section of a book store, please know that someone was confused, as people are at times. This is a work of fantasy, although there are zero dragons and only a few real-world potions. Nothing that occurs in this story was impossible at the time.

That brings us to sex, which is always possible at all times. Some early readers were disappointed that a book with "harlot" in the title isn't filled with sex scenes. If you picked up a book about chemists, you might expect there to be nothing but laboratory scenes. It would be a relief to find something else, I'm sure.

This story is in that spirit, in that it's about the people more than it's about what they do. You may assume that there's loads of sex going on, just not in focus. For the sake of my more tender readers, whenever the sex is going to be in focus, there will be a mention of pomegranates. There are not many pomegranates, and certainly not in the first few pages, so you can disregard the mentions above and just relax and enjoy the lies.

Introduction

In 1895, the town in the midst of our story was dying or already dead. Like so many wonders of human endeavor, it failed and left a confusion of rubble that its residents mistook for a township. They stubbornly imagined their home could be more than a tainted playground for their wealthy neighbors, but in time the Port became so much less.

The Port had a long, peculiar past that no one person knew. The songs and legends of its original people were lost, along with all of their jokes.

For those original people, the fishing was always superb and the climate, while swampy at times, was rarely severe. The river could be tricky and rough, but it was ordinarily a placid place for fishing and more protected than the wide Chesapeake Bay.

Over time, people murmured the Port was cursed. The evidence of some dark spell piled up, until only the most deluded would argue there was no curse.

When the Port was thriving, crops had shipped out nearly every day of the growing season. Feisty stevedores and tea merchants had secretly participated in a revolutionary Tea Party. It was much like the one in Boston, only more sordid. George Washington was said to have supped in the Port, although there was only the vaguest confirmation in his diaries.

The Port was slowly superseded by the newer, greater port to the north. Their tobacco negotiations failed, and so much worse, the harbor was relentlessly filling with silt from the farms. Finally, the large ships could no longer reach the harbor at all, and to its embarrassment, the Port was then a port in name only.

The original people would not have recognized their home. None of the ancient trees remained, since all of them had been harvested for lumber long ago. Great sections of forest had been cleared for farming. Even the enormous stones that had marked paths and magic places had been disturbed and broken and utilized.

A few wars had touched the Port, but none marked the current populace as much as the Civil War. No fighting took place nearby, no piles of bodies were left on the roads, but the town was changed completely by the exit of all its brightest women and able-bodied men. Over four years, they returned in much smaller number, many of them missing limbs.

Technically victorious, with the Union, their hopefulness was hollow compared to before. As they returned, the things that truly interested them were prosthetics and a means to dull their pain.

The underground railroad of little General Tubman passed through regularly, even throughout the war years. As viewed from the outside, the abolitionist network seemed entirely fortified in the Port, but the truth was entirely more complicated. Confederates mingled quietly there, too.

Many of the passengers of the underground railroad returned south after the war, only to be terrorized and run back to the north when they attempted to secure political office or any other ordinary endeavors of citizenship. The Port became home to them on their return; its Negro School was as attractive as its sense of relative safety.

The local newspapers of the day listed racial designations like a title, but only when the person was unknown and likely to be mistaken for someone else. "Mrs. Marchbottom, colored" was kept distinct from "Mrs. Marchbottom, white." Help-wanted and position-wanted ads would likewise list races to avoid misunderstandings. A "respectable colored doorman" avoided answering an ad where he wasn't expressly requested, for his safety. The many disadvantages of this practice hadn't been revealed or brought to courts just yet. At the dawn of the 20th century, the "good intentions" of the editors were only warming up for the road to hell.

Once compared to a "facetious pettifogger" by an Illinois newspaper, and having transformed into "The Great Emancipator," Abraham Lincoln was photographed under a great oak at the Port after the war was all but won. His speech wasn't regarded as one of his best. He'd had some bad shellfish and was unusually curt.

In the historical record, there might not have been proof Washington ate at the Port, but it was beyond dispute Lincoln had spewed there.

The loss of the shipping business had led to a thriving trade in gambling and prostitution. Their professional pandering ranged from the routine to the most esoteric of erotic whims.

Even as the town excelled at vice, violence was not routine; people had had their fill of killing.

The earliest railroad line had originally ended at the Port, so travelers to the capital were forced to hire a carriage to complete their journey. The business owners crafted an unnecessarily indirect route from the station to the livery, and somehow the carriages were never waiting for travelers at the station. They had to pass all of the attractions in order to continue their journey. They couldn't get away without at least a glimpse of the shooting gallery, a few brothels and other games designed to lighten their wallets.

State authorities ignored the Port. They were occupied with installing water works in cleaner towns and keeping other places safe for upstanding citizens.

The few powerful types who took an interest were content to keep the town limping along in the shadows. It became a haven for their own scandalous wants, where anonymity was prized and protected.

Despite all the industrious grift, the residents didn't make enough money to inspire the county to bother with them, either. Most of the men there couldn't afford a family and all the women had a profession. If they weren't educated or otherwise skilled, only one profession remained to keep them well fed.

When the railroad completed trestles and extended through to the city, the trains didn't stop at the Port on schedule any longer. The "grand march of progress" swept up all the municipalities around them and still skirted the Port.

The surrounding towns, if they regarded the Port at all, considered it a place that had died but didn't quite yet recognize it was dead.

Chapter 1—Helen
1883

No reasonable person would have looked at eleven-year-old Helen Driscoll and thought, "Why, there's a future undertaker." She was too disheveled and too female for such a vocation, and her liveliness would never suggest such a livelihood.

Helen burst into the front room of her home where her family was quietly gathered, to insist they look at the sunset. She didn't wait for an answer, and she did not appear to notice when only the children followed her out to the wide wooden porch steps.

"It's like the world is on fire," whispered Helen's little brother. The sunset was a strange, vivid red and the vermillion light ringed all of the horizon they could see.

She stood with her arms resting on the shoulders of her transfixed sister and brother. "I think it's a very good omen," declared Helen, with the certainty that children often decide such things.

Helen could not have been more mistaken. The weird sky was, in fact, a token of horrible disaster. Ten thousand miles away, Krakatoa had erupted with such vast destructive power it had altered the islands, the sea, and the sky around the world.

"Did you know she was outdoors?" asked their irritated father, speaking in the direction of their mother. "It's a never ending ruckus. I have been telling you she reads too many adventure books meant for boys." Their mother only sighed in reply. The sigh signified every debate they had ever had about latitude bestowed on children.

"Reading about it will keep her from sailing off for treasure," said her grandmother, Gertie, her voice holding a conviction she did not feel, "Unless you want another pirate in the family."

Gertie, who was not very reasonable on the subject, might have seen the future Helen would claim. She watched her, as Helen listened to terrifying bedtime stories meant to mold her into a dutiful and moral citizen. Her grandmother saw the sparks in Helen's eyes. They weren't only thrown from the flame in the lamps. This girl, whose strong and tiny hands pulled at her grandmother's skirts and begged, "More about the goblins, please;" this girl was made of wonders.

***

Helen and her siblings enjoyed more freedom than their peers. They were tasked with incidental farm labor intended to build their characters, and they attended lessons at the little country school, but on long summer days they ranged much farther than their parents would have guessed. They seemed heedless of their mother's laconic warnings from her sick bed about tramps and bear traps.

They charged through the shimmering fields and climbed unsuitable trees, bothered the neighbors' weary livestock and lost shoes in the river. They lied and said the shoes must have been eaten by goats.

Helen's sister, Fannie, liked to eavesdrop on her family, creeping unseen under the furniture, imagining she was a barn cat set on stealing scraps. Wally, their younger brother, struggled to keep up with the girls and was never, ever able to triumph at a day-long game of hide and seek.

Their father was stern and more than a little frightening to the children. They were grateful that he was usually distracted by delegating his responsibilities. He had a chief hand and a business manager, both of whom he was required to manage, and they in turn had staff to direct and complain about.

So as Helen's father, also the *paterfamilias,* sat back in his favorite chair, comfortably engrossed in his newspaper, he was not inclined to look up as the children ran past him. He was focused and intent on enjoying a hard-earned moment of pure contentment. As they bolted through the front door again, their passage ruffled his newspaper, but still, he did not look up.

It took five tries before they disrupted his attention and caused him to rise and furiously shake the newspaper after them. They heard him bellow, "What in thunder does a man need to do for some peace!" Scared, yet satisfied, they hid in the hay loft until their grandmother called them to dinner.

While their father grumbled, he was rarely roused to action by these rituals. Ahead of his time in many respects, he preferred to leave all things parental to his wife and his mother.

The children's mother, Margot, recognized that a lack of fearfulness was at the root of their unruliness. She watched Helen carefully during dinner. She believed that if Helen were more cautious, the other children would follow suit, as they followed her in everything else. Margot decided on a scheme and felt very satisfied with her inspiration.

When Helen came to her mother's room to bid her goodnight, Margot had a word with her. It had been one of her best days and she was relatively energetic. On her bad days, Margot stayed in bed and refused food all day, lamenting that nothing was worth the chewing. On her good days, she spent most of her time in bed but allowed the meals to keep her company. On her best days, the family wheeled her to the porch for fresh air and to the table for dinner.

Her mother stroked Helen's cheek affectionately. "I don't mean to alarm you," Margot lied, "but you must not allow yourself to become too excited, you know. Ever."

Helen peered at her quizzically, asking why. Her mother's eyes were dark and serious with worry.

"It's your heart," Margot said. "It's not strong and I am afraid for you, the way you're always running and climbing. Living with a terrible illness means that you must forego many sorts of entertainment and many sorts of strain."

Helen was confused. Her mother often remarked bitterly that Helen should never become a farmer's wife, it was too much drudgery and despair. The despair was evident, but her Margot didn't engage in any drudgery that Helen had observed. For years, Helen thought that "drudgery" was another word for "delegated."

Despite the complaining, Helen adored her mother. Unlike other adults, Margot listened patiently and Helen always knew where to find her.

So, she wondered, was her mother saying that Helen should avoid strain as she did?

"Do you mean I can't jump rope?" The thought made Helen suddenly terribly forlorn. Jumping rope was her favorite occupation.

"You *may,*" Margot replied, "but only a little. Too much excitement could be deadly."

Helen had a brief bout of despair of her own after that.

She lounged on the porch steps the next morning, and when it was time for children to churn the butter, she told them dramatically, "Mother says I'm not to strain myself."

Hearing this, Gertie stopped with her hands on her hips, "You had better churn," she said, "otherwise, you had better fetch a switch and then you can churn after your beating."

Helen was moved to forget about her health for a little while.

Chapter 2—Heart

Helen doubted her mother's warning. Her heart sounded very strong to her. Its pounding could keep her awake at night, beating into her pillow and echoing right through her ears. If it were weak, wouldn't it crackle and sputter?

She had observed in her short time on Earth, the worst things that could happen never came with a warning. When she worried about one of her hens, with its lame foot, in the end that wouldn't be the trouble at all. Instead, a completely different chicken would be carried off in the jaws of a bobcat. She became certain that if she worried about goblins all the time, goblins would never get her. That was just the way things worked.

When her mother died, Helen was completely taken by surprise.

She might have worried if she had known Margot was "in confinement" but she didn't see any difference between her mother's usual confinement and the expectation of giving birth.

Helen knew babies were dangerous and twins were doubly so, but until then, the extremes of suffering surrounding births had been unknown to her. Childbirth could not have made a more terrible impression.

She burst into the room, as she so often did, only to encounter a dreadfully gory scene. Gertie was there, with a strange woman Helen had never seen before. They seemed to be in the process of butchering her mother.

Helen shrieked and her grandmother barked at her to get to the corner and be still. Helen froze instead, and while she kept quiet, she could not make her feet move at all.

Impossible waves of blood covered the bedding, the women's arms were bathed in it as they worked. Tiny feet and ropes came into view. Helen thought of goblins as her vision blurred and she thumped to the floor.

No one could bother with her, and she roused with her face pressed into the cool wood of the floorboards. Gertie's bare feet shuffled into view and out of sight again. Helen wondered if her heart had failed her. It hadn't, but it was about to be broken for the first time.

***

Helen watched the midwife rub one of the babies to wake it up to meet the air, while Gertie worked on the second hairless little rabbit. The room took on a terrible quiet, as if the babies had pushed all the sound away.

That was how Helen realized that her mother wasn't breathing, in that quiet. Her mother departed without ever knowing that she had brought two more lives into her family. Helen had no warning at all and withstood the shock as an older child does, growing a bit older and a bit more closed into the sheath of adulthood.

When Bonnie and Beanie started to cry, it ended the last quiet any of them would have for a long while. Their tiny voices rose to fill the room with their raspy demands.

Helen didn't mind their noise. She was fascinated and could not stop staring at the babies. Gertie would have to show her how to hold them and how to keep them warm. The wet nurse was a day away and it was going to be a very long day.

Helen's father arrived too late. He met them at the cemetery. She was very glad to see him until she realized that he seemed angry. His face was taut and his eyes looked too small. He paced as they waited for the hired men to return with the coffin.

Daddy was dissatisfied with the grave, so the children took turns digging it further, while their father absently supervised. Wally clowned around in the deep hole and Helen scolded him, "We're not building a dam, Wally. We need to do this properly." His lip trembled as he recalled their purpose and she tried to calm him then. "You're a very good digger," she said, more gently.

Helen remembered the relief of seeing the neighbors peering over the edge. They reached to her and pulled her out of the hole while she clambered up the sides with her muddy shoes. She remembered a brief warm embrace but not whose it was.

The first funeral that Helen could have remembered wasn't a real funeral at all. The wrongness of that was lost in a sea of wrongness. She saw the shrouded shape of her mother, she saw the lid fastened on the pine coffin and she saw the coffin put under the earth, but it happened so quickly and strangely. It felt like something happening to someone else.

The family felt their world tilt and shift, and they were unable to find a new center that was unchanging in the same way her mother had anchored them from her sickbed.

Helen's father was gone more and more and she felt doubly bereft by his absences.

Gertie was distracted and struggling with the babies. She became a dervish of diapering and swaddling and would superstitiously avoid sitting still at all.

From that point forward, Helen was raising herself and her siblings, as much as they would let her. She didn't complain about the ache of her mother's absence; it was soon a fact of her life and so not remarkable.

Gertie grew bitter in general, and she was specifically irritable toward her son, Helen's father. She fussed at him to re-marry, but he said he never would. Helen thought she understood; he had loved one woman to death already.

Helen still loved her home and cherished the unchanging fittings of it even more. She was comforted by the squeaks of the porch swing and the heft of her iron. Helen loved the smell of the old oak furniture and the feel of its cool, worn surfaces. She liked knowing that she could reach out a window and crush a handful of mint that had grown too high in the summer sun.

The house was not emptier in her mind. She and Fannie could sit and read on the wide front porch and hear the footfalls upstairs when the twins awoke from their nap. They could discern from the slam of the oven door exactly how grumpy Gertie was. They knew that Wally would always try to steal a marble if they overshot, just as they knew they could catch him and make him give it up, as long as he hadn't swallowed it.

Chapter 3—Incentive

Their home shifted again when Wally turned sixteen. Over that one summer, he had grown to be more than a foot taller than Helen and Fannie. His sisters knew he spent every spare cent at whore houses and they marveled that their father and grandmother didn't seem to notice.

"Can you imagine the germs he drags home?" Helen whispered to Fannie. Fannie only wrinkled her nose. Who would ever roll around with Wally?

He demanded they call him Wallace, and he expected to be treated like a man now and not like the whiny little brother he was. "Of course, Wally," said Fannie, with the same expression she offered in the discussion of germs.

Helen and Fannie were less wild, having steadily taken up more and more of the work that sustained the family business. Helen's father liked her gumption and her quick thinking, and he would praise her problem-solving to others when he thought she couldn't hear. Even as he regarded her as his brightest daughter, she was still not due the regard of a son.

After the harvest, the pair now known as the Driscoll men went to market with feed corn and played at auctions when the hogs looked healthy. When they returned home from a day of pipe smoking and reconnoitering at the market, Wally was usually at his worst. He would swagger as if he had absorbed some masculine fuel from the day.

Wally resembled his father only in profile, and his bluster made him very distinct from Ephraim's measured demeanor. He became what Gertie referred to as "something else."

One such evening was the tipping point for Helen, and the comfortable familiarity of the farm became something closer to suffocation. The women had spent the entire day canning the last of the tomatoes and Helen had burned her hand preventing Beanie from a worse scalding at the stove. Her hand was bandaged at

Gertie's insistence, but neither of the men noticed it nor took note of her fatigue.

"You should have a look at that sow we got," said Wally to Helen as he hung up his things. Helen didn't answer, but let her shoulders fall at the sight of his muddy boots.

"Wally!" she scolded, "Just look at the muck you are tracking in here!"

He stomped his feet, freeing more of the mud and bits of straw. "It's Wallace," he growled. The twins vanished to the back of the house, as if they had been blown away by an ill wind. Their father perked, however, turning his gaze with mild interest.

"Just so, Sir Wallace McMudmaster," Helen said. Her voice rose despite her haughty intentions, and she could feel her throat tighten with anger, ruining the joke.

"Wash it up."

"I will not. It's your mess."

"Wash it up, now," his growl returned. She had never feared Wally for a minute, and this minute was no exception. Instead of addressing him again, she turned to her father for support.

Ephraim studied her in return, his expression mildly inflamed. He jerked his head. "Do it," was all he said.

"I'll do it," said Fannie, rushing in, "She hurt her—"

"No," said their father, "It's for Helen to do. Not another word from either of you."

Wally sat down and extended a muddy boot toward Helen to complete the humiliation. She kept the tears in, even as they prickled to get free. Slowly, because of her stinging hand, she worked her brother's boots free.

He realized, belatedly, he had created a cruel chore. With a pang of regret, he started off to get the broom in his stockinged feet.

Ephraim stopped him. He believed that this was an important lesson. The sisters must accept their place. One day, their brother would be in charge of them, just as surely as he would own their home.

Helen knew what her family expected, of course. She should be grateful to have a home and to have a place to serve. Her own feelings ran entirely contrary to that expectation and they came into flawless focus.

Helen could see herself, detesting and deferring to Wally, dear dull Wally. She could imagine years of scheming circles around him and she could see him preening and taking credit for her efforts.

Helen began to plot a means of escape. Staying was impossible.

Chapter 4—School

By the time she was twenty years old, Helen's plan neared fruition. She campaigned for a year to persuade her father to enroll her in nursing school. She could not enroll herself in the school, but he could make the arrangements for her, if only he were willing.

It was a delicate and gradual process and she congratulated herself on her tact and steady persistence. She said she didn't want to establish a nursing career—if he thought that she was moving on to a professional life, he would be dissuaded. Instead, she told him that it would be good for her to learn the new methods they were teaching. She said that with proper training she could be of better service to the family.

A sprinkling of frightening medical facts crept into her conversations. She told them about the man who had been accidentally boiled and then delicately and antiseptically skinned alive. "It took the bellies of a bushel of frogs to cover him back up!" she exclaimed.

"How big were the frogs?" asked Wally. Fannie just stared in dismay at her sister's bizarre interests.

"Two—"

"—a bushel is a bushel," interrupted Gertie. "It doesn't matter how many frogs it fits."

Two-pound frogs did matter in Helen's thinking, but she wisely kept that to herself. Her siblings might disapprove of her brand of curiosity, but their father approved and even encouraged her.

It was never overtly discussed among the family, but they dreaded the next personal calamity. Another serious illness among them was a certainty. Still, her father hesitated to send her to school.

"Who will help if Wallace is hurt?" she asked. Help was miles away. Helen let that suggestion stay without stirring it for two days.

***

As the whole family strolled to church, her father walked up behind her to resume the discussion at last. "I will make some inquiries," was his answer, which was as good as assent. The school fees and lodging were modest and it was only a short train ride.

Triumphant, she tried not to sound too excited when she told Fannie. Of course, Fannie wanted to go with her to school. Their father dismissed that notion and ignored her echoes of enthusiasm.

"You aren't as studious," he said, "It would be a waste."

Helen didn't plead for Fannie, even though her sister wilted with disappointment. Helen didn't want to risk his change of mind.

She need not have worried. He had his own reasons for consenting to help with her plans. Silently, he hoped that Helen would meet a proper husband before the two years were over. Marriage was the real solution to her future. He believed that, and he believed she needed fresh air and firm handling just as she always had.

***

Baltimore was more of a change than she imagined. Helen felt out of place. People were courteous most of the time, but occasionally someone assumed she needed to be reminded of her place and they barked at her. These people weren't accustomed to having a woman meet their gaze or question them with an assured voice.

For her part, Helen wasn't accustomed to people assuming she was dim-witted. At home, she was treated with a bit of deference by the people in town. As a Driscoll daughter, there had been a different sort of barrier that supported her. She felt protected. They had just enough fear of her grandmother and respect for her father that the folks in town would not pick her pockets or offend her otherwise.

These city people were different, and their reactions puzzled her and made her anxious. She had read all sorts of volumes about far-off places and peculiar customs, yet none of them were very useful now. She wondered how she might find the roadmap that she needed to get along with these new people. She began to practice a sort of experimental anthropology, carefully searching for a way to fit herself into her new life.

The night courses were one of the many novelties she tried to understand. At home, evening instruction was shoddy and only for children who worked during the day. Here, the school doubled sessions for a completely different reason: to insure the white students were not taught alongside their colored counterparts. The school believed it was in everyone's best interest not to "complicate" the classes by mingling the students.

The clerks were uncertain how to classify Helen, so they put her with the white students. Her father, who delivered her to school, looked white to them, and he had a gentlemanly way about him, which made them fear to offend him.

This separation of students seemed nonsensical to Helen. At home, people were classified in her mind as trustworthy and untrustworthy and there were very few of the former—of any variety. Wally was deceptive, as was the white dry goods peddler, who would feign surprise at a challenge on his skimpy measurements. The colored ministers and teachers were some of the best people in town, but then there was the colored woman who picked pockets and claimed rewards for finding the things she stole. She appeared respectable to the uninitiated, and they thanked her as they forced the reward coins into her perfect hands.

Helen believed that if someone encountered a wolf in sheep's clothing, they should have been more careful about the sheep in the first place. The color of their wool was entirely irrelevant; bitten is still bitten.

She wished she could tell Fannie about the casual cruelty of the city, but she didn't know how to explain it. It was as if she had scaled a huge wall only to find herself on the edge of a canyon she could not cross. It was a fascinating canyon, but there was no way to move on for a woman. She was just a witness, kept to her seat.

Uneasily, she went about her school days, walking from one huge brick building to the next, each of them designed to dwarf the student into a state of awe. The gigantic white columns were intended to represent ancient learning somehow, but Helen only wondered how they could be cleaned.

Students were free to observe any procedures and attend any lectures as a general rule. Women were included, unless space was a problem. Helen was pushed out of the gallery during one such lecture, steered roughly by her elbows and shoved into the corridor. She saw that other women were allowed to remain, in male disguise. That was clever, she thought. Perhaps sometime she would masquerade for an education, too.

During her time in the hospital, it was quickly discovered that Helen had an intolerance for the sight of blood. As a woman, she had a regular acquaintance with small quantities of blood, and as a person, she was accustomed to the concept that she, herself, was full of the stuff. The problem lay in the large quantities of free storming blood that any medical student routinely encountered.

At her first operation, standing high up in the gallery, she was able to see perfectly well when the operating physician nicked an artery. Before he had completed his swearing and commanding his assistants to get back to assisting, Helen hit the floor with a thud.

She was embarrassed by this turn of events, but that didn't stop her classmates from teasing her about it in the very persistent way anxious people do such things. They could have seen her face go gray, but they could not have felt the singular electricity in her knees that had been her only warning.

When it happened again, she was observing an attempt at caesarian delivery. The mother was gently put to sleep with gas and released from her pain. Helen sighed, feeling some relief of her own and was quite sure this operation would be one she could withstand. As the scalpel drew across the woman's skin, *thump* went Helen again.

She could not account for it, although her grandmother Gertie would have had an idea about it if she had been asked. Helen speculated to herself that this was a manifestation of her bad heart.

Afterward, she artfully avoided any occasions when arterial spray might be demonstrated. It was a very sensible solution for anyone, really.

Autopsy was a much more calm and predictable procedure. She gravitated there and observed the slicing and measuring of organs without the slightest twinge of difficulty. Innards were part of the scenery on the farm, after all. She had seen the inside of sheep after predators had dined on them. She preferred this clinical and measured dissection. She appreciated the quiet politeness of the coroners, too.

She didn't like loud characters, and so when her boarding house proved very unruly, it was unpleasant for her. Sleeping was impossible in a room with a dozen girls, giddy with new freedom. Among them was Alice, a little miss who had evidently never been taught any modesty. Alice sat up in bed at all hours and masturbated aggressively while conversing with her roommates. Helen, who was impressed by the girl's lack of shame, caused a torrent of hilarity by inventing a rhyme for little miss Alice: "Mind the malice, you'll get a callus."

Despite the entertainment, Helen fled the low boarding house to a shared room in a wide, dilapidated town house. She found her roommate was a rather small-minded and squeaky character, but Helen could sleep at last.

It took some months, but Helen was a bit more at ease when she found the track she was to follow to avoid creating a ruckus simply by existing in the city. Evidently, she was expected to follow orders, never be other than cheerful, and avoid the operating theater.

She was determined to make the most of her time and studied ferociously. Responding to her intensity, her teachers gave her encouragement and more and more challenging work. Lazier sorts would press her to tutor them—or other students. She learned to elude them by walking on and waiving, "Tuesday is no good," she exclaimed, pretending that she didn't understand what they wanted.

Her roommate, like so many of her classmates, was most intent on flirting with any doctors or professors who crossed her path. Helen didn't criticize, but only smiled at the way the girls lavished themselves on even the silliest men.

She had pangs of loneliness, but Helen only cried at night.

Chapter 5—Port

Helen didn't pine for the farm and she certainly didn't miss the Port while she was away at school. The Port didn't miss her; the Port didn't miss anyone.

She dutifully returned home to the farm after her training was completed, and a few people were surprised at the way she picked up the threads of her old life. It seemed to them she quenched her ambitions in the years away.

The familiar family dinners were louder than ever. Bonnie and Beanie were ten years old and boisterous, so the jostling and competition for portions was intense and maddening. Helen wondered if the kicking and bickering wasn't somehow intended to make sure she did not become too comfortable.

Fannie was disappointed her sister hadn't obtained a situation in Baltimore, or anywhere else. If only she had found work, Fannie could join her and make her escape too. When she probed Helen about it, Fannie found nothing but a wall of evasion. "No regular nursing for me," was Helen's only clear statement.

Something terrible had happened, Fannie concluded. Something had frightened her sister into retreat. As if bolstered by her sister's imaginary terror, Fannie decided to find her own shocking ordeal and ran away to the District.

"She's repairing umbrellas!" announced their father. Ephraim was distraught more by the work than the shabby boarding house where Fannie had settled. Helen took note—even knowing where she was, their father did not interfere. Fannie was twenty-one now, but he could have made himself a nuisance. "She will get tired of it soon enough," he said. He said it many times, even after the chant was clearly false.

Helen wrote a few letters soon after, and her words echoed her mother's.

March 31, 1895

My darling squirrels,

I have taken a position in the Port! The Widow Kate has asked me and I have accepted as quickly as a mouse would dart for a doorway. Please don't be sad about missing me, I will see you at church every Sunday, just like today, and I will make you some lovely things at the dress shop.

Listen to Grandma and do not make her chase you too far. Stay away from the hobo camp and do not cross the railroad trestles, even a short one. That poor jockey was struck by a train on Friday, and there was not the slightest chance to save him. A train is much quicker than you think!

I am writing to everyone, so stay out of sight until Daddy has a chance to collect himself. One day, when I have a house of my own, you can come and stay and I might not make you do the washing.

Your devoted sister,

Helen

Chapter 6—Samuel

Samuel's first sight of the Port gently deflated his hopes. The place seemed nothing more than a very old traveling carnival that had long overstayed its welcome.

He had imagined a busy little port with a sturdy row of store fronts. Even from a distance of nearly a mile, he saw instead the splattered aspect of the main street, and the closer he drew toward it atop his hearse, the greater his dismay.

While he could see a few fine houses and a large mill as he descended the slope approaching the Port, he could also recognize a great many hastily constructed buildings. There was shouting and clanging that sounded more like trouble than the routine noises of a smith's shop.

Shots rang out, but they were only feeble shooting gallery rounds that plinked against targets and caused a few congratulatory roars. Farther out, toward the water, he could see the puzzling sight of a lone mast; a stranded schooner lay tilted stubbornly in the silted landing.

The road was less muddy and pitted than he had any reason to expect and he was grateful on behalf of the horses. He worried a bit for them since there were a number of dogs that seemed quite at home in town. The dogs also appeared to have a sense of traffic, however, and tamely let the horses pass.

Stopping by the livery stable, he left the carriage and began a walking inspection. He searched for evidence that his hopes for a future in such a place were not completely mad.

As he reached the main crossroads, in sight of the train station and the remains of the once-great port, he could see the place was both derelict and yet lively.

The sturdiest buildings were the tiny bank and the baker's shop, while the majority of the other structures were worn wood in need of paint. The grocery had a garish sign declaring that spirits of all kinds were available, alongside a smaller placard promoting their dry goods and hardware.

Persons of all sorts walked and staggered on the streets. They were primarily men, but there were some women and little brown children as well. No one seemed to take much notice of him.

One old man grimaced at Samuel as he passed him. Samuel excused himself, realizing too late he had been obstructing the man's path. The man made his way into the store on worn crutches; one of his legs was missing below the knee.

A smoky odor clung to the air, and as Samuel approached the train station, he arrived at a recently smoldering ruin, presumably the remains of a house.

It seemed lucky to him the entire town hadn't burned, but he would learn later, it was not just a bit of good luck but a matter of amazingly good luck. The fire brigade was shamefully ill-equipped and notoriously slow to react.

The train station was in fine condition but devoid of any activity. Its little post office was vacant also. He thought of how much simpler a train journey would have been, instead of riding all the way down, persuading the sometimes-stubborn carriage horses and listening to the incessant squeak that came from some support under the hearse. He had asked the livery man for his opinion of the problem and he had grinned, "It sounds expensive to me, undertaker."

Beyond the station were houses that were little more than shacks along a narrow road that curved away and paralleled the river. He turned and walked back toward the crossroads.

His mild excitement was giving way to a sense of fatigue. He would need to find a room to rent, as the hotel appeared to be far too festive for his disposition. Fancy young women eyed him from its porch as he passed. One of them giggled as he tipped his hat.

Piano music started to emanate from the tavern, and more laughter met his ears. He paused thoughtfully and looked at it from across the street. The saloon was large and prominently placed and its name was emblazoned on a huge wooden sign that declared it "Hideaway House."

He smiled then, feeling a glimmer of happiness. As peculiar as this place was, he could make himself at home.

Chapter 7—Hideaway

Hideaway House was larger on the inside than Samuel would have guessed from its exterior. It had room enough for more than a hundred revelers, if they were friendly. Paneled partitions suggested that there were indeed places to hide away if needed.

Some men stood at the long bar and others perched at tables while carrying on negotiations that seemed friendly enough. The place was experiencing a temporary lull before the evening was underway.

There was a fascinating variety to the patrons, and Samuel was pleased. This was more interesting than the sort of watering hole he was accustomed to visiting.

In Samuel's experience, a tavern would not contain multiple languages, and if you didn't hear your language, you wouldn't linger there. His city was divided into sections of ethnicity and within those were pockets of kinship. Other neighborhoods weren't a place for a cautious fellow to visit; the poorer ones were far too dangerous with the terrible fevers haunting them.

Here, the piano was in excellent tune and being masterfully made to put out a cheerful song that Samuel recognized as the "Sheriff of Nottingham." He resisted the urge to sing out *I've never yet made one mistake, I'd like to for variety's sake...* He could not resist humming, however.

The barman was a dark-eyed Irishman with a serious face, "Ahoy there. You're the new undertaker? Care for a whiskey?"

"Yes and no," said Samuel, affably. "I'm Samuel Keegan," he said, taking a seat. "I'll have an ale, if you don't mind."

"Pleased to meet you, Keegan," the barman replied, still not appearing pleased. "I'm Gannon."

"Thank you, Mr. Gannon." He settled himself more comfortably at the bar. "I've done just about enough travelling for the day." He savored the ale. "I was wondering at that burned plot up the way. No loss of life, I hope?" As soon as the words left him, he chastised himself. The question could be considered quite rude for a man in his position.

Gannon shook his head, "That was the undertaker's place; the *former* undertaker. He's moved across the river. Good riddance, too. Not one Irishman in the county will hire him, anyway."

"No?" asked Samuel. He hoped he sounded encouraging.

"We would never consider him after the business with Mother Dalton. Such a disgrace," Gannon said. He stopped long enough that Samuel felt a pang of disappointment there was no more of the story.

He need not have worried. Gannon continued, "The entire clan gathered to say farewell to the old gal. They had been at it for days." Gannon looked both wistful and disgusted, shaking his head. "Then who should come knocking, but Old Digger." Gannon's expression emphasized that this was a very poor decision by Old Digger.

"They'd seen her fetch the night before," Gannon said. Samuel knew *fetch* meant an apparition of her person; the German would have called it *doppelganger,* a bad omen in any language. "She wouldn't linger for long, but so terrible was the shock of hearing that Digger came calling — the poor old thing lost the last of her spunk. Tremendous was the fooster." Gannon shook his head again and Samuel mimicked him sympathetically. "Her sons chased him off the property and went so far as to advertise that Doeger was digging up business."

Gannon smiled just a little. "All his luck was destroyed after that. Worst, everyone heard he used his hearse to haul fish when the business was slow."

"Is that true?" asked Samuel. One had to occasionally press an Irishman on his stories, he believed.

"About the fish? Likely not, but it soured his business just the same. They'd rather just be sunk by their cousins than call that German in."

This was good news for Samuel. He felt a burst of glee that his competition would be so limited. He had other concerns about the endeavor, but this was excellent luck.

"You should be introduced to Mr. Eggers," suggested Gannon. He served two more men at the bar and then returned to Samuel and shouted past him and across the room, "Say! Eggers!"

The target for this greeting sat up and reared back just a bit from his scribbling at a compact table. "Eggers considers fleeing the scene!" narrated the man, who apparently was Eggers.

He pushed back his chair and approached Samuel with an outstretched hand, "How do you do?" He said it as *howdooyoodoooo*.

Gannon went on to explain that Odd Eggers had worked for Digger for some time, but had quit. He was now one of their odd job men, more fitting his name.

"Ah, that old degenerate," Eggers said in a mock wistful tone, "One day I woke up and knew I could not look at his ugly face one more time."

"So you were apprenticed?" asked Samuel.

"Oh no no, nothing so fancy; I was an assistant, only an assistant. He wouldn't share his trade craft with anyone but his sons, but you know—he was not so very crafty at hiding his craft." Odd Eggers winked.

"Are you over-occupied or would you like to apprentice after all?" Samuel asked.

This was as bold and dishonest a question as he had ever asked. He didn't need an apprentice. He needed a teacher.

Chapter 8—Eggers

Samuel joined Eggers at his table, remarking on it and the other handsome and sturdy woodwork. Eggers shrugged. "Amish," he said, pointing out the joining in the wood.

They discovered they had furniture-making skills in common—with each other and with the Amish.

Eggers explained his drawings as he put them aside. He was planning some modifications to the henhouse for the Countess. "She'll be quite pleased when I'm done," he predicted. "This bit here," he pointed, "acts like a chute. The eggs will roll down and collect here," he pointed again.

The Countess, Samuel learned, was a Madam who presided over an old, great house up the hill. She was a fearsome and fabulous lady by Eggers's account. She had a large collection of hens, and that was not a euphemism for her staff—she actually had a great many chickens. Many of the folk still traded in livestock it seemed, and Samuel wondered what sort of services one would get in trade for a chicken.

Eggers told him there was a room available there for rent, but Samuel said he was interested in finding something a bit more private.

Samuel didn't specify that he would prefer not to room with harlots. He didn't want to begin by hurting Eggers' feelings since he was clearly fond of the place.

They talked and drank and supped on oysters, standing at a high table to have room for shucking the shells. "That'll put lead in your pencil!" Eggers said to Samuel as he swallowed. They ate the oysters raw with a dash of spicy Dumas' sauce.

Samuel choked with laughter several times, since Eggers jabbed him with jokes and kept catching him with his mouth full. His jokes were terrible, but his timing was perfect.

Eggers was, as it happened, quite a talker. He had come over from Norway as a galley boy. Afterward, he worked in a hotel kitchen in Baltimore until, he said, he decided cooking was not his calling. It seemed to Samuel that instead of the personal decision Eggers described, someone may have told Eggers rather forcefully that he needed to leave town. Eggers' details were a bit light on the departure part of the story.

Some years after that, Eggers worked with Doeger, the German, preparing bodies for burial. "You know the way it is," said Eggers. "The work gets you traveling and there's always something new to untangle, but it's not enough work to keep very busy unless there's an outbreak or a flood." Eggers wrinkled his nose.

Samuel asked where he had learned the woodworks and Eggers shrugged again. "Here and there," he said. "I'm not going to claim that I am very good at furniture, but I can whip up a coffin in a jiffy," he boasted.

Eggers cocked his head at Samuel, considering. "I think we could salvage some tools from that burned-up mess."

Samuel hesitated, thinking about the burned house. "I'm not sure it's worthwhile." He had no idea what sort of tools Eggers had in mind. "Won't he want whatever is left? It's his property."

"He had insurance on his insurance," replied Eggers. "Besides, I'd be frankly amazed if we ever see him on this side of the river again."

"What happened, anyway?" asked Samuel, curious about the fire. Gannon approached them with two more drinks.

"Bolt out of the blue," said Gannon, setting the mugs down. "All the family was in church when *blam!*—lightning strikes and the house explodes in flames." He leaned toward Samuel and continued, "There were chemicals, you see, and he's a son of a bitch." Gannon smiled. Samuel wished he wouldn't smile.

Gannon's explanation made little sense to him. Was he saying Doeger had tempted lightning with his poor character?

"Much as I dislike him," said Eggers, "he isn't careless with his chemicals. He's very tidy and not likely to go down in vapors or leave a potion laying around. Such a tidy bastard."

"You mean 'lying'," suggested Samuel.

"Tidy *lying* bastard," Eggers corrected.

"Don't let the bastards get you down," said Samuel cheerfully, "Let's have a look at what's left."

They made their way to the burned house, both of them with the genial mood of new friends sloshing around with a pleasant quantity of brew in their bellies. The light was fading, but Eggers exclaimed it was "fine light for tool spotting."

"Sonofabitch." Eggers pointed at a large stack of burned lumber at what had been the far wall. "We are too late."

They prodded the site with the toes of their shoes, reluctant to get filthy with soot for a picked-over site.

"Tell me," asked Eggers, casually, "What was your worst body?"

"My father's," answered Samuel, plainly. "It was very bad, in every way," he continued. "The lockjaw ruined him with agony."

Eggers squinted at Samuel then. He hadn't expected that sort of answer; it wasn't the kind of thing a professional would offer. "Terrible," he muttered, reaching down and retrieving a small metal instrument. He blew on it and dusted it a little, gently with his thumb.

"So tell me, what do you make of this?" he displayed the tool and studied Samuel's bashful reaction.

"A tiny hog tamer?" suggested Samuel. "A sort of piglet tamer?" He actually had no idea what he was suggesting. He was reminded of a catalog illustration, the memory of which had stuck because of its peculiar description.

"It's a mouth-closer," corrected Eggers as he mimed putting the tongs in his nostrils. "What sort of undertaker are you, anyway?"

Chapter 9—Explanation

"Go on," encouraged Eggers. "Explain yourself. Why would you play at undertaker? I cannot imagine why. It's all very peculiar."

Samuel took a deep breath, and then launched into his story in a rush, "I came into a bit of money—a good bit of money—and decided that I needed to make a change, to make a mark in a new place," he could feel his face flushing. Saying this out loud made him feel even more ridiculous than the situation did. "I don't want to go west—I suppose I don't want anything quite that new."

Eggers look was encouraging and Samuel went on, "When I won the hearse, it seemed like a natural choice. Wherever there are people, there will always be a need for an undertaker. Soon everyone will be using them, if you think about it."

Eggers laughed and reared back a little on his heels as he did so. "Ah, the appeal of the endless market. So, you won a hearse? Gambling!" He laughed again. "What was it, poker?"

Samuel grinned back. His embarrassment was easing. "Indeed. It was a miraculous flush. I won the hearse and the two horses. And now, I will never gamble again."

"So," Eggers said, "You are ready to set up a flourishing business with no notion of what it entails, but you are not ready to gamble again." Eggers waved his hand in the air. "Hold your story, as I cannot hold this piss any longer," and he deftly stepped around a low wall to relieve himself. He sighed vigorously.

Eggers moved back toward Samuel warning quietly, "You mustn't mention the money to anyone. This place is full of sharpers with brigands for cousins." He told Samuel the week before they had a problem with an angry farmer who had accidentally signed a promissory note when he thought he was only signing a receipt for a dollar. "If they start talking fast, you'd better start listening fast."

Samuel considered this advice while recognizing that Eggers was a very fast talker.

As it became too dark to see in the shadowy rubble, Eggers lamented that they had found nothing more than the mouth-closer.

Samuel said he would be going back to the livery to collect his Gladstone bag, and Eggers rejoined that he was going in the same direction. The street lights were being lit, so they waited and watched and chatted as an ancient little man climbed up to each light and performed the rituals of his vital calling.

"You heard about Digger's hearse? The fish-hauling problem?" Samuel nodded and said that he had heard a little about it. "Foolishness," Eggers said, "There wasn't any smell at all, but somehow the very idea of fish having been in the carriage utterly put people off of using it, as if it could be haunted by fish." He made a *pfft* noise. "Jesus wept."

The lamplighter arrived at the nearest lamp, positioned his ladder, climbed up, polished the glass a bit and tinkered with the adjustments. The lamp emitted a series of whooshing noises and sprang to life.

They moved away, along the street, carefully navigating the puddles of shadow that might conceal actual puddles.

The watchman at the hotel nodded almost imperceptibly at Eggers as they moved past. The warm smells of tobacco smoke and savory pork roasting blended with sour horse sweat and an edge of mildew. Music spilled out of the doorways and windows and swirled around them in the cooling evening.

Samuel was not prepared for the change of turning the corner.

The lights blazed much brighter there, as mirrored gas lights hung between the street lamps to light the street nearly as well as a full moon.

People gathered on both sides of the street, cheerfully engaged in games and amusements. The shooting gallery targets whirred and plopped, bowling pins thumped.

Two boys passed them, moving purposefully with heavy-looking lanterns. Another pair of younger boys were chased away by a woman wearing a teetering hat. It was obviously not a place for child's play, but just the sort of space that little boys would be inclined to investigate.

The train whistle sounded, announcing the only northbound stop of the day. Eggers told him this was typical since the Port was considered little more than a whistle stop. He opined that no one wanted to be seen getting on and off the train here, and Samuel was beginning to see the reasoning in that.

The crowd was mainly, but not all, male. Some of them were grubby from manual labor; others, while dusty, were clean-shaven and dressed more for presentation, with the occasional shiny buckle or tall, bright white collar.

They congregated near the games but Samuel also noticed more than one narrow alleyway that promised a puff of opium smoke or some other more serious and private diversion. An empty wrestling pen sat opposite an open-air theatre space that was oddly angular and somewhat un-safe looking.

A round old man sat playing a marching tuba. He paused here and there to listen for the melody from the tavern piano and added his festive punctuation of low tones. Beside him was a wooden figure of a French soldier and a sign that read, "Finest imported jackets for your soldier, 15 cents." Beside him was a basket of condoms.

Eggers was enjoying Samuel's interest in the proceedings. "This isn't even a company payday," he said. "But there is something for everyone, even if you fancy sword swallowers."

A woman exited the dress shop clutching an enormous skirt so that it was high above the dirt. The door of the shop *snicked* shut decisively, and the shopkeeper turned her sign in the window to "Closed." Sam's gaze moved up catching movement in the upper level of the shop.

He saw a young woman leaning on the sill of the open window. Her face was warmly lit by the gas lamps below. She regarded him directly and he began to feel that he was staring. Even so, he continued staring. He thought she was very lovely.

"Don't spend your notions on that," said Eggers, clapping him on the shoulder to turn him away. "Believe me, you do not have the time." Samuel looked back anyway and Eggers tugged at him again, "I know, I know, the face that launched a thousand skiffs," They steered to the upper end of the street to collect Samuel's things.

The livery stable was hosting a card game and seemed to act as a refuge for old men who had no interest in drinking, smoking, or broader society. Samuel checked his horses and showed Eggers how fine they looked. Eggers stepped up to inspect the first brown mare. She sniffed him in an approving manner, and he stroked the blaze on her nose as if he knew her.

"How much do you reckon your win was worth?" he asked Samuel.

Pleased, Samuel rubbed his jaw and said he thought it must be worth seven hundred dollars, aside from the horses.

"Not here, my friend," said Eggers. "Around here it is worthless."

Samuel stared at him. The old men shifted and began to release all manner of stored chuckles and guffaws.

"You won yourself the fish hearse."

Chapter 10—Brothel

Samuel and Eggers made their way up the hill to the home of the Countess. Eggers had a few ideas about the hearse problem and sketched his schemes as they went along. For his part, Samuel was happy to see that Eggers intended to help him in any way.

The paving on the long drive to the house was very smooth and Samuel found the tapping of their boot heels on the old stones comforting in the dark expanse. The long house lounged at the crest of the hill, more than a dozen windows winking and blinking at them.

He was curious about the vintage of the house. There was a sturdy, colonial aspect to it, and yet it had contemporary Victorian flourishes, with its inviting porch and scrolling wooden details. He asked Eggers what he knew about the house.

"It was built by some tycoon or other more than a century past—I misremember the name. It burned down, was built again and then—see how that center section is separate? The wings are newer, but the Countess didn't do that. She put the porches on. Or rather, I put the porches on for her."

"She owns it herself?" Samuel was impressed. "Is she an actual Countess?" This was a lot of acreage and a lot of mansion for a madam, he thought.

Eggers laughed, "Indeed, the house is hers and the title, well, who knows?" They could hear a piano, now that they were almost to the porch. Samuel didn't recognize the waltz; it was a little sad, not quite Strauss, he thought. "There are rumors that she is a runaway princess and others that she is a Spanish assassin or a spy from Hungary."

"What do you think?" asked Samuel.

"I think she started all the rumors," Eggers said. He knocked gently on the wide front door with his rough knuckles. He did not use the brass hand knocker he had installed there.

The door was opened by a tiny woman, who smiled at them without showing any of her teeth or her lack of teeth. She put her hands out for their hats and other burdens and tiptoed away without speaking.

Samuel had decided long ago, he did not want to be the sort of man who visited brothels, so this was a novel experience. He was delighted by the elegance of the room as they stepped into the salon. The Countess had acquired many lovely things to display and she evidently took very good care of them. The wood gleamed as did the crystal pieces. Burgundy and gold upholstery echoed the colors in the enormous woven rug.

The piano was played by a very young man with a round face. He played with the kind of assurance earned by relentless practice. Portraits of semi-nude young women smiled down on him from the walls.

Facing him from a side table was a large hoop filled with boldly colored lilies and needlepoint words. It looked complete, but it was arranged on its stand as though it were a work in progress. Ordinarily such a project would be a favorite prayer or psalm. At a glance, this one looked like a list.

Soft words
Gentle hands
Whispered wishes not commands
Secrets kept and pleasures made
Behave yourself or get the blade

Overstuffed chairs and chaises around the room were empty, except for a wingback chair that formed a soft golden frame for the Countess. Eggers approached and kissed her hand with a bit of flourish. Samuel found his sudden courtliness amusing and simply bowed in her direction.

She was tall, he could tell, even though she was seated, and the arm she reached out to Eggers was quite long. Her dark hair was arranged with precision, and while she was not imperious she was a presence, to be sure. He felt her take him in with her shiny, brown eyes. He could not guess at her age. It wasn't a skill he possessed ordinarily, and she was far from ordinary.

"Dearest Mr. Eggers, I see you brought me the undertaker, but I have nothing for you." Her voice was husky and low.

"Countess," Eggers smiled at her broadly, "May I present Samuel Keegan. Samuel, this is The Countess, the jewel of the Port." She gestured for them to sit, and Samuel took a seat, gratefully. "I will be assisting him in setting up his venture," Eggers continued. "It's sure to be quite the undertaking."

She chuckled politely, "How many ventures can you manage, my dear?" Samuel could feel there were some obscure layers to their communication that he could not follow and it was an uncomfortable awareness.

"Always room for one more," said Eggers jauntily. "When there is no business, Keegan can help keep the watch. I thought he could stay in the other room." He gestured beyond the back of the house.

The Countess did not appear persuaded. "That would be… an exceptional arrangement," she said, "We have never…" she turned her gaze to Samuel, "I would rely most forcefully on your discretion." There was no question now, she was not pleased.

Samuel opened his mouth, but he was immediately cut off by Eggers, who was not slowed by her vexation. "We can't very well shun him to the straw mats in one of those houses." Eggers said this as if it would be a disgrace and he also pretended that the hotel didn't exist. Eggers was nearly pouting and Samuel was embarrassed for both of them.

"I wouldn't want to impose," Samuel added finally, "but perhaps just for tonight?" He was very tired.

She nodded. The girl returned to bring them a heavy tray with a teapot and cups. "I heard about the fish hearse. I'm very sorry," the Countess said as she poured their tea.

"Thank you, but my goodness," said Samuel, "Is there anything else the whole town knows that I should know?"

"Indubitably," she smiled. "I also heard you're from the land of Poe, but that cannot be a surprise to you."

"I suppose I'm from the land that killed Poe," Samuel said. He remembered his father telling of the paltry funeral for Poe. Only a few people were there, and two of them were the undertaker and the minister.

Samuel recited a few lines of Poe's poetry.

"...Bells, bells, bells," she finished the line for him, pleased. "It really is a shame about the hearse. What will you do?"

"Eggers and I think we have a solution. As soon as we have an out-of-town client, we'll trade this hearse for another, something with a distinctly different profile. The horses are very fine and haven't given me cause to trade them," he continued.

"I wonder if you might not talk to the lawyer," The Countess suggested. "He's been a great help to me with the vandals." A few years before, she had successfully sued a gang from a neighboring village who had attacked her house in a drunken fit of moral outrage. Her business was not illegal, after all, and their raid was most certainly against the law.

As they talked and became more acquainted over tea, Samuel described the poker game to them. His opponent was evidently one of "Digger's" sons who they agreed would be facing a great deal of trouble with his father about the matter. Samuel said he didn't believe the fellow knew the Port was his destination. Eggers offered that Samuel hadn't been nearly fleeced as much as unlucky in his luck.

The boy at the piano played on as Samuel studied the room and they talked about more pleasant things. He asked the Countess about her paintings, shyly. He hoped she was warming to him, just a little.

She told him about her paintings. They were mostly gifts, as were her late-blooming roses. She had an entire rose garden, she said, filled with sought-after varieties brought to her by thoughtful clients.

A clear rapping came from the brass knocker on the front door. "Time, my dears, to skedaddle," she directed. Samuel had no idea how to exit, since there were doors in every direction. He wished her a hurried farewell and followed Eggers out one of the rear doors. As they left the library through a low window with a worn sill, they could hear quiet conversation and a bell ringing somewhere in the upper level of the house.

They made their way past a watchman rocking amiably with a shotgun across his lap, past the stone cookhouse, and went inside a smaller building. Eggers explained they had what used to be the old servants' quarters. It was now split into two bedrooms with a small sitting room between; the bedrooms were surprisingly spacious and the beds were first rate, as Eggers had promised.

Samuel's bag was waiting for him in the farther room. As he lit a lamp, Eggers explained to Samuel that the Countess was suspicious of anyone she didn't employ and distrusted those she did employ. He said that as long as Samuel rose to any trouble he'd do just fine. "Say, if you hear anything on the roof, worry not—it'll be me."

And that is how Samuel found himself in an agreeable room, and quite contrary to whatever he had imagined at the start of the day, a part-time watchman of a whorehouse.

He removed his boots and placed them beside the wash stand. He had no interest in sleep, but felt a rush of gratitude as he stretched out on the feather bed. As he began to construct a mental list of tasks, he drifted into a dreamless sleep. He didn't hear Eggers on the roof or anything at all, soundly asleep on top of the quilt.

Chapter 11—Tools

In the days that followed, Samuel kept very busy acquiring space to work and tools of his new trade. He and Eggers fell into a routine of having breakfast together at the Countess's house during which they would plan their day. Often, he didn't see Eggers again until late evening, as they struck out in separate directions on their various missions.

He was perturbed at the thought that he might not be prepared for a client in time, but Eggers seemed confident the instruments and chemicals he ordered for his kit would arrive before they had to wrangle with a body.

The majority of people were still most comfortable with having their dead tended at home. An undertaker would appear—not too quickly—with his implements and be given privacy in the parlor to attend and embalm the customer. Of course, no work could begin until everyone was thoroughly satisfied that said customer was really and truly dead.

Samuel was familiar, as everyone was, with the worries of being buried alive. Lurid tales of live burial had been a favorite sort of horror story for decades, and for good reason.

Samuel had asked Eggers if he'd ever had a live client, and Eggers shook his head. They compared remembrances of the supposedly true tale of the man who sat up during his embalming only to become so terrified that he genuinely died a short time later.

Eggers said it was an utter fluke and the fault of a truly terrible doctor.

Fortunately, there wasn't a lot of dying in the Port and none at all while their early preparations were underway. They could expect a few elderly customers each year, they thought, and possibly a very few children; very few because there weren't many children in town to begin with.

The greatest variable would be the manslaughters and murders. The Port was not home to murder often; the neighboring city had much worse trouble with that sort of thing. They read the news of a woman who shot a child for stealing fruit—or attempting to steal fruit—and were disgusted to learn she was likely to be exonerated due to her excuse of poor eyesight.

The people of the Port were not inclined to pull a gun when someone annoyed them. They just weren't that fashionable.

Lynching was very much in style also, but not for them. The one lynching that got some momentum was stopped when all the citizens who possessed the proper type of rope refused to provide it. The little mob still managed to string the man up, but the inferior rope broke and he escaped in the chaos. It was a doubly fortunate turn, since he was the wrong man, after all. The truth of the story was accepted, because of the earnestness with which it was most often told.

While the violent crimes and accidents of the Port were relatively rare, they were spectacular when they occurred. As a general rule, if there was a shooting, it was a massacre; likewise, a mishap with the railroad crossing involved a train plowing through the hotel lobby. There were terrible casualties and everyone in town claimed to have witnessed it, even though most of them had only vivid memories of the newspaper sketches.

A particularly gory tale was offered up one morning by Myrtle, one of the professionals of the house. Samuel found Myrtle so entertaining that he wondered that no one paid her to simply talk. As it happened, she did have significant trade in talking services of the whorehouse variety. He just didn't know that yet.

Myrtle appeared early and hungry and tiptoed into the morning room where they were eating. Her red hair was sloppily braided and her feet bare. She resembled an unkempt child. She had a habit of wearing fingerless gloves, possibly to cover some scars, and she pulled at them and sometimes scratched in a very distracting way when she talked.

She gnawed on a slice of ham and listened to them deliberating about which one would ride across the bridge to see about some lumber.

"That bridge is haunted, you know," she said. When Eggers scoffed, she continued hurriedly, "No no, don't doubt me. I'm not speculating specters, I have seen them with my very own eyes."

Samuel encouraged her and she went on, "When they used to run a stagecoach through to the city, there was a terrible, dreadful accident." Myrtle leaned in to the story and her eyes were wide with blarney. "There was ice on the road and treachery in the wheels of the coach that night," her voice hushed with drama. "While the ladies and gents were tucked in their furs and still shivering at the chill that seeped into the carriage, the driver bravely pushed the steeds to go on. He had some notion of getting home to his own warm bed before midnight..." she paused and looked at the men in turn, "but it was not to be."

Eggers snickered and she raised a gloved hand to stop him. "On the bridge, the horses startled as the wheel slipped and failed. An icy screech and the carriage tipped—the horses panicked completely as the people scrambled and flailed to abandon their conveyance. The entire contraption crashed into the ice—" Myrtle slammed her hands on the table, "—horses screaming now, helpless to free themselves from their deadly anchor." She stopped to breathe and sip her tea. Composing herself with flourish fit for the stage, she continued, "They struggled very briefly, and before a crew could be assembled for any kind of rescue, the horses froze solid. They became statues of beastly, twisted terror."

"So you've seen the ghost horses?" Eggers asked politely.

"Aye," she said, "You wouldn't forget it if you saw them, either." She sighed. "They say the removal was much worse."

Samuel nodded. Removing dead horses was very serious work and he couldn't imagine how they would even attempt it in the ice and said so.

"Well, they weren't going to try it at first, but the ladies were upset by the sight of those horses in the ice, day in and day out. They complained enough that a gang of husbands decided to try to cut the horses out so they could at least sink them under the ice and hope the river would take them away. After hacking and sawing away at the carcasses, they could not get any progress before everything began to freeze again. Bloody parts littered the ice into a hellish tableau." She pushed back from the table, satisfied.

"Ah, Myrtle," said Eggers ruefully, "I can always rely on you to affect my appetite," as she began to move away, he reached for her hand as if he would try to kiss it.

"You're better off with my feet," she said and quite swiftly and acrobatically pointed her toes to him instead. She giggled and skipped off when he demurred.

They looked at each other in silence for a few moments to let the images dissipate before going on. Samuel squinted uncomfortably at Eggers and Egger squinted back, mocking him.

After a bit more discussion, they decided Eggers would inspect the lumber and arrange the delivery if he was satisfied, since Samuel needed to visit the bank to finalize his purchase of the old mill.

Eggers disliked the bank. He liked the dogs that lounged there well enough, but he despised the banker. Eggers never believed it when the banker refused to honor his notes, and more than one heated debate about proper arithmetic had resulted from his skepticism.

Samuel decided to trust the bank with his account anyway, partly because it was the only bank in town and partly because of the way the Countess had dismissed Eggers' concerns as only more of his jocund playfulness. Her business instincts must be reliable, Samuel reasoned.

Once the deal was completed, Samuel walked from the bank to the mill, now his mill. He was enjoying the cool, cloudy day. An orchard cart was parked along the road, and he bought an apple for his lunch.

In the late morning, the crossroads area was nearly unrecognizable from the evening; he mused the difference was indeed night and day. There was a slow, but steady flow of customers to the bakery and casual repairs and adjustments were quietly being made to the other shops. A wide-shouldered man walked with a discouraged slump, removing manure. When his cart was filled, he could rest, uncomfortably, riding out of town to dump it. And then he would come back again. And again.

A child Samuel recognized rode by in a handsome, green dogcart, and he was clearly delighted to be running on dog power for a change.

"That's a fancy rig you have there, Patrick," exclaimed Samuel, "Mind you don't put any fish in it." Patrick laughed a hoarse little laugh and rode on. The huge brown dog that pulled him seemed no less delighted than he.

Patrick Allen was, at least for the moment, a bit more fortunate than his peers among the messenger force. A dog would naturally avoid ruts and bumps in the road that would ruin a bicycle, and having a happy beast do the running was a marvelous thing.

The messengers were kept busy running messages around town, since there was currently only one telephone at the telegraph office.

The city people, and the Port folks to some extent, were skeptical of the telephones. They preferred to send and receive signed notes as they had always done.

Some people refused to touch the devices, even when they were available, worried the electricity would bite them or cause some malady that was yet to be understood. In case telephones might be proven to cause deafness or idiocy, it was best to be cautious.

At the Port, however, only the telegraph operator was vulnerable to the dangers and delights of the gab box. He would take the calls and transcribe the messages, sometimes quite poorly, and give them to the boys to deliver.

Patrick's latest message was, "We needs some eager milk, please bring it with you." It should have read "Eagle brand milk," but the recipient would know what was meant. The proprietor of the shooting gallery was always getting such messages from his wife. His mistress preferred letters.

Chapter 12—Murder

Samuel arrived at the mill and took it all in, envisioning it as he would like it to be. He imagined a shop to construct first-class caskets and a small show room and office for the sale and discussion of them. He would have storage space on the lower level and might use the upper loft for a reading space, since it had excellent light.

The mill was derelict, having been abandoned for more than a decade, but it was not a ruin. It had long ago been a center of commercial activity, with farmers and merchants and teamsters converging on it to meet and greet and cheat.

The mill's usefulness dwindled with the grist market in the county; its race had silted up so that the broken wheel was still and sunk in the earth. It had been a proud stone structure, though, and its walls were still true and tall. It had been built by people who understood the peril of flooding and it would be able to weather many more floods, Samuel believed.

The reality of the mill was far from his idea of it. Any working machinery had been pilfered long ago, and still a daunting quantity of debris remained. Broken windows would need to be replaced, years of grit and grime cleaned away, and decades' worth of useless record books and memoranda removed. In spite of the mountain of work it represented, he felt thrilled by the challenge and anxious to get started.

He worked for hours clearing debris and was pleased to find no hidden defects in the flooring. The mill was as sound as he'd hoped. There was a musty, dried insect odor that clung to his nostrils and he hoped that once all the paper was removed the smell would go with it.

He found an iron pump handle on a shelf and went back outside to look for signs of a well. Even though the blackberry bushes had stretched to disguise it, he found the well pipe without much trouble. He half-heartedly secured the handle to the mechanism and primed it with water from his canteen. He began pumping. After several gushes of rusty smelling fluid came up, he was rewarded with clear, cold well water. He splashed it on his sweaty neck and went back to fetch his jacket from inside.

As he was closing up to leave, one of the young men from the school shouted over to him, "There's a body on the road, they say, just over the bridge and up the hill!"

Samuel froze. His mind started racing. He was not ready for this. The student continued, "No one can find LaFevre, but we're trying all the joints." Benjamin LaFevre was the town constable, known mostly as a fixture of the tavern and occasional problematic drunkard.

Samuel grabbed his bag and began to trot toward the bridge before he stopped himself. It would not be dignified for him to run to work. He paced himself at what he believed was a business-like march. The air was breezy and held the promise of autumn, even though it clung to warmth.

Cresting the first hill after the bridge, he had begun to think that the student must have been mistaken, but no, there was an ugly scene in view as soon as he looked down the dusty lane.

A dead horse lay crumpled at the edge of the road, still harnessed to a driver-less cart. A few men stood nearby, but not too nearby. They looked a bit like they were supervising the dead horse.

He could smell smoke and sulfur and the tinny odor of blood grew strong as he approached. In the ditch was a man. He would have assumed the man had fallen at first glance, if not for the situation of the horse.

Samuel picked his steps carefully and quietly. He did not even nod to the spectating men as he passed them. "It's a murder," said the first man.

"Fine work there, Mr. Holmes," said one of his companions.

Eggers had warned him that death scenes were often populated by idiots, and he consciously ignored them as he'd been advised to do.

It appeared that the man had been struck by a bullet in the head, and one of his eyes was completely obscured by blood. His clothes were rumpled and buttons looked to have been torn off.

Samuel wondered what the man could have done to inspire such violence. He may have deserved it, but the horse clearly did not.

He pressed his budding anger back and started considering the problem at hand. He pulled a woolen blanket from his bag and gently covered the dead man.

As Patrick arrived in his dog cart, Samuel began to worry about the crowd this poor fellow would inspire if he didn't remove him soon.

"Any sign of LaFevre?" Samuel asked.

Patrick shook his head, looking down to inspect the horse carcass. "They look so much smaller on the ground," he said sadly.

"I need your help," said Samuel. Patrick snapped out of his reverie and looked very alarmed. "Not anything difficult," he continued, "We need to send for the dead-horse wagon and I need to get this poor fellow indoors."

"Well, I'm not putting him in my cart," said Patrick. Samuel briefly imagined propping the dead man up in the tiny seat and escorting him back to town pulled by the dog. He had to smile.

"Of course not. Now, go on and get to Sutton. Have him call around and locate the wagon—"

"Someone's for an earth bath!" Eggers interrupted as he hopped clumsily off a bicycle and joined the growing crowd.

Samuel pulled him aside. "The fellow is rather small. Do you think we could manage with a stretcher?"

"He's not so small," said Eggers, "they just look small on the ground." Eggers pulled back the blanket and peered at the victim, critically. "Bad luck again, Undertaker!" he declared, "This one is not for you," he reached down and pulled a displaced kippah from behind the man's head. He held the cap out for Samuel to see.

"Patrick will need to fetch the Rabbi instead," he directed, "That's all the help we can offer. The horse can wait."

***

After the Rabbi arrived with proper help of his burial group, Samuel and Eggers walked back home in glum spirits. Samuel allowed that he wasn't fully prepared for a customer, but he was definitely game for the challenge.

They passed LaFevre on the way and told him that he'd missed his murdered body. LaFevre countered that he'd already alerted all the merchants in the area to watch for a big spender, the rumors of robbery on the road having already reached him.

LaFevre was an ugly, misshapen man. When people met him, they would try to recall if they had ever met one uglier. His mottled complexion and uneven features resembled something a child might mold out of stale clay, in a hurry.

He bellowed at them that he had no time for their nonsense and proceeded away from them to investigate what remained for him to investigate.

Samuel whistled the *Sheriff of Nottingham* tune softly and Eggers laughed. He clapped Samuel on the back as they made their way, and he nearly lost hold of his bicycle. "Cheer up old chap," he said in a very poor English accent, "Someone is bound to die again soon for ya. Let's wait for them in the tavern!"

Chapter 13—Trouble

The wind began to pick up at twilight and Samuel shivered a bit as they walked first to the mill and then on to Hideaway House. It wasn't cold enough yet to nip at the fingers and nose, but just enough to remind them that it soon would be.

He told Eggers about his survey of the mill and then listened to Eggers' account of his day in the city.

Eggers believed that he had an understanding of the way traffic should be managed, and it was a favorite topic. "Those city people are barking mad," he said. "You would think the sight of a bicycle has them overflowing with wrath. I wouldn't be surprised to hear that there are sermons against the likes of my lovely machine." Time and again he said the city people had tried to kill his bicycle and him along with it.

The rules of the road were so rapidly changing that no one seemed to agree on who should yield to whom. Should a laden carriage give way to a tiny two-person tricycle? Should a fire cart have precedence over all others? The newer machines truly were eyed with irritation and the European horseless carriages hadn't even made an appearance yet. Eggers exaggerated, as usual, but he wasn't entirely off the mark saying that the buggies and horseback riders wanted to kill him.

Samuel knew that all this murder talk was intended to cheer him, and it helped a bit.

"You recognize that every soul in town is a client," Eggers had said, "Not one other establishment can say that. Not even the brothels."

"Even the Germans are clients? I suppose the colored folks?" Samuel inquired, dipping his eyebrows at his friend.

"Ah, well, the Germans I would say yes, all of them," he said, figuring in his mind. "The emancipated darkies, well, some of them may want to be shipped to Richmond if they have the funds.

But you'll still be invited to the party, even if you aren't the band leader."

Eggers would have guessed that half the folks in town could afford to have their bodies sent back to their hometowns, and many of their hometowns would have them. Shipping meant embalming fees and a coffin at the very least.

Samuel was willing to accept anyone as a client, he said firmly. His challenge would be to inspire them to accept his final hospitality.

"Don't lose heart," Eggers said again, "How long will your funds last if we don't see any profit at all?"

"Just over a year, I'd say," Samuel replied.

"Oh, then there's nothing to worry about," Eggers said cheerfully. Eggers thought his confidence was misguided, but cheered him on anyhow. "All we need is a good solid outbreak of fever, and that is all but guaranteed!"

They reached the crossing and it was busy as usual. News of a murder did nothing at all to dull the merriment. Old Fabian chose to drag out his accordion instead of the tuba, possibly lacking the wind for a horn. He shifted his polka tune to a dirge at the sight of Samuel and he laughed at his own cleverness. His jowls shook twice as much as his shoulders.

Samuel veered into the tavern and Fabian went back to his polka. No one ever asked Fabian anymore, but he had learned all his instruments sailing about with a musical troupe. He could play most of his instruments lying on his back or blindfolded, and some even upside down. He had never wondered if he might have put all that boredom to more beneficial use. He firmly believed that his musical offerings aided the sale of his condoms and as he felt he was a good Samaritan, Fabian was a contented man.

"Whiskey for me and my boy here, if you please!" shouted Eggers as they drew up to the bar. Samuel shook his head slightly but significantly at the bartender, and Gannon slid him an ale instead.

"The killer is in the city jail," Gannon announced, "Did you hear?"

Samuel was taken aback, "That's fast," he said.

Gannon went on to tell them that an idiot had been apprehended. He pronounced it *idjit*. The idiot, after tossing around a great many silver dollars and bragging that he had magic abilities, essentially confessed to the killing. He said that a horse had told him that he should ease its burden and take all its silver. Because he was clever, he thought, he would not let the horse fool him further and killed it to be sure.

"I don't suppose LaFevre will slow down to take credit for that," commented Eggers sarcastically. "Pour me another one for the horse!"

Samuel was a bit concerned. He hadn't seen Eggers behave exactly this way. There was an edge of recklessness that went beyond his usual.

Samuel hastily ordered some food, hoping to divert Eggers' attention from the whisky. This was not very successful, since Eggers made a mess of his fish, irritated the barmaid, and hardly slowed his drinking at all.

His friend's speech grew louder and although his English was ordinarily excellent, it was becoming difficult to make out what he was saying at times. Drink by drink, his Norwegian was taking the lead.

He stomped and clapped exaggeratedly and leaned in to shout close to Samuel's face that he should enjoy himself more. This just made Samuel the more miserable.

Eggers' eyelids fluttered as he shouted at the fiddle player in what was probably Norwegian. Whatever he was trying to communicate, in English it sounded something like, "Lying rascal!"

If Eggers had been in sensible condition, he would have noticed that all three of the one-eyed men in the tavern were now turned with their respective good eyes toward him.

Several things occurred in essentially the same moment.

First, Gannon motioned to Samuel vehemently that he needed to remove Eggers. He was sensing the impending collision, albeit a bit behind the best timing.

Second, the fiddle player stopped, lowered his instrument and rose to his full, impressive height. "Back up you filthy, stupid Swede!"

Now, Samuel knew this was very bad indeed. He had no idea what sort of tribal squabble had caused such strong feelings in his chum against all things Swedish. Frankly, Samuel wasn't certain how one could tell them apart; for him, Scandinavians were like bees—all very much alike. He did know that there was nothing more insulting than to connect the words "stupid" and "Swede" in Eggers' direction.

Instinctively, Samuel dove to grab Eggers, but only managed to catch a handful of his trousers. Eggers had launched himself toward the musician, his arms flung wide as if he were a large drunken bird of prey. The fiddler deftly stepped aside and Eggers landed, hitting a stool with an outstanding *thwack*. The sound was like the collision of two blocks of wood. One block of wood was Eggers' forehead.

Gannon wasted no time in hauling Eggers out into the alley, while Samuel rushed to assist and to make sure there wasn't more injury on the way. Eggers' face was covered in blood, but he was moaning about his suspenders, which were half torn away. Gannon threw a rag to Samuel and stalked back indoors with a disgusted shake of his head. "Take him to the gal at the dress shop," he said before slamming the door. He opened the door again and added, "And clean him up a bit first!"

Samuel wasn't entirely certain from here which of the doors in the alley were what, but he thought they were close to the dress shop.

"Come on, you ruffian," he said pulling Eggers to a leaning position. Without cooperation, he would get nowhere. Eggers was a solid fellow, and while Samuel had a height advantage, he imagined they weighed the same.

"What has happened to my trousers?" Eggers moaned.

Chapter 14—Stitch

Helen had her hands full, even before the knock on the back door.

Her employer was sobbing in a strangled, partly muffled fashion, stopping only to tear at a handkerchief in frightening, angry spasms.

"I will never escape this horrible place!" Kate screeched, before veering into another series of sobs.

Helen stood over her, not unsympathetic, but feeling a complicated mix of pity and fury herself. "You'll scare the children with that noise," she said with a gentle tone that did not communicate her feelings at all.

The space between the two women would appear small to an observer, but to Helen it was a growing chasm. They could have avoided so much aggravation if they had begun their arrangement with more clarity. Now it was a conversation they both imagined as entirely fruitless.

Kate had employed Helen without proper negotiation, and now both of them were disappointed and nourishing resentments. For her part, Kate expected an assistant who would also be something akin to a servant and even a sort of friend, in that order.

Since her husband had been struck and killed by a train, Kate found herself not only a mother and seamstress, but an ill-prepared business owner in a place she distrusted, surrounded by people she despised.

Church was her one safe haven, and there she had been introduced to Helen.

Reverend Price had extolled Helen's abilities, pointing out to Kate the lovely robes Helen had donated to his tiny choir. He didn't know, and Kate didn't ask, what actual situation Helen was looking for.

Helen had only two conditions, aside from proper pay. She wanted to room away from her father's farm and she would not be a servant. She would sew and keep her own things tidy, but she would not cook or clean, and she most definitely would not tend to children.

So, their uneasy arrangement had limped along for most of a year. Kate would ask Helen, for instance, to dress one of her boys, and Helen would shake her head, "No, ma'am," she would say, continuing to propel her sewing machine. Kate would pout and sulk, but she would be sure to ask again for the same service in a day or two. They both believed they had the worse part of the bargain.

Kate had not felt comfortable complaining about it in church, but she was becoming so accustomed to being dissatisfied, that it was just one more item on her growing list of grievances with life. Her real displeasure was with God, but she was too much of a lady to say so.

Over the noise from Kate, Helen heard a man caterwauling about trousers and flung open the back window. "Stop that this instant or I'll call for the fireman!" she commanded.

The fireman was a much better threat than the police, since he would almost certainly turn up. He was just up the street and was rumored to be routinely consoling the widow Kate. He would have said he was just attentive, not quite ready to admit that he would press a suit on so fresh a widow. In any case, he was a formidable hothead and no one would be pleased to meet him in a dark alley.

Helen caught sight of Eggers and rushed to open the door with a greeting of, "Oh." She felt a tiny flutter in her knees and steadied herself. His clothes were bloody and he held the rag to his head. This was going to be a trial on her nerves.

"Can you stitch him?" asked Samuel. He felt a flush and assumed it was the burden of Eggers, and so he eased Eggers clumsily into a chair.

She nodded, serious and composed. She leaned hard on the table as she studied the patient and whispered, "I think we still have some ice." She moved to the back door to check the tiny icebox cabinet. Returning with a chunk of ice and some rags, she fashioned a compress and pulled Eggers' head back and placed the cold cloth bundle on his head wound. The bleeding was slow and swelling was beginning to deform his forehead. "Hold this here for a bit," she instructed Samuel.

Kate staggered into the doorway and barked unintelligibly at the sight of blood, clearly not pleased. Her eyes were red and swimmy. She then staggered away, back to her divan to resume her swoon.

Samuel patted Eggers pocket and pulled out a flask. He waved it at Helen, raising his eyebrows in question.

"Marvels," she said and added a healthy jigger of fluid into a tea cup. "I'll get my kit," she said to Samuel and went in to Kate with the whiskey-laced tea. She stole a nip of her own once she rounded the corner. The warmth trickling in her chest distracted from the tingling in her knees. *Steady, steady*, she told herself.

When she returned, Samuel could hear the fervor of Kate's sobs diminishing; she was only letting out some exhausted mewling sounds. "I want to be in New Jersey," she whimpered.

"What on Earth has happened?" he asked Helen.

Samuel thought he could see her mouth tense, but he wasn't sure. "The man who was killed was on his way to buy this shop," she said. She didn't elaborate that it was a complete surprise to her that the deal was afoot, but it was.

Kate, who could not keep her outhouse adventures secret, had managed to keep this business arrangement entirely covert.

Helen washed her hands and then proceeded to wash Eggers' forehead as they talked. For his part, Eggers was still muttering and seemed content to be tended, for the moment, with his eyes closed and his jaw slack.

"The money was recovered," Samuel told her, "so the purchase would still be possible."

"She has already had word from his people that none of them will ever set foot in the Port again," she said. She did not say that the selfishness of Kate's reaction had unnerved her, or that she found her brand of grieving revolting.

"The killer was caught?" she asked, washing her hands again in the basin.

"Oh yes," Samuel replied. "The city police clapped him directly into the asylum."

"I have never even had a mild attack of nervous trouble!" bellowed Eggers, inspiring Kate to whimper from the next room.

"Shhhhh," admonished Helen. "Mr. Eggers, you will have to be very still while I patch your head. Do you think you can do that?" She did not say *stitch*, but if he had he opened his eyes, he would have seen the needle at the ready.

"I have a rumpus in my chitterlins," he said, "but my head is frozen." He shuddered. "Do it," he concluded.

Swiftly, she flipped the needle through and pressed his head as she drew the stich.

"Gah," said Eggers.

"Once more," she said, "It's not bad at all."

"Easy for you," Eggers tapped his boots together and Samuel had to smile, suddenly imagining him a little boy at the barber shop.

"Done!" she proclaimed. "Keep it clean." She turned to Samuel, "If he's still reeling after he sobers, take him to the doctor in the city."

Samuel nodded, looking directly in her brown eyes. He struggled to think of a question; he felt a pull to prolong this strange encounter just a bit more. He wanted to know… everything.

Chapter 15—Tomfoolery

As they made their way back to the house, Eggers leaned on Samuel less. After he stopped to vomit energetically, he was much sobered and walking unsteadily on his own. He pushed Samuel away and held his trousers up, since his suspenders had partially ripped away. His steps were irregular, but as he held his pants with one hand and extended the other hand, he looked like he was performing a slow, trousers waltz on the road.

Further along, as Eggers became more steady, Samuel asked him about Helen. How did he know her? What did he know of her? Eggers groaned.

"I've fetched some dresses for the gals and I must say she is never friendly at all," said Eggers. "I'll take a friendly girl over a pretty one every day."

Eggers went on to say that her lack of friendliness was partly that her father owned the largest farm around and because she was a serious "Methodical," his off-hand term for Methodists.

"I cannot abide that superiority," he said.

"That's because you fancy yourself superior to all the church people," commented Samuel.

"Just so," Eggers agreed. "I can get much more done on a Sunday."

Samuel had seen Helen's father around town and had gotten the sense that he was a sort of unofficial mayor. People deferred to him and sought his support for their grumbles. He was not a client at the Countess's house, although he might have frequented one of the other, more ordinary brothels. Samuel didn't like to speculate on that.

Samuel wondered why Helen wouldn't live at home with her family, as he began to imagine her as a sort of adored princess who could enjoy a quiet pastoral life of leisure. Samuel had no understanding of real agriculture or farm life to interfere with his fantasy of regal picnics and twirling, pastel parasols.

When he and Eggers arrived home, they didn't stop at the front of the house, but went directly toward their rooms.

Conrad, the watchman, was horrified by the sight of Eggers. His hat lost, the large bulge of his forehead and bloody clothes made him an awful spectacle. "What befell the other fella?" Conrad asked and Samuel motioned to let him know that was a poor choice of a question.

"I dispatched him to Hades, I am sure," Eggers lied. "And now I will dream an angelic feather-bed jig with a tender celestial being."

Samuel remained outside with Conrad, unwilling to end his night just yet.

"His foe was a piece of furniture," he explained quietly.

Conrad chuckled. "The Countess will want to have a look at him, and that knot." Samuel nodded and asked if they had many customers. "The usual tomfoolery," Conrad said, "And Juniper is providing a little high stepping." Samuel cocked his head skeptically. All he could hear was the undulating buzzing of the cicadas.

"The fellas are all deaf, so there's no need for musical accompaniment. Even so, I thought I may have heard a tambourine," Conrad explained.

Samuel knew there was a deaf college in the city, but he'd somehow never considered that they would travel out here for entertainment. He valiantly tried not to imagine Juniper dancing a strip tease in virtual silence. He failed.

Samuel appreciated that they were not supposed to discuss the "tomfoolery" at the house, still he had learned far too much about the proceedings of the past weeks. The instructions to keep mum about all of it didn't slow the crew when talking amongst themselves. After all, they were entertainers and little was more diverting that a wink and a bit of nattering about the naughtiness.

There was a very particular rhythm and order to the running of the business. While it might appear to be casual, that was only artifice for the sake of hospitality. Day to day, the house ran much like the intricacies of a music box, and it seemed to Samuel to be nearly as complex and still mostly predictable.

As a rule, the Countess didn't take random runaway girls in, as the hotel and the other houses did. She recruited rarely and would never hire anyone in whom she sensed an appetite for destruction.

An optimistic disposition seemed to be her only firm requirement. The hotel girls were young and pretty and inexperienced. They might pick a pocket or incite a fight out of boredom and their brand of mischief was not welcome with the Countess.

She made sure her employees looked after their health and that they spent their spare time practicing and preening. They were to think of themselves as professional *artistes* and to avoid melancholy unless it was by special request from a client.

The clients were courted and questioned when they arrived, their desires probed gently and tactfully. The Countess would determine the entertainer and the form of entertainment for their appointment and would accept payment in advance. The rates were prohibitive and still, the clients were grateful to pay.

The artistes were accustomed to playing parts and could easily slip into the role of disciplinarian or precocious student; they could inhabit anyone or anything the Victorian male could concoct.

Samuel was only aware of the louder scenarios that went on when he was keeping watch in place of Conrad. He would be warned that there might be harmless shouting, as in the case of the old chap who had a fascination with steamship explosions.

Said chap could only afford to stop in once each month, but he always turned up in his best finery with his picture book tucked neatly under his arm. He enjoyed explaining the steamship disaster illustrations to idle young women on the train. They would wonder at his shortened breath, having no idea the excitement the exercise brought him.

In most respects, he was a very typical case.

There were foot men, blind man's bluffers, bathers, big babies and peepers. All manner of tastes would be serviced, but there were a few limits the Countess would not yield.

No spirits or opiates were allowed on the property; cigars and sherry and a few fancy wines were permitted and stocked for the clientele, but that was all. If a customer wanted to drink to excess, there were half a dozen other places to do so in town.

No services were provided outside of the house. This came up with some regularity, but the Countess always said no. She'd even been offered a shocking sum by a client who wanted her to participate personally in a scenario in which he chased her through the woods. She could carry a pistol, he said. No, she said. She could chase him instead, he offered. No, she said.

She did attend to a few clients personally, and this was just another peculiarity of her management. "Sometimes there's no other way to give them what they need," she explained, breaking her own rule about discussing it.

The night of the fight, Samuel went to the side door and let himself in and made his way quietly through the darkened morning room. The lights were very low and the ferns cast shadows that made the room feel jungle-like and dangerous. He saw the Countess at her piano, playing quietly to pass the time.

"A moment?" he asked.

"Of course," she said, playing a prematurely conclusive chord and turning toward him with a gentle smile, her teeth gleamed with her pearl earrings, the only brightness in the room. "How is poor, dear Mr. Eggers?"

"He'll live but may wish he hadn't in the morning," he replied.

She shook her head, "He's so disturbed by the violence, being such a gentle fellow."

Samuel laughed, startling her. After all, Eggers had launched himself at a giant. She corrected herself, "A gentle fellow in sobriety."

Samuel considered her comment about his gentle nature. Eggers was so bombastic and energetic that it might escape notice that he was a tender-hearted man, cloaked in all his bluster.

Samuel felt a sense of shame creeping up as he recognized his error. Eggers had been quite upset by the murder scene, he realized. He was so caught up in his own exhilaration that he had overlooked the way Eggers hands had shaken and how his voice had become high-pitched and tight.

Samuel sighed then, "I am a poor friend to poor Eggers. I didn't see it."

She leaned in to catch his gaze, her eyes kind and understanding. "This is how we become better friends," she said. "You cannot know a man's heart without time and attention. We have to consider people with fresh eyes and even then, you will be surprised by their fears and needs."

Her eyes were sparkling with mischief as she moved next to him on the divan. She held his gaze and he felt both lulled and uncomfortably exposed. Her skirts rustled as she settled into place. The upholstery was rough, and it felt like the skin of a pomegranate under his nervous fingertips.

Samuel was completely unprepared for the sensation of her hand in his lap. It was not an unintentional motion. She continued looking at his face, smiling, as her hand moved expertly into place to find his erection. He gasped just before his throat snapped closed and he skittered backward away from her on the now tiny divan.

"Don't be afraid," she said, not moving toward him but maintaining her playful tone. "You like women. Older women?"

"I... I don't know," he said quite hopeless and swooning. "I was raised to, uh, conserve." He could not imagine why she was behaving this way. He couldn't imagine anything but escape.

She clucked her tongue, "Oh dear." The Countess was sorry for men like Samuel. They were taught that their seed was not to be released, made to feel guilty for even the accidental spillage. In her view, it was a very sad state. Only men with a milder disposition could escape a terrible cycle of guilt and punishment. She judged Samuel to be one of those milder types, which was fortunate for him. The serious cases inevitably became poisonous in their self-loathing.

He avoided titillation, she had noticed, and was at this moment more embarrassed that shamed, as he should be.

"You have been touched by a kind of madness, you know," she said.

He looked down in confusion and she laughed much more genuinely than before.

"Everyone has a madness to harness," she continued. "Those who cannot harness their own madness will suffer from other people who can."

"Samuel," she pushed his chin up and he shuddered, "I will help you, but you need to listen and do as I say. Make yourself comfortable when you leave and know that any method you choose was first designed by God.

"He wants you to be happy and enjoy your life and he would never have given you man parts if you weren't expected to master them.

"Tomorrow, I want you to think about which one of the ladies you most fancy. I know you have avoided any notion of the kind, but I insist that you make a selection. There's no hurry, but you must begin tomorrow."

Samuel fled.

He imagined he heard the Countess rustling outside his bedroom door and he bit the blankets like a child might. She didn't enter, but he thought he heard her cooing over Eggers in the next room.

Relieved, he slept and dreamed of dancing harlots whirling in and out of a massive cuckoo clock. A cuckoo was not what popped out of the top, however.

Chapter 16—Mending

Eggers healed with a speed that amazed Samuel and he had no need of the doctor. The next morning, he was devouring everything set before him and hollering out the news headlines as usual. The Countess even made an early morning appearance, which was unusual. She sent the maid to the dress shop to deliver a small pile of coins for Helen and some pastries for Kate and her boys, in thanks.

Eggers read from the newspaper, "The Japanese legation are back from an extensive summer tour to the watering places through Canada. They found but few of their countrymen located in Canada; only one Japanese living in the large city of Montreal, where he had been alone for ten years."

Eggers tisked, "They just couldn't leave that fellow alone. Had to barge in on him all the way across the world."

"Wouldn't you be pleased to have a pack of countrymen arrive?" asked Samuel.

"Not at all! If I had a yearning for them, I know where they are." He commented that it hurt to furrow his brow, and so he hoped Samuel would be taking care of any matters that might require more concentration than the newspaper.

So, although quick to heal, Eggers was not very industrious that week. Samuel left early each day and busied himself with assembling his first few caskets. He wanted samples to display and if he made good use of his time, he could have a variety to show.

He had one of maple completed, and one of oak and another of walnut in progress by the end of the week. The space smelled of magnificent, woody destruction. He could taste the walnut dust and enjoyed the sense of swimming in his work.

He was very happy to shake the saw dust out of his hair and look around at his wonderful mess of a shop. He didn't mind working alone, but he found that he welcomed some form of companionship after many hours of sawing and sanding on his own.

At the end of every day, he would take his bag and walk up the road to the springs and bathe. He felt it necessary to be seen as a dusty woodworker as little as possible.

After that, he would have supper at the tavern, clean and presentable in his best black cutaway suit.

The working people in town were becoming accustomed to him, but kept him at a distance, with few exceptions. A couple of the fellows referred to him as Conrad's ghost, but generally, the younger men seemed to feel a superstitious itch in his presence, and would avoid referring to him at all. The elders were more at ease. To them, he was just a boy who dabbled in death and they would comfortably joke and say, "See you soon," with a smile.

Hops, the postman, was one of those who didn't feel perturbed by Samuel. He regularly appeared at the springs or the tavern when he knew that Samuel would be there, in order to bring him a package or two that might contain coffin handles, small tools or a smattering of other mail-order items. Hops quickly became the kind of pal that would let him know if his tie fell off.

One evening, Hops presented Samuel with an elegant wool blanket that had been mailed to him by the Jewish burial club. It was far finer than the one he had left with the dead man. Hops smiled at Samuel's delighted reaction.

A note was in the box, the seal on its envelope marked in wax with a symbol that Samuel assumed was some ancient message of its own. The note thanked him for his prompt kindness in assisting to return their fallen son to his family. Samuel felt quite moved by the gesture.

"Your people are too kind," he said to Hops. His friend's smile did not falter, as he knew Samuel intended a compliment, even if it was a clumsy one.

Later, Samuel put the package away in his wardrobe with the note still in the box.

The Countess eyed him that evening as if she might remind him of his task, but he only blushed and looked away. He had not forgotten, of course, but only allowed himself a tiny slice of time to mull over the candidates.

He found all of them wonderful in one way or another, but to consider them as desirable creatures he would have to approach the problem in a less neighborly frame of mind.

His only sexual experiences had been alarming and sudden, and he could only recollect a jumble of sensations, chief of which was pure panic.

The first time, he had been at work in the theatre. A young actress, overexcited by her stage murder, had accosted him. She pressed Samuel into a space behind the stage in a ferocious, silent bout of kisses.

He remembered being tangled in her limbs, driven by waves of impulse that seemed to come from some place outside his own body and yet from his very center. He also remembered being left breathless and covered in stage blood.

He had never initiated such a scene behind the scenery, but he had found himself bewildered and trouser-free on two other such occasions. It wasn't the reason he left the theatre, although the embarrassment had been tremendous.

For all their theatricality, none of the Countess's girls reminded him of that "Emilia." She had been very lanky and rough and moved like a hectic puppet. He had been a little afraid of her, even before she bit him.

Cherry was perhaps the least like her. She was round and soft and maternal. She had a slow, musical voice that was a delight to the ears. Still, Samuel found no enticement to touch her and would worry about being smothered by her powdered flesh.

No, he thought, not Cherry; he would prefer to picnic with Cherry and gossip about people they didn't know. He would like to see her smile when she realized he had brought her special oranges to share, but that was all.

Juniper, well, she was wonderfully graceful, but as soon as she spoke, he would wish she hadn't. Her voice was very high-pitched and her speech was slushy. He envied the deaf students experience of her, come to think of it, and he would have to lose his hearing to enjoy her company that way.

Then there was Violet, who the others called Wee Vi. No no, certainly not Vi. She was young enough to be too young for the business, at least it seemed so to him.

The entire exercise was terribly uncomfortable for him. It wasn't just that it was an unwanted assignment from the Countess, and not just that he was indisposed to consider physical female companionship. It was also, he realized, that he had a distaste for picking and choosing amongst women as if they were peaches in an orchard.

He supposed that it was the most natural way for a man to decide such a thing, and yet it was as if he was being manipulated to force himself to go against his nature.

Perhaps his abstinence training suited him after all.

Chapter 17—Church

Helen continued, but barely, to keep her temper with Kate. They had been busy with dress orders and even had some work trickling in from the city, as autumn parties and fairs were carrying on in the exceptionally hot weather. The watermelon vines had sprouted anew in seasonal confusion.

Helen was pleased to have a pair of mourning doves settling in on the roof where there had only been a gang of pigeons before. None of them were homing pigeons, she was sure; they were only rootless, wandering pigeons.

Helen was careful not to mention any of the birds to Kate, and she discretely carried feed to the roof. Kate would have wanted to eat them come winter, she was certain.

Helen would eat pigeon if it were a practical necessity, but she had no taste for pets as a rule. She liked the way they, and now the doves, would mill around her calmly as she sat very still on the old wooden bench. They would peck and coo quite contentedly, but then would burst into a flurry of flying panic the instant she stood. It always made her smile.

She would be sorry to leave the birds, but it seemed that with the impending sale of the shop, it was going to happen sooner than she planned.

Her sister sent notes filled with enthusiasm for city living, but Helen didn't like the crowded, swampy boarding house where Fannie lived. She thought it was a temporary fascination and that her sister would soon give up on the umbrella repair business. The umbrella gang was surprisingly wily. They didn't suit Fannie, she thought, and they definitely wouldn't suit her.

That morning, like every morning, Helen stood on the roof and watched the sun come up, uncertain if she'd ever do so again from that same spot. As the birds began to stir, she shook off her doubts and went about her day.

Church was the same as ever, although it was a bit worse for her that Sunday. Helen went early to avoid traveling with Kate and was captured by her family ahead of schedule. She had stopped to put flowers on her mother's grave and weeded a little, apologizing softly for the state of the blooms, when she heard her brother's voice.

He complained about the hot weather as if it were conversation. "I will be very glad to see the harvest moon, just to work without this awful heat," he said. "Come on, Helen, let's move along."

The twins echoed him, "Move along, Helen! No time for fussing with flowers." Their faces were angelic, but their voices carried an irksome tone.

Irritated, Helen rose and adjusted her bonnet. No one else tended Margot's grave, she was certain. Now they didn't even acknowledge that it was right there, quite literally at their feet.

She had expected the twins to take an interest by now, to ask questions about the mother they hadn't known, but they maintained their odd detachment and behaved as if they had sprouted up from the farm without assistance or pain.

Helen and Fannie mistakenly believed that they had been far less bothersome as girls than their little sisters were now. In fact, they had been models of annoyance.

Gertie would readily remind them given a chance, "Oh, you would make me drag you out from under the house, playing at making ghost noises and terrifying your little brother. You two were something else and don't you forget it."

Helen's father greeted her warmly and asked her if she would be coming home, now that the dress shop would be sold. Patiently, Helen explained that it wasn't necessarily so, and that she was content to wait and see what happened.

Ephraim was always, always asking the same questions, no matter what words he was using. All the messages were versions of "You should come home," or "You should get married and then come home."

The sermon was "Who is on the side of the Lord?" and it was a little melancholy, Helen thought. They sang "O For a Closer

Walk with God" and her brother's voice boomed powerfully through the little chapel. The choir had tried to recruit him, but he wouldn't take the time.

She loved that hymn and the longing it conveyed. The tune had a lilting sweetness that veiled the desperation of the words. The choir was dragging the tempo, however. She thought it could be called "A Saunter with God," today.

She recognized that she was feeling a bit too churlish for church. "It's good thing you are here, then," her mother would have said.

The little church had often felt like another home to her. While other churches in the county were splitting and joining to separate their congregations, hers still stood welcoming all. Some might believe it was the best way, and others might secretly wish they could afford a second church, but it was the way it was. It was a little beacon of the divine in the midst of a bit too much human frailty.

As they filed out of the entrance, Reverend Price took both of Helen's hands, wrapping them up in his big, dry paws, remarking on how well she looked. Her father scowled a bit and moved away.

The Reverend was habitually attentive to the elder Driscoll daughters, and Helen knew that she provided a little, very little, obfuscation of his true affections. His attachment to Fannie was proving to be the longest, slowest, dullest courtship ever, Helen believed.

He asked after her sister and Helen lied smoothly that Fannie was not enthusiastic about the city church she had been attending. The Reverend could not conceal that this news pleased him. He hurried to change the subject.

"I've had word of an upholstery position," he said. "It shouldn't be too much of an occupation, but I hear you may need a new situation."

"Upholstery?" she said, "I think I'd like that." Something new! She was frankly delighted.

"You should be able to find Mr. Eggers at the tavern tomorrow evening," he suggested.

"Thank you!" she said and whirled and ran to catch up with her father as they all went home for their customary Sunday supper.

She kept her prospect to herself through dinner and played cheerfully with the children after they had done a great deal of canning. This time of year was a time for exceptions, a time when everyone was a bit of a farmer and a part-time preserver, even on Sunday.

It was too dark—at least in her father's opinion—for her to walk home alone. He assembled some jars for her to take along, and she grinned as she added an extra jar of peaches to her basket. "I knew you were the peach pincher," he said, smiling back.

He didn't ask about her conversation with Reverend Price and she was relieved that he didn't seem curious. This way, she could enjoy thinking about her opportunity just a little longer without addressing his disappointment at the same time.

The evening had cooled only a little, and as they rode along, her drawers clung uncomfortably to her skin. She had no way to adjust them once the carriage was underway, so she was glad it was a short ride.

A few late and very lonely fireflies blinked in the branches of the trees, their mating race now almost certainly lost. The sky was dark and opaque as if all the humidity clung there to blot out the stars.

Her father talked about his labor problems, not complaining he thought, but educating her in the intricacies of seasonal employment. He believed he must prepare her for the day when she would help manage the farm. She listened politely, equally certain that she would never need to learn one thing more about farming.

Chapter 18—Curtains

Eggers was pleased that Helen was interested in working with them. "After, all," he said, "I know you can sew!" Her laughter surprised them both.

"The undertaker is dreadful with fabric," he continued, "Don't hurt his feelings by telling him, but you'll need to rework all the linings and whatnots." He asked her to come to the mill the following afternoon, if she could get away. She was now curious to see what the *whatnots* might be.

The whatnots, she discovered, were satin pillows and the beginnings of some curtains to be used for improvised privacy during a house call.

Samuel showed her around the rooms he created in the mill, explaining the way he envisioned the operation. Her work area would be in one of the small offices, he said, and opened the door to display the room that held the sewing machine.

"This is a very good one," she remarked, pulling at the cabinet drawers to inspect the supplies.

"It's complete," he said, "It has all the ruffle-fluffily attachments." She nodded. "It operates smoothly, but it can't make me a qualified operator," he said, lowering his voice, "Don't tell Eggers, but I know my efforts are horrible."

She smiled back at him, conspiratorially, "Everyone is telling me secrets lately. I have a very bright future in blackmail." He blushed, but she didn't see, having already swept out of the little room.

"It's wise that you have an embalming room," she said directly, "I think I should start with curtains in there." He nodded. The windows were tall and narrow, and gave the illusion of being inside a castle. Even though the small glass panes were far from clear, covering the windows was logical.

"Very good," he said determined to win another of Helen's dazzling smiles. "It's curtains for you."

Chapter 19—Strategy

The next morning, Eggers grinned broadly at Samuel as he came in for breakfast. "No woodwork today?" he asked.

"No," said Samuel. "I was thinking that you and I should spend some time on our, uh, procedures."

Myrtle, who had been dawdling with Eggers, sipping some morning chocolate, raised an eyebrow at Samuel skeptically and said, "I have no interest in hearing another word of this. Either it's something very naughty or something very nasty that you have in mind."

He did not object as she flounced out of the room. Samuel moved her cup from the table to the sideboard and took over her place at the table.

Eggers pondered, looking past Samuel, "Perhaps an animal carcass?" The lack of human bodies was a barrier to teaching by demonstration. Samuel had started to collect a reference library and studied it in the evenings, but that wasn't the way he understood things best. They talked through the preparations and ways of embalming, but only practical application of the tools would serve to instruct him. "I think we may be able to get ahold of... something."

"No," Samuel said, "I'd just like to have a sort of practice with the instruments in hand. I must be more ready than this when the time comes."

Eggers said, "Very wise and prudent as ever. Will we have Miss Driscoll along again today?"

Samuel found the way he said her name irritating. Eggers misunderstood his expression, "Oh dear, you don't like her after all. She is a little haughty, I suppose."

Samuel sputtered, "No, no. You mustn't." He collected himself, uncomfortably aware that he was becoming cornered in a kind of conversational mire. He was not very good at this. "I thought nothing of the sort, my friend. She will be an asset to our operation, I'm sure." He looked directly at Eggers for emphasis.

"Certainly. Certainly!" replied Eggers, not the least ruffled. "You're already fond of her, I understand."

Samuel sighed, miserably. He would rather not discuss his feelings. Eggers was disdainful of romantic ideas and often proclaimed with a bit too much insistence that his goal was to die a bachelor eccentric. "One has to be quite rich to be eccentric," he always added.

Eggers seemed to sense the need for kindness, and he offered Samuel a nonsensical exit from the conversation in his inimitable way, "I may complain about the ladies, but where would we be without their gentle charms and clever wiles? We would be too savage to know we were unhappy without them."

Samuel laughed because he had no other possible response to the remark.

Chapter 20—Practice

That bright morning, Helen set out for the undertaker's shop with a purposeful gait. She would start on curtains and move on to work on all the little things they would need.

They should have a few wreaths on hand to put on mourners' front doors, and black arm bands to provide if anyone lacked supplies to fashion one on at home.

She had the sense that these men didn't know precisely what they were doing. That didn't worry her; she relished sorting things out and righting things that were askew.

Brown leaves swirled around her as she walked. Autumn was beginning to tiptoe in. Even though the season had always meant long hours, she loved so much about it. Her siblings had teased her when she would collect leaves on her way back and forth to school as a child.

She would pick up one perfect, vivid, scarlet dogwood leaf at a time and tuck it carefully in her pocket. If later she found one that she deemed more perfect, she would replace it, and once at home, she would put her selection in her tiny bible.

Because he teased her, she never explained to Wally that they were magic leaves. She wasn't sure how to use them, but she had been confident that collecting them was a very good start to her magic career.

When she arrived at the shop, the door was standing half-open, as if they wanted the air, but hadn't blocked it open properly. She crept in, cautiously. She could hear movement.

"Right!" Eggers exclaimed from the embalming room, "First of all you need to be entirely certain your client is dead." His voice would have filled a lecture hall. "Hold the mirror under the nose for a full minute, while sensing the temperature at the back of the neck," he continued. "Good God! Your hands are cold!"

Helen could see the client stretched out on the table was Eggers himself. Samuel was bent slightly over him, as if concentrating on the position of the completely fogged mirror.

Helen tilted her head, craned her surprised expression toward them and said, "This is not what I expected to find."

Samuel started and nearly crashed into her in his surprise.

"Second," continued Eggers, ignoring them both as a good teacher should, "you must have a peek at the tallywacker to establish his identity and rigor."

Samuel guffawed and lurched backward again. "I will not."

"That is not the way at all," Helen interjected, crossly. She wasn't at all bothered that Eggers was talking of tallywackers in front of her, but she was very bothered that he was doing everything wrong.

"Why don't you move along and sew something, Missy!" Eggers rejoined, "We have important instructional activities to conduct here."

Samuel was embarrassed his ignorance was so easily revealed to her, but she didn't seem interested in that aspect of the scene at all.

"You cannot play at such a disrespectful pantomime!" Her tone of authority was remarkable to them, and they gave up the exercise. Eggers sat up to accept her scolding. "It's a horror," she explained.

"What do you suggest?" asked Samuel with genuine curiosity.

She sighed, "You need a real body on the table, of course. You, Mr. Eggers, are far too full of comedy for the job."

Eggers sat up and cocked his head, "We could claim a hobo from the city mortuary, but it might be rather nasty."

"They keep them on ice, don't they?" asked Helen.

"Yes," Eggers replied, "but that way some of them are both cold and nasty."

Samuel thought a moment and then nodded decisively, agreeing with himself in advance, "We'll offer discounted fees to an unfortunate. I'm certain that will work. Let's go right now and get a client. We have everything else we need."

Helen looked around the room, uncertainly. "I don't see any jars."

"We have everything except a body and jars," he amended. "We'll collect them on the way."

Eggers shrugged and followed him to fetch the hearse. They had replaced all the ornamental parts and the supports so they could almost honestly claim it was a different conveyance.

Helen got busy on curtains, smiling whenever she imagined their mission to the new city morgue. It was so eerie there, Samuel might die of fright.

Chapter 21—October

Samuel had considered trying to obtain a body from the city, but was naturally reluctant to do so. Sentiment was very negative about trafficking in bodies and body parts. Such traffic had never been precisely popular with the public. Even decades after the lurid details of the murders done by Burke and Hare were absorbed by the English-speaking world, it was a sensitive subject.

Burke and Hare had not been found out for nearly a year, a year during which they ran a brisk business of murder, butchery and cadaver sales. The legendary horror of their crimes was only magnified over the many years since.

Anyone trying to simply buy a dead body would end up in a police interview at the very least, and they would waste a day verifying that they weren't involved in some medical school mayhem.

Extending a humanitarian price cut however, well, that was a perfectly reasonable idea. Plenty of families weren't able to afford more than a burial, and the coffers of the burial clubs had not caught up with the tremendous new array of options for sending the departed on their way.

As they ascended the broad white steps to the morgue, a worried-looking young couple emerged, bookending an old woman who was in a wobbly state. She drew in her breath sharply when she saw the men, inhaling her black veil, and then commenced coughing largely and violently. Samuel thought the sound might be mistaken for a bear with bronchitis. The young woman, somehow not terrified, murmured about finding a bench for her as they moved away.

The city morgue was very modern and imposing. The marble steps led into a lofty, spare lobby. The polished white stone walls had no ornamentation. The only embellishment was the carved arch, high overhead.

It was disorienting, stepping inside. Cold electric light shone up from windows in the floor. As they walked between the two rows of windows, their steps echoed in the white void.

Samuel imagined that this was some architect's concept of the afterlife. He was sure that the living would be glad to exit rather swiftly.

Each window held one body for display, although not all of the spaces were occupied. They peered down at each side in turn. Only the faces were exposed for some, their bodies swaddled in white fabric. Others were displayed in their clothing, presumably to aid in identification.

All races were represented on this particular day, and nearly all of them were men. One man's face was shrouded, a note pinned carefully on the fabric that read, "Unrecognizable due to trampling." His hands were exposed and showed a strange tattoo that would be recognizable to someone, just not to Samuel.

How sad, he thought, to come here looking for someone who's been missed at dinner. How discouraging it would be to stop in for the sake of curiosity, only to find a favorite tavern mate had drowned.

Samuel cleared his throat and called out, to whom he didn't know, "Hello? Is anyone here for arrangements?"

A head with shiny dark hair peered sideways around a white wall at the back of the lobby and promptly disappeared again.

Eggers took the lead. They had found that people responded better to him in the front, with Samuel standing behind looking serious in his long black suit.

They rounded the corner to find a man at a broad white desk, his work area illuminated by the strange steady electric glow of suspended lanterns.

The man frowned back as Eggers explained that they were experiencing a lull in business and wanted to extend some help to the poorer patrons of his establishment.

He supposed it would be all right as long as they weren't competing with Doeger. "I have one the German refused to take," he said. "He's a Pole. The family only has enough for a burial and have just left to try to drum up support from cousins in Baltimore."

They thanked him and hurried out with the description of the widow and her entourage, who they had passed on the way in.

The little family was sitting on a city bench just around the corner. The mother was collected, now that she had pushed back her veil to breathe, and the children were discussing who would telephone and who would travel personally to get what they needed to get their papa's body home. The brother stood, leaning on the back of the bench, smoking a pipe, while his sister waved away the smoke as they talked.

Time was the enemy in funerals. He had gone missing two days before. He was in the city looking for work and had died during dinner. The shabby tavern where he had his final supper was owned by shadowy types who naturally did not want to be investigated. They had his body swiftly moved to an alleyway to avoid any involvement. It said something about their confidence in the chowder they served to strangers that they threw out the chowder as well.

The entire story of his death was unknown to the children who found him as they made their way home from their factory jobs. His story was typically anonymous to the coroner's wagon team who retrieved him, and his family knew almost none of the story of his mysterious end.

The family's relief at Samuel's proposal was visible. He would accept whatever they were able to pay and would arrange to get Mr. Gasnik prepared for travel and on the train with them by evening. Samuel clumsily offered his arm to Mrs. Gasnik to escort her back to the clerk while Eggers scurried to find a couple of helpers for loading the body.

Chapter 22—Preservation

Helen sat outside despite the chill. There was a very old and complicated sassafras tree next to the mill building, which had a low branch swooping out from the trunk at an improbable angle, forming a comfortable perch. She sat there and swung her feet back and forth and gazed up at the leaves at the top that were becoming a wonderful burning orange color.

She nibbled on blueberries from a jar and tossed one to a nearby mockingbird. It had stopped its frantic calling in order to inspect her, a newcomer to its domain. It rejected her offering.

She watched the comings and goings at the school without a thought that they were watching her too.

Her mind was occupied in its own battle. While she was confident in her ability to embalm whomever the men brought her, she was also shrinking from the idea in a tiny fit of cowardice. She had attended only one body from start to finish; who would consider her qualified to instruct after that minor experience?

She was practiced at pressing past her self-doubt, however, and she reminded herself that she would have to over-reach if she was ever going to expand her place in the world.

The mockingbird swooped down and collected the blueberry and she smiled.

Her worries had cooled and she had moved on from being bored with arguing with herself by the time the hearse arrived. Samuel jumped down from the carriage as she jumped down from her seat and he hailed a passing student to help them unload the body.

Eggers flung open the large doors of the building, and the four of them proceeded to work on transporting Mr. Gasnik. They chattered quietly about the circumstances, Samuel urging everyone to hurry, but not to rush.

Samuel thanked the student and ushered him briskly out the doors and closed them firmly. "We have the perfect coffin size for him," he remarked to Helen as he breezed back into the embalming room, "so that won't cost us any time. He's been on ice."

Eggers unwrapped the oilcloth around the body and the shriveled face was revealed. "Very dry," said Helen clinically. Samuel blanched a little as the sight of the body set in, and he was happy that Helen couldn't see his discomfort.

Mr. Gasnik was naked and very gray. His eyes and cheeks were hollow-looking and he appeared withered, as if he were formed of ancient driftwood instead of flesh. His jaw hung slack in a way that no sleeping man's could, falling down too far to his neck.

Helen took the lead, showing Samuel how to bathe the body. She explained the large dark bruises they found on the back of his legs, telling Samuel, "It's ordinary—the blood collects there after death, like a puddle in the skin."

She worked quickly and Samuel hovered, ready to assist but tentative and queasy. "We need to roll you back over now," she said, "Mr. Keegan would surely appreciate it if you were quiet." Eggers snorted and Helen shot him a warning look. "Don't pay any attention to Mr. Eggers," she continued, "he doesn't know how to behave."

"I know that I don't need to reassure a dead man," Eggers countered.

She gave Eggers her undivided attention as she spoke steadily, "Your joking is just a way to pretend this isn't happening. It has happened to this man. We owe him proper care. We owe a witness."

Samuel looked from one to the other. Helen was now standing with her hands on her hips and one might imagine that she was close to pulling off her apron and walking out. Eggers was leaning on the door frame, smirking.

"Eggers, old chap," he said, "I am glad that Miss Driscoll is so kind to instruct me too, so please be more serious and don't interrupt."

Helen tried to conceal her gratification at that, and mostly succeeded, although Eggers saw it and winked at her.

As they rolled the body onto his back, he let out a whistling groan. Samuel whimpered in reply and recoiled.

"Mr. Gasnik," Helen chided, "you're a joker after all." She washed his face and combed his hair into a likely shape, a not-so-fashionable style. "We're going to take very good care of your body, you know. You can move along whenever you are ready," her voice was soft and friendly. She demonstrated closing his mouth so that it would stay put, and she seemed pleased with the result. "I think Mr. Keegan should shave you now."

Samuel moved in and carefully gave the body its final shave. "I think you might leave his neck alone," Helen cautioned, finally speaking to Samuel instead of the corpse. "Old skin is very fragile. We can fold his collar up."

Samuel was relieved when it was done. He had expected the body to stay still, but he wasn't taking anything for granted. He stepped back and took a deep breath and set the razor down on the tray with a muted clink.

Eggers demonstrated the embalming, draining the blood to replace it with the chemical mixture. He had only a little difficulty.

As the preservation progressed, Samuel was frankly astonished at the change that was taking place in Mr. Gasnik. His face was filling out and a subtle pink hue began to color his skin, replacing the gray shrunken thing he had been with a life-like model.

Helen let Samuel work on the cosmetics, and he seemed to have a knack for it. She only directed him on how to fill the eyes. Sweat was pouring from Samuel's forehead and his concentration was making his head pound.

"You are doing just fine," Helen said. Samuel was fairly certain she was still speaking to Mr. Gasnik.

He stepped out to fetch the suit that Mrs. Gasnik had provided for her husband and suggested that they work together to wrestle him into his shirt. Helen smiled, explaining that they should cut the cloth and tuck it around him instead. "He won't mind," she declared.

It seemed to Samuel that they had been at it all day, but the late afternoon sun streamed in as they fetched the coffin.

As Samuel completed smoothing the man's clothing for the final time, he fancied a sensation in his middle. It was abrupt and alarming and a bit musical, like tiny men were moving a piano in his stomach.

"Pa-ha," he said.

Samuel burst out the side door with only enough time to regret his rushed snack of stale bread and cheese. The snack left him with another *pa-ha* and a splash.

He pulled his handkerchief and dabbed his eyes and mouth and then blew his nose with a tremendous honk. A chorus of laughter answered him and he looked too late toward the school. He had interrupted a hectic game of croquet, and the children whistled and waved as if he had scored a point in their game. He took a short bow and fled back into his shop.

Despite his detour, the team managed to have the body ready to meet his family at the train station with time to spare. The railroad would make an exception for picking up a deceased passenger ahead of its scheduled daily stop.

Samuel and Eggers drove the hearse. Helen walked home alone, pleased and looking forward to a nice bath of her own.

Mortician's work suited her infinitely more than nursing. As a bonus, there was no chance of killing the patient.

Chapter 23—Deception

It's too bad we'll miss the ceremony," said Samuel a bit wistfully as they drove back to the shop. "The Polish hymns are beautiful."

Eggers nodded. "I suppose it's not the same as the usual Irish nonsense."

"Yes, well," he replied. He reflected silently for a while on the things that constituted the usual Irish nonsense. "You know," Samuel continued, "the priest doesn't ever try to round me up. Suppose it's because of our accommodations?"

Eggers chuckled, "I don't think Father Kenneth would be keen on visiting a whorehouse, even on a mission. He has a hope of getting ahead, you know."

Samuel didn't think it was funny. Father Kenneth surely had no professional prospects if he was assigned to a tiny forgotten town. It seemed more likely to be punishment. "I have no patience for priests," said Samuel.

Eggers was surprised by this tiny burst of bitterness. "What's the matter? Did Mama steer you toward the seminary?"

"Oh yes," said Samuel, "My brother was to be the mogul and I was to be the spiritual talent." He sighed.

Somehow, this admission was a slight relief. He wondered if Eggers shouldn't have taken up taking confessions.

Eggers was truly interested and he asked him about his heretofore obscure brother. Samuel rarely mentioned his family at all.

Samuel told him about his older brother, his voice tight and his phrases abrupt. Matthew was frankly preferred by their father. He was quicker, stronger and even taller.

As a boy, Samuel sometimes had imagined that he preferred his brother to himself.

His mother had been the only member of the family that didn't make him feel that he was just a lesser echo of his brother, and once she was gone, the matter of his inferiority seemed settled.

His father had taken to calling him simply, "You there," which did not alleviate his sense of being the spare son.

Still, Samuel met the challenge with good humor, signing letters to his father with a "Yours truly, You There."

Samuel had struggled mightily with school work and would often complain to his father that he could not do it. This answer was never acceptable. His father would always say, "You mustn't say you can't do a thing, only say that you don't know how to do it *yet*."

All of his little family worked with Samuel in turn to develop him into a literate young man. His marks were never better than average, despite all the hours of effort.

His father quizzed him relentlessly during chores with math questions. "If a tree stands fifty feet, how many six-foot lengths does it have?"

With all this effort invested, his disappointment was very extreme when his father told Samuel that the family could not afford his further education at school.

Matthew was receiving very fancy legal training and Samuel had assumed that he would have his turn at higher education. What had all that tumult and frustration with school work been for otherwise?

Instead, when his father fell ill, Samuel began working in his place and he did so for years. His father secluded himself and was only physically capable of planning and bookkeeping, and sometimes even that proved too tasking.

Samuel's brother did not visit or contribute to their situation. Their father excused this reflexively—Matthew was building a practice, Matthew was handling vastly important legal matters, Matthew would become a very young partner in his firm at this rate. Any of these reasons would be propped up at the slightest provocation.

Meanwhile, their father's health declined and Samuel worked feverishly to make the most of the booming demand for the cabinet business.

His resentment wasn't jealousy, he insisted. He wanted good things for Matthew too. The resentment wasn't from working so diligently and so… solo. Hard work was a blessing.

The resentment came later, when their father died and Samuel discovered that his father was secretly a very wealthy man. The story that tuition was too expensive for Samuel's education had been a lie all along.

His face burned with stifled fury as his brother genially pointed out that the old man had never expected Samuel to learn to read, much less pursue higher education.

Samuel told Eggers that he could have traveled the world and could have studied at an esteemed university instead of burying himself in ten years of sawdust.

"Why not travel now? You could get your highway education or steam to Europe and range about the continent!" exclaimed Eggers.

"It's what I wanted, not what I want now," said Samuel matter-of-factly. He went quiet and then spoke again, "You understand, I'm sure. When you desire something feverishly it's not the same once you have it handed to you. All the luster is off.

"I am a sour-minded sinner on the subject, just the same." He sighed and then sneezed mightily, interrupting his somber reverie.

Eggers offered to buy him a drink. "Only if you're not drinking too," was the reply.

Chapter 24—Temptation

Samuel was beginning in earnest to consider moving to another house. With some regularity, the Countess began making morning appearances and he felt that it was specifically to interfere with him. This morning was one of those.

"Not all temptation leads to evil," she said to him rather than, "Good morning." Iris was drinking coffee and peering at him over the newspaper.

"Good morning," said Samuel, anyway. The Countess smiled.

"What's the bad news, Iris?" She poured herself a cup and offered Samuel another pour companionably.

Iris yawned and set down the paper, stretching like a lanky cat. "There was a murder spree in Constantinople and a man named Moe gunned down his wayward wife at a hotel. They called her a *wayward wife* without naming her. That wasn't in Constantinople, though. That was Chicago, I think."

Samuel found Iris intriguing, but intimidating. She was in some ways the most like the Countess out of all the girls. She had a real taste for her work, which wasn't unheard of, but her gusto was unusual.

Cherry had told him that newer girls generally had to be given some time to get command over their nerves, but she specifically mentioned Iris as a naturally gifted practitioner. "She really, truly enjoys it," she said, "and she doesn't get bored with the work, at least not yet."

The Countess was a bit disappointed, however. Iris had originally been part of a sister team that would have been an excellent novelty for their menu. Iris's sister was dismissed during the first week, because she failed the pickpocket test.

Once she was caught, she was swiftly put out of the house. She was given a little bit of money, enough to get far out of town, which the Countess considered a penalty for herself at having misjudged her. Along with the money, Iris' sister was given a small traveling case of essentials and that was that.

The Countess had very sternly questioned Iris if she would rather go with her sister, since their parting would be a condition of her employment.

The story was that Iris shrugged a bit sadly, but didn't honestly seem to be bothered to say goodbye. "She's an odd one, that's for certain," Cherry had said quietly.

Samuel thought he understood how that could happen. He mused that when those closest to us disappoint, it really deserves a completely different word.

Iris was looking at him again, frankly, blinking slowly at him rather than reading the paper now.

"Pardon," he said, "What did you say?"

The Countess leaned toward him, a bit touchily, "I said, there's a nice big room at Mary Crocker's that I think you should consider." She wasn't exactly making a request, he realized. "Now that you're in business, we don't want everyone to have to call here for the undertaker. They wouldn't like it and we don't need the fuss of mourners at all hours."

Samuel nodded solemnly.

"Don't worry," she continued, "You are welcome for breakfast in perpetuity."

He chuckled softly as she patted his hand with her offer of eternal breakfast. He was wondering how she read his mind, again.

Without even speaking to Mary Crocker in advance, he composed a note for the Countess, thanking her and assuring her that he'd be back for the rest of his things. Then he packed a little bag of essentials and left the place without fanfare, rather like a snatch-and-grabby whore.

Chapter 25—Moved

That same week, Helen quietly moved her things from the dress shop to a room at the Admiral's house. It was a relief to be away from Kate and into a house that was not full of nonsense. That wasn't precisely fair, but the Admiral's place had a different brand of nonsense.

She would keep working at the dress shop some mornings, but she wouldn't have to live there and contend with Kate's moody afternoons or her sons' bedtime rat-chasing antics.

The Admiral had several boarders already and he seemed content to accept whatever she wanted to pay. Possibly he was more interested in the company than the profit. His staff clearly adored him and created a warm and welcoming atmosphere.

Had his house been plucked up and re-planted a day south, scandal and uproar would have met the arrangement. Men and women of three races under one roof would have attracted terrible attention and retribution.

In wider society, thoughtful and educated people were debating quite frankly that measures of separation were necessary for everyone's safety. Why, if you had a house with black and white boarders, who would be presumed responsible when things went missing? Former slaves were hounded everywhere and should not be made to endure such a delicate situation, they said.

Helen viewed that as an insidious argument, although she would not explain further if pressed. It seemed to be from the same species of argument as saying women should be protected from independence and its responsibility. Many thoughtful articles decried the use of bicycles by women, too, along with the devastation caused by dancehalls.

Those writers would not have approved of her housemates. The residents included Fabian the musician, two young teachers from the school, Madame Grace the fortune teller, and usually

Thomas Jefferson. With the addition of Helen, the house had fewer white inhabitants than most of the old houses in town.

Mr. Jefferson was a great favorite of the Admiral's. Helen did not know his history, and so, during her first night, the other tenants told her the tale of his famous jailbreak. It was a treat to get good gossip that was completely new to her, even if it was a very old story.

Many years ago, Mr. Jefferson had been apprehended as a chicken thief. The frequency of missing chickens was plaguing homes all over town and he'd been seen fiddling with a coop and could not explain his activities. He also could not explain the cage in his hands.

The old jail where Mr. Jefferson was locked up was in terrible disrepair. Since the town had not had funds to maintain it, the structure had started on the path to dilapidation just as soon as it was built.

He was put in the crumbling jail to wait until the circuit judge came back to town to hear the evidence against him. The wait could have been weeks, but it was not. During the very first night, the outer wall fell away and Mr. Jefferson tumbled into the street.

He got up and nonchalantly walked away from the incident. The judge wasn't amused, but the less respectable citizens were charmed by the story.

Jefferson enjoyed the reputation of a beloved rascal and the image of him simply falling out of the old jail endeared him even more. In the end, the chicken owner declined to proceed with testimony and the legal case dissolved.

Unfortunately for Mr. Jefferson, he didn't have long to enjoy the freedom and notoriety of his jailbreak. Soon after, he was kicked in the head by a horse and thrown into a long coma.

When Jefferson awoke, he was quite changed. He spoke with a different accent and fancied himself a business man rather than a vagrant and petty thief. He would dress in a too-small suit and visited around town on "business."

At the bank, he had a desk where he was allowed to nap as long as no one else needed the chair, and the various shop keepers would slip little treats into his pockets while he was distracted with small talk.

He had become something of a living good luck charm for all of them and the Admiral in particular had taken a fancy to him and quietly paid his meager expenses.

Mr. Jefferson didn't always return home, and the assumption was the he lost his way and forgot where he was going when that happened. After so many nights of his non-appearance, like this one, the Admiral didn't fuss or worry.

Helen was sure she would like him, just as she liked her new housemates and she liked the new place. The Admiral gave her a long-winded but incomplete tour of the house and the grounds after dinner.

There was a broad patio out back and a kitchen garden. Beyond that was an arbor and a bench swing tucked into one lovely corner. A ragged stretch of re-grown woods extended beyond the yard, all the way to the railroad tracks.

***

On her first morning, Helen awoke to a cacophony of crows. Their calls frantically swirled all around the house, all around the town perhaps. It was a sure sign that autumn was landing at last.

She opened her window and placed the peg to hold it open, in spite of the noise and the chill. She saw the way the birds dotted and smeared every tree limb, like carelessly drawn musical notes. They could behave like this when signaling a predator, but she knew that this time the predator was the advancing, bitter winter weather.

Chapter 26—Moon

Helen and Samuel didn't realize that they had become neighbors until the Harvest Moon.

They had worked into the evening on a challenging charity case. The body that they had collected was that of a young woman who had been strangled and lay unclaimed at the city morgue.

Samuel would not give up on the idea that he was a complexion specialist and kept trying again and again to cover the bruising on the woman's neck with makeup.

Eggers became very impatient with him and finally stalked off, saying that no one was going to appreciate his Sistine Chapel and besides, they could finish the job in the morning.

Helen observed good-naturedly, wondering when he would realize that it was never going to have a natural-looking result. The marks were just too livid.

They had no knowledge of a family to present her to, but they would have photographs made for the morgue and the other authorities before she was buried, so Eggers was only mostly correct.

"Well, my dear," Helen said to the victim's body, "You have had our best efforts," and she gently pressed past Samuel to fold her own lace kerchief around the woman's neck.

He stepped back and made a small sigh of acceptance.

They transferred her tiny body into a cooling casket and determined that the evening air in the room was just chilly enough to leave it at that.

Without speaking, they washed up and hung their aprons, a bit somber about this latest case.

The rituals of putting the work area right were an important transition to leaving all traces of morbidity behind. Samuel typically took a moment to step outside and retch at the end of the day, but on this occasion he was calm of constitution and was not troubled by his tiny piano movers.

He hoped, in error, that he was finally past his nervous troubles. His funds were dwindling and he was vexed by midnight bouts of restless arithmetic, but he found it easy to put his upsets aside in agreeable company.

They stepped outside together, very ready to forget the day.

Helen was pleased to see that the sky was almost perfectly clear in the twilight. Looking east, they had a wondrous view of the rising full moon. It seemed to chase the fading pink light out of the sky.

Full moons were a delight, particularly for people who still did not have reliable electric lights, like the people of the Port.

With a full moon and a clear night, one could travel the side streets and fields without fear of getting lost or anonymously molested in the dark. People everywhere would be working at or reveling in their harvest, dancing by fires and drinking too much. Going to sleep would only ensure that a wayward friend would be banging on your door in the wee hours asking where you were and whether you had more mead.

Helen enjoyed watching the merriment, but she wasn't generally a participant. She suspected that Samuel was a watcher too.

They didn't say much as they made their way into the middle of town, where it was already getting noisy. When they passed the dress shop he hesitated and then followed a step behind her, eyebrows raised.

"Where?" he asked.

"I moved to the Admiral's place," she told him.

"We're neighbors!" he exclaimed with happiness. She smiled at his frank delight.

Samuel's new home was nestled in a group of houses and small shops, nearly all the way down the side street, while Helen's house stood across the street, proud and relatively solitary.

He had admired the steep roof and tall chimneys before and asked her if all the fireplaces were sound.

"I have no idea," she said, "but mine works, they say." Just keeping the wood supply for the large home was a significant job of housekeeping. It wasn't cold enough to light all of the fires yet, but it would be soon. "Would you like to see the garden?"

Samuel said that he would, but he really didn't have much interest in gardens. He merely had no wish to move on from this part of the day; he'd be content to delay parting as long as she would allow.

She pointed out the broad door at the back of the house that opened into the colonial kitchen and pantries. "They told me that this was an Underground Railroad station," she said. "Slaves could hide in the pantry or the barn or maybe some tunnels that are lost now. No one seems to know exactly what they're talking about."

They sat on the bench, swinging slowly and companionably.

"It's a good story," he said. "It would be a thrilling feeling to risk so much to rescue people. I like to think I would have done it."

She looked at him with a bit of appraisal, as if she was trying to decide if she believed him. He was certainly a Yankee by birth, but he seemed not to be strongly opinionated on the things that divided people. Race and class were not things that he mentioned in conversation. She suspected the omission was an effort to be polite.

Some men could ignore the subtle racial boundaries of life in the Port in a way that others could not afford. A person of color was compelled to be unobtrusive and expect less from every situation than a white man.

Women of every shade were pressed into their particular corners. Helen enjoyed a bit of protection from her social position as a Driscoll daughter, but she had her sharp memories of mistreatment, too. She wasn't willing to discuss any of that with Samuel.

"Why do you think our customer was strangled?" she asked.

"I was wondering about it too," answered Samuel. "They said she was found with no money or valuables."

Helen nodded, "But why murder her? She was so slight that I think that even I could have robbed her without any trouble at all."

"Maybe she resisted?"

"Pfft," Helen smiled a slight smile. "Resisted without getting another bruise? Or a scratch?" Looking at him sidelong she asked, "You know why he did it, really, don't you?"

"Because he could?" he offered, looking at his own long hands with a hint of borrowed shame.

"Maybe he just didn't want to pay her. Instead, he decided to take everything she had," She sighed, leaning back. "Everything."

Samuel felt a wave of disgust that matched hers. "Let's make sure the photograph is perfectly clear." He was becoming anxious to put the subject aside, and really, all that they could do for her now was to properly document her identity.

They sat long into the evening, content to exchange stories. Samuel learned that Helen had not taken a single official course in mortuary work, but had instead learned that and many other skills from friends while she was away at nursing school.

She didn't confide that some of those friends were lovers. It didn't seem necessary to tell him anything that specific.

In turn, she asked him what it was like at the Countess's place. He described the architecture. Helen began to laugh as he talked, and he couldn't understand why she found that so funny.

She waved off his inquiry. "Should we be worried about Mr. Eggers?" she asked, her mirth subsiding.

The last time they had attended a violent case, Eggers had been extremely emotional and needed stitches. A clear moonlit evening would give him ample opportunities to pick another fight.

"We should," Samuel replied, "We could also worry about supper while we check on him."

They set off for the tavern, enjoying all the mayhem along the way. From the street, there was the effect of a "Dutch Concert," and every instrument seemed to be playing a different tune. Someone sawed on a fiddle, while incompatible drum beats emanated from another direction and Fabian picked enthusiastically at his mandolin. Samuel thought it was all marvelous.

Revelers danced in and out of doorways, some with corn husk crowns and others with old fur hats and horns. Their stomping feet were in no way coordinated with any one tune. Horseshoes clanked, bells wrung and the erratic noises of the shooting gallery contributed to the auditory chaos.

When Samuel realized that Helen couldn't hear him, he swept his hand through her elbow and pulled her into the tavern to look for Eggers. Just as she was about to protest, he let go and shrugged an apology. She assumed that he wanted to touch her and just didn't know how to go about it properly.

Eggers wasn't there and Gannon said he hadn't seen him all day. They companionably piled in with a long table of diners and enjoyed some magnificent fried chicken along with boiled corn and potatoes.

Afterward, Samuel suggested that Eggers may have called on the Countess and asked Helen if she wouldn't mind walking with him there before he walked her home again. She shook her head as if to say no—but then she said that she could hardly decline getting a better look at the architecture.

She smiled at him then. Thrilled, he thought that there were not many things he would rather see than her gleaming smile.

They worked their way back through the crowd, and when they could converse again, Samuel told her that he had always wanted to see a Chinese Harvest Festival. The accounts in the newspapers were amazing; stories of dragon parades and rockets on balconies and sparks and even flames amidst the feet of the people roaming the streets.

"It makes our celebrations seem very tame," she said.

Helen supposed she shouldn't ask him, but she was very curious on a particular point that had nothing to do with architecture. "What do you think of the Countess?"

"I don't like to gossip and I'm bound to avoid gossip about her or her business," he said.

"Your opinion isn't gossip," Helen said matter-of-factly. "I'd like to know what you think."

He was quiet, considering how to answer.

He told Helen that Eggers had jokingly said to him that the Countess treated her staff like livestock and the comment took root in his mind.

He had been bothered to see that while she was generous, she was always handling them and wrangling them. Even though they lived together, the familial feelings were strictly amongst the girls.

He had asked her directly if she thought of them as cattle. She had said, of course.

"Even though you are also a woman?" he asked.

Clearly pleased by the question, she had said, "Yes, because I am a *business* woman." She went on to say that she nurtured and developed them and protected them, just as a farmer would mind her crops. The intention of selling them for the best price is the whole point.

Helen took in this information, nodding. "I think it's better to let your ideas direct your business than to let your business direct your ideas," she commented.

"I agree," said Samuel. "Who said that? Benjamin Franklin?"

"I believe that I just said it," she replied, amused.

Samuel was embarrassed into silence.

"It's important to have respect for the labor of other people," she said, "There can be real honor in all sorts of work."

Samuel scoffed, but he decided to test her idea. "Alright. Take Fabian—"

"Must I?" she asked with amusement. "Alright, let's take Fabian then," she went on agreeably. "He provides a valuable service to the girls and to their customers. It's not as if one can get condoms in the mail the way we get our tools."

"Oh," said Samuel, uncomfortably. Her lapses into frank nurse-like conversation always gave him a turn. "I didn't know that. They cannot be mailed?"

"No no, it's a Federal offense," she replied. "He is part of a network of messengers and merchants. I suppose it was intended to make them scarce or very expensive. Anyway, he does a respectable service for the disrespected. Quite an honorable thing, if you ask me."

They arrived at the house and she told him she would wait at the road while he checked for Eggers. He disappeared around the back and she felt suddenly quite uncomfortable and almost superstitious. The house seemed to be staring at her, but she knew that was foolishness and that the eyes she felt were certainly somewhere in the dark windows. She shivered a little, just the same.

The moonlight illuminated the drive and the yard, enough that it cast wide shadows in contrast to the silvery light. The dark spaces were what drew her eyes now.

Samuel appeared around the other side of the house and waved to her as he approached. She felt her face smile in response, unbidden, and she realized that in that instant she liked him more than she had imagined. Until that moment, she had considered his awkward attentions an irritant. Maybe the irritation could become more pleasant, she thought, and blushed in the dark.

"He's here," he said of Eggers, rejoining her at the road. "I hated to think he was out there sulking about the strangler all by himself."

"I'm glad we found him," she said.

They made their way back toward her new home and Samuel wished it was a longer trip. "Tell me about the Admiral," he suggested.

"I haven't spent very much time with him," she replied, "but he seems to inspire great affection and loyalty in people." She thought of the fortune teller, who rarely had anything kind to say about people but was warm and almost fawning with the Admiral.

"He tells astonishing stories about his time at sea, but really, I'm not sure that they are all exactly his stories."

"What do you mean?" asked Samuel.

"I'm sure I've read one of them in a book," she explained, "So maybe he's just confusing legends with his memories. My grandfather used to do that." She sighed, "Anyway, he likes to banter and tease, but no one really understands most of his jokes. At least, we suppose they're jokes because he laughs at himself so much."

"Does he claim to have hunted a white whale?" asked Samuel.

Helen laughed then, "I don't think so, but I'll be sure to ask him about whales very soon."

As they moved through town they saw that the revelers' numbers had swelled. The field workers were beginning to join in; the only duty they had left for the day was to celebrate that all their work was done.

Helen saw Kate. She was sitting on the steps of her shop talking to the fireman and adopting a flirtatious pose as she did so. Helen smiled to herself, feeling just a little bit sorry for the fireman.

When they returned to her walkway, she thanked Samuel for the company and he said, "My pleasure," in earnest reply. "It's very warm tonight," he observed, stalling. It wasn't truly warm, but the air felt oddly humid and unstable and the trees were still heavy from the earlier rain.

"Life in the swamp lands," she said casually turning toward him again. "Oh," she looked in the direction of his ear with concern and he pulled his chin back in alarm, thinking something must be crawling on him, unfelt. "Don't move…" she reached toward him and he felt warmer still.

Instead of rescuing him from a stray insect, she pulled hard on a small skewed branch, creating a tiny rainstorm on them both.

He squawked and she turned away, skipping to her door, laughing over her shoulder. "That's better, isn't it?"

He grinned at her retreating figure.

Everything was better.

Chapter 27—Lovers

A woman who has one lover is an angel, a woman who has two lovers is a monster, and a woman who has three lovers is a woman – Attributed to Victor Hugo, who learned this actress's proverb from his lover, Juliette Drouet

Helen had three lovers in her two years away at school, but her mortuary student was the one she had most admired. All three of her young men were pretty and socially advantaged beyond anything she had ever imagined, but he, he behaved as if rules were for other people.

He wooed her relentlessly, popping up when she left a classroom and then delivering her little gifts a bit too late in the evening. As a stranger in a novel town, she didn't fret about being seen walking alone with him. Instead, she basked in the attention, amused by the show.

He had taken her to the morgue where they practiced, and she experimented there too. She liked the cool of the mortuary space and its modern trappings. It had none of the urgency of a crowded operating theatre. Even the echoes in the place were austere.

Those visits were by far the riskiest pastime that they shared. He wasn't bothered, but simply confident that while other students would never dare such a thing, he would do as he pleased with no trouble.

His flouting of caution appealed to Helen, but she worried that he would not only steer her into danger, but that she might find herself in some peril entirely unintentionally.

She preferred to appraise things and decide on risks for herself. This beau refused to understand that, even a little bit.

"Surprises are good for you," he would say. She was not convinced. He kept saying it, anyway.

He boasted that he did not drink or smoke or chew, although he helped himself to chloroform, she knew. She did not know he dallied with other numbing agents that would eventually cause him great pain.

Helen allowed him to visit in her room when her roommate was away. It wasn't much of a feat for him to enter through the large ground-floor window, but it was a thrilling deviance for her.

She grilled him with questions about *rigor mortis* when he demurred and said he was not going to answer her questions any longer.

His breath was hot and rapid, and as he moved her hand to his own example of rigor, she was certain it was pulsating like a living being, quite on its own. What should have been frighteningly unfamiliar was instead fascinating to her.

It was just the sort of surprise she should have expected from him.

She felt later that she had misjudged his appetite, and that she should have foreseen that afterward he would leave her aching and jumbled.

In the moment, she was caught up in her own desire. For the first time, she felt the madness of a kind of passion that risks everything. No thought of reputation or danger, no fear or guilt would stand against the hunger she felt for him in that moment.

Helen confided to her sister later that she felt she had been infected by a kind of fever. It didn't make her feel more like an adult, she told Fannie, but she felt more powerful. She could make crazy things happen if she wanted to and she might want to do that again sometime.

Fannie just nodded, thoroughly appalled.

Chapter 28—Photographs

In the late morning, Hops arrived with his gear to photograph their unidentified client and Samuel helped him to wrangle his tripod into the entry.

Hops was usually resentful about people's attempts to help him, but he liked Samuel and accepted the assistance without a fuss. For his part, Samuel was impressed that Hops could get around so efficiently and accomplish so much.

In some ways, he had a lot in common with Eggers, and they both would deny their similarity with equal strenuousness. Hops was always in motion, restlessly working at deliveries or photographs or tending to his pocket watch collection. Hops had at least one broken pocket watch to commemorate every disaster he had ever witnessed, and several more for remote tragedies.

"It's very good of you to go to this much trouble," Samuel said.

"Not at all," replied Hops. "My only trouble is that I'll get behind on the mail, but there's no alternative. We need this good light to get a good photograph." He looked around the shop, appraising. "We should set up by that window."

They walked around the shop, deliberating a bit more about the setting and Hops told Samuel without a hint of humor that dead subjects were the best models.

His photography device was an older type. It wasn't as fussy as a daguerreotype, which had required subjects to remain motionless for minutes. Even so, he'd had problems with fidgety portraits and blurring.

Memorial photos might try to imitate life, but they had no need for such pretense with this woman. This was strictly record-keeping. No one knew who she had been in life, and possibly no one from her family would ever know what had become of her.

A coffin photo would be adequate, although they agreed it was important to make it dignified and for it to be set apart from some front page gunslinger photograph.

In the end, they tipped her coffin and Samuel held an arm across to keep her in place. Hops handed him a white reflector to eliminate shadows. Samuel struggled to manipulate the reflector with his weak hand while protectively bracing the body and silently cursed Eggers for gallivanting.

The exposure was quicker than he recalled but Hops assured him it would be fine. He asked Samuel to turn her slightly so that he could get a picture of her ear as well. He didn't think her profile was particularly distinctive, but ears were considered excellent identifiers by the police who kept up with modern methods.

Hops said he would need to get back to his work and should have the pictures ready within a week. He promised to try to do it very soon.

He waived away any discussion of cost, pointing out that he was just an amateur after all. It wasn't like he would use crayons or any fancy extras, he said.

When the photo was done, it was a small but enduring advertisement with a caption that read, "Jane Doe, Washington D.C., slain October 2, 1895. H. Tyler Photographer."

Chapter 29—Burial

Helen and Eggers walked behind the hearse as Samuel set out to deliver Jane Doe to the edge of the Methodist cemetery.

The Methodists could be counted on to donate a grave now and then, and they had plenty of space. It was much more convenient than going back across the river to the city's so-called pauper's field.

As they reached the cross roads, something peculiar happened. A few of the hotel girls began to file in behind them. They walked behind Helen and Eggers, not speaking. The sounds of the gear and hoof falls of the horses mingled with the swishing of a great deal of fabric.

This late in the morning, one would expect to see people in the street but no one else was evident. Curtains were drawn and the street was otherwise deserted and turned away from the procession. Eggers was unnerved and felt the flesh on his neck twinge in reaction to the eeriness of the scene.

At the next intersection, most of the gals from the Countess's house waited, whispering amongst themselves and shivering; the Countess, the housekeeper and Iris were absent.

They joined the procession silently and Helen shivered too, but not from the cold.

Finally, Fabian and the fortune teller joined them.

Fabian played the melody of a Purcell funeral march. It was intended for a quartet of horns, but he managed to make it very lovely and dignified with just the one horn. He had to stop playing a few times to catch his breath. Samuel thought the pauses made it more regal.

They passed the church and marched on around the cemetery to the far side.

Only four of them were needed to place the modest coffin beside the grave. It looked tiny opposite the mound of damp earth.

They circled the grave and waited, while the horses were sighing and anxiously nickering in waiting.

Reverend Price strode out to meet them, very surprised to see the number of impromptu mourners. Most of the professional women, who he would refer to as *nymphs*, were unknown to him. Even without their acquaintance, he was comfortable concluding they could all use a bit more Jesus.

He wouldn't normally be there for a minor anonymous service, but his junior attendant was away at a convention of colored divines and he was the only person available.

Awkwardly, he cleared his throat and recited a short prayer. After a long pause, he began to sermonize a little about the life and wages of sin. Sensing that his audience was not appreciative of the gentle scolding he was lapsing toward, the Reverend halted.

He said, more conversationally, "You know, according to the Dominican order, Mary Magdalen was called by Jesus from sinner to saint, and such a miraculous transformation is a beacon to all women-"

Eggers interrupted and stepped forward to shake the Reverend's hand vigorously, "Thank you so much for officiating, Reverend Price, we know you are very busy with your regular duties." He steered the minister away from the graveside and walked him a short distance toward the stone church. The entire group sighed with relief, especially the Reverend.

Helen asked if anyone else had anything to say. Did anyone know her at all?

"We all know her, even though we don't know her and we don't have her name," said Myrtle, quietly. They all nodded. Her life was familiar to them, and that was why they were in attendance. The idea that she would pass on without observance was unbearably sad.

Fabian stepped forward and said simply, "Me mother was a whore, so I 'as told. Don't know more than that about 'er."

Juniper placed a bunch of heather on the plain coffin, and resting her hand on the cool wood she said, "Bon voyage, little flower." The others muttered farewells and at least one "Amen" was said.

The fortune teller pulled a coin from her bag and pointedly put it into the Reverend's hand. He wordlessly made his escape. The horses shifted, sensing that it might be time to move on soon. They didn't mind the cemetery, but they didn't care for the sadness.

As the girls walked on, Myrtle reached to Juniper and clasped her hand as they walked. Their murmured discussions moved away.

Samuel circled the deep grave and walked over to the workers who had dug the hole. They would need to be paid, too.

The diggers were possibly somber or maybe just patient about getting on with the work of finishing the burial. They stood with Samuel and watched as Eggers and Helen drove the hearse away and the parade began to reverse itself.

"Mighty fine coffin you did there," said one.

"Thank you," said Samuel, affably. He reached over to brush a fallen leaf from the short edge of the coffin. As he did so, he had only the briefest moment to show surprise at his error. He popped upright, his mouth formed a tiny circle and his arms clapped to his sides, offering no practical help before the ground gave way and skidded him into the grave, feet first.

"Lordy, fetch the straps!" exclaimed the second man, "You've kilt the undertaker!"

The parade stopped to spectate as the first man peered clinically down at Samuel. "I say he's not even half killed. He looks alright." Samuel looked up at him with a dazed expression and the man began to laugh more and more fully with the recognition. His enjoyment of Samuel's distress would only grow in the retelling of the scene. To Samuel he said, "If you're done your inspection, sir, would you care to join us up here on the lawn?"

The men pulled Samuel out of the grave. His black suit was mostly brown with mud. Other than a crushed hat and the echo of all the future jokes at his expense, he was unharmed.

"Mighty fine digging you did there!" Samuel said cordially as he swiped at his dirty trousers.

***

The afternoon party at the tavern caused quite a stir. It was unheard of to have so many *nymphs du pave* assembled off-duty and aggravated.

"The trollops baint so pleasant in themselves," commented the bartender glumly.

Conrad kept watch over the herd, since the Countess allowed their little mutiny, but did not wish it to go on unsupervised. The undertaking crew was not in attendance, but Fabian and the fortune teller tagged along to the tavern; Fabian because he fancied a drink, the fortune teller because Fabian fancied a drink.

Madame Grace did not imbibe, but she would occasionally keep a vigil for her fellows. She remembered how wild and belligerent Fabian could become when he lost his teeth and she intended to get him home with all his accessories intact.

She sat with complete composure, but would occasionally adjust the position of her rings, unnecessarily. No one could guess that she enjoyed this variation from her routine as much as she did.

"Will the police chase them off, do you think?" Fabian asked her, referring to the harlots.

"No," said Grace, definitively.

"Are your prophesies always correct?"

"No," said Grace, with a smile. "But I would venture this one is. The big fellow will have them out of here beforehand." She nodded toward Conrad.

The trollops toasted each other more merrily and feasted without concern for the thoughts of the onlookers or the potential of meeting the police. As Grace had predicted, they moved along after their meal, just like regular patrons.

Most people in town were amused by the story of the clumsy adventures of the Keegan fellow, but they disagreed about the meaning of the funeral parade. Some were bitter about the procession, and expressed annoyance that some little nobody had a larger funeral parade than they could ever expect for themselves.

Others had taken notice of Helen and that she walked at the front of the parade, like a dignitary. She was obviously in charge of the funeral business now, they said. That awkward chap would do well to let her get him in hand.

Whatever their interpretation, everyone agreed it was best not to mention the affair to Daddy Driscoll.

Chapter 30—Visible

Helen was relieved and surprised that apparently no one had related her part of the events of the Jane Doe funeral to her father, at least not yet. For a town that was fueled by gossip, this was an astonishingly sensible secret to keep.

Her grandma Gertie was aware, but all she said when she saw Helen at church was her standard warning, "Don't get into any trouble," which was her well-worn shorthand for "Don't get pregnant," or occasionally the more emphatic, "Don't ever have any children."

Gertie was small like Helen but twice as fierce. When she was younger, Helen longed for a gentle grandmother who would hug her and braid her hair. What she got was a hardened and unsentimental grandmother who did not tolerate nonsense from other people.

At the age of eighty, Gertie was in full possession of a brilliant mind. She was merciless with people, calling out inconsistencies to the point of being rude; and she seemed to remember everything she had ever seen or heard with supernatural clarity. While these attributes might make her obnoxious to the uninitiated, people who knew her over time found a great deal in her to appreciate.

Gertie's laugh was large and warm, revealing her largely hidden generosity of spirit. She cogitated at length about the problems that plagued her loved ones, and she would employ her genius to finding unexpected answers. When she bestowed an elegant solution, she would be dismissive of any gratitude or fuss. What else was she supposed to do but provide her best guidance?

Helen's grandfather died when Helen was a teenager. Deep mourning would not be the correct description of Gertie's demeanor. She did seem sad to Helen, but she doggedly maintained all her rituals and routines, and more than anything Gertie seemed annoyed by the whole thing.

Her husband had been absent for many years, and he rarely visited home after their son was able to take over running the farm. Helen had only vague memories of him and the way he seemed to blow into their lives and out again, like a summer storm.

One afternoon as Gertie and Helen were poking around at the creek side, looking for jewel weed, Helen had the courage to ask Gertie about him. No one ever spoke of him around her grandmother, but Helen hoped that, now that he was dead, there could be less mystery.

"Where did he go?" she asked her grandmother.

Gertie knew who she meant. "Oh, after your father took over, he went off to pursue his first love," she replied with a whiff of irritation in her voice.

"The sea?" suggested Helen, stopping to study Gertie's reaction.

"Gambling," said Gertie, with a snort. "He got all my money and now he's left what's left to your father," she sighed, "Pretty presumptuous for a guano merchant."

"He wasn't a pirate?" asked Helen.

"No, of course not."

He had enjoyed the mystique of a retired pirate, but Gertie wasn't going to let that seep into the family legends any longer. She had another legacy in mind.

She often told Helen to never marry. Her warning amplified the one Helen's mother had given her, years ago. "You may never inherit as it is," said Gertie, "but if you do, and you are married, it won't matter. Don't impoverish yourself with a husband."

Gertie told Helen more on that day than she had ever heard on the subjects of Jamaica and the speedy romance that had delivered Gertie and her money to Maryland.

Helen's curiosity had never been so well rewarded by Gertie. "You never talk about the old times. What was he like when you met him?" Helen asked.

Gertie stopped and seemed to come to a decision about something before she spoke again. "He was a fine-looking man and he had a gentle way of attending to me." She looked at Helen then and seemed to disapprove of her expression. "Now you know there's nothing a man likes better than a woman who likes him and doesn't demand very much of him. I wasn't hardly at all as smart as I thought I was." Her tone was becoming gruff, but the she softened a little again. "I remember waiting to see him all day and feeling as if I was waiting for the most momentous thing, like expecting a sunrise. Or maybe an earthquake. At any rate, it was a boatload of bosh."

Helen pouted a little at this and tried to pry more out of her grandmother. "He courted you for a long time?"

"Oh yes, he had everyone bamboozled. He would bring me wilted roses he had probably stolen from someone's garbage and carry on about how they must have faded from being near my beauty." Gertie chuckled then, surprising Helen. "He did make me laugh like no one else.

"My father was easily won over. They gambled together, you see, and he always let my father get the better of him. As soon as he began to view him as a son, it was the most natural match anyone had ever seen."

"Us, I mean," she added.

Gertie stopped again. Although she didn't seem to be brooding, she seemed unwilling to continue the tale and Helen prodded her again. "How did you learn he was a faker?"

"Oh that was a fast discovery after the wedding," Gertie sighed. "He started ordering me about and all his nice manners vanished. We were sailing north, to come here, and he spent the whole voyage attacking my beaches. The crew thought it was very amusing, all his grabbing and pushing. I heard them joke he was likely to mount me on the rail while I was seasick." She looked at Helen again, with a stern expression. "There isn't anything less funny, is there? At any rate, that was the beginning of a terrible disillusionment."

Helen felt tears stinging the back of her eyes. "Oh, grandma!"

"Pfft!" Gertie said. "That's ancient history. He's dead and gone and I'm here with you. He has done all the damage he can and he can do no more.

"That's why I tell you not to marry, of course. And if you must marry a man, don't take an interest and don't read his diary."

Helen didn't want to know more about him now. Her thoughts were of a version of young Gertie that was difficult to comprehend. "It's odd to imagine you being foolishly in love like that."

"Well, I was," she replied straightening her shoulders sternly, "Besides, whatever gave you the idea that you ever knew everything about me?"

"You'll use up all your 'evers,'" Helen said, smiling. Gertie smiled back, and gave up the scolding to concentrate on their foraging.

Helen would never repeat Gertie's story. She felt a possessiveness about it, as if it were her own bespoke fairy tale. She felt a kinship of a greater sort for this little woman, along with a trust that followed it, naturally as light came from a flame.

And now, Helen was discovered to be working with men and dead bodies. Helen believed that her grandmother wouldn't spread the word about her new situation to the rest of the family. She knew, even so, it was only a matter of time before she was found out and would be faced with at least one very difficult conversation.

Chapter 31—Visitors

The next Tuesday morning, Helen saw that the rain had washed away nearly all the leaves from the trees overnight. Only a smattering of golden maples held tight to their foliage and the fog curled around as if determined to take them away too. The sudden change was both eerie and magical.

She settled in to work on some bunting. It was serviceable as it was, but Helen had found some gold-colored ribbon that she thought would add some austere contrast to the black. Over the weeks, she had generated enough drapery to convert a large parlor into a funeral parlor.

They hadn't used any of that handiwork yet, and as she continued to make it more lavish, Samuel had commented that it was well on its way to being fit for a monarch.

Helen wasn't reserving it for a dignitary; no one could remember the last time a notable person had visited the Port openly, anyway. People of note, quite literally, would never be caught dead in the Port.

Eggers arrived earlier than usual, since he was avoiding the Countess for the time being.

He recounted to them that the Countess was very unfairly put out at the mess she believed he had created with her hens. That morning, the housekeeper, Dora, had stopped in during breakfast to ask him what he thought was the matter with the hens, or rather to tell him what she thought was the matter with the hens.

"They don't like your contraption, Mr. Eggers," Dora said, "They haven't laid for four days, since you moved all the boxes around and put that chute up."

"Nonsense," grumbled Eggers as he pushed back from the table and set off for the yard with a wealth of purpose in his gait.

He found the chute still attached to the side of the coop, and he wiggled it to verify that it was connected securely overhead. Hens could be eccentric about laying in new places or onto new materials. He aligned his mind that Dora should have searched through the straw on the ground before bothering him about such trifles. Surely the eggs would be there, if they were anywhere. As he shuffled in the straw, he further aggravated himself with thoughts of how inconsiderate lazy people could be. He was still hungry! She had interrupted him eating his eggs to look for other, less important eggs. Ridiculous!

His shoes would be hers to clean, he decided. He rolled up his sleeve, muttering about his grievances and reached into the nearest nesting bin and groped overhead to see if any eggs were there. The chute was supposed to make such fumbling unnecessary, he thought bitterly and he reached into the thin straw. He moved to the next bin and reached in. It was not a success. An explosion of flapping, angry cackling and sharp pecking at his hands were his reward.

"Back you devils!" he shouted at the indignant chickens. "You should be up and about with the rest of them!"

He went back around to the outside and thumped the chute again. It abruptly detached from the roost and crashed down to the ground with approximately two dozen eggs in pursuit.

"The hens got very excited and ate all the eggs," he told Samuel. "Vexatious cannibals!"

Samuel covered his smile with his hand and merely acknowledged him with "Mm-hmm."

Before midday, Eggers, Helen and Samuel received a surprise delivery. Until now, they had only collected bodies from the city morgue for their cut-rate services and practice. Having a body delivered to their doorstep was something they should have been prepared for, but certainly were not.

A farmer brought them a body that he'd fished out of the river. He explained that he had been looking for his best milk cow and had spotted this body at the riverbank.

"Still haven't found my cow," he remarked, dryly. "Suppose this fella here is an oyster pirate."

Eggers scoffed. "Unlikely," he said, "Whoever would mess about with oysters up here?"

It was a sad fact that, along with its many other former virtues, the river had once been an excellent home for oysters. Now, between the heavy silt and the city's decision to drain all its storm water and municipal sludge into this poorer-side waterway, any oyster found there was likely to run away on three legs.

There were reports of oysterman mischief in the area, however, and it was not inconceivable that this fellow could have run afoul of oyster pirates. Armed conflicts occurred with regularity between the pirates, the authorities and territorial oysterman who were trying to protect their own oyster beds from the thieves.

"Why did you bring him here?" asked Samuel, immediately regretting the silly question, but not fast enough to stop himself from asking it.

"Well, you're the closest on this side of the river, aren't you?" came the reply.

Eggers and Samuel rolled the body onto a stretcher, with difficulty. Despite the squelching noises and tremendous stench, Helen stepped forward to offer assistance and the farmer objected sharply, "Kenneth!" he shouted to his helper, "Don't you dare let that gal hoist this man!"

Kenneth hopped between Helen and the stretcher amiably as she cut her eyes at the farmer. She was offended. *That gal*.

The farmer continued, addressing her, "I don't want you to hurt yourself, Miss Driscoll."

She was still offended, but she let it go.

"Perhaps I can be of assistance," said a new voice. A tall gentleman had appeared unnoticed in the tumult. He looked to Helen like a medical man. He stepped up and took a stretcher handle and the four men wrestled the body into the shop and then onto the table.

The farmer tipped his hat and drove away the instant Kenneth rejoined him. He was off, presumably, to resume the search for his wayward cow.

They regarded their new client with dismay. This man may have been shot, stabbed or strangled, but his body was so discolored and bloated that it was difficult to say what exactly had happened before he spent many hours getting waterlogged.

As to their live visitor, Helen had guessed correctly that he was a medical man. He told them that his name was Anton Cook, although he pronounced it *Eendawn Kook*. His accent was quite distinct, even after many years in America.

It took a long sideways conversation before Samuel could wrestle the nature of his visit from Professor Doctor Cook. As they talked, Cook wandered about in a manner that suggested he had stopped there to examine the premises. The inspection was making Helen just a little nervous, although if anyone had asked, she could not have said precisely why.

He leafed through their copy of the *Tabulae Anatomicae* handling the old volume with proper gentleness. "Who reads Italian?" he asked.

"I do," said Eggers and Helen in unison.

"Excellent," remarked Cook.

Finally, Professor Doctor Cook said, "Finding donations for a medical school is terribly difficult these days." He sighed, replacing the anatomical textbook precisely where it had been on the shelf. "One must travel farther and farther if the local, eh, resources are, eh, competitively sought." Helen understood he was asking for bodies without ever using the word.

He went on to lament the shortage further, and said he was sure that they, when they had been trainees, had had the benefit of real body parts for technical instruction. He said he was happy to have met them and would continue on his quest.

This was how he discreetly let them know he was "in the market," while preparing to leave the shop.

Eggers blurted, "You can take our oyster pirate right now for free!" Eggers was enchanted by the entire thing and was not about to let Cook make a clean getaway.

"Ridiculous!" exclaimed Helen. "You know we can't do that."

Professor Doctor Cook smiled down at her, approvingly. "Of course, you have a duty to deliver it to the authorities."

"Just so," said Samuel, and he led Cook toward the exit, thanking him for the visit, without suggesting he return another time.

Unlike Eggers, Samuel was not charmed by the man or by the distinctly unusual experience of socializing with a doctor who seemed friendly and even admiring of their occupation. But then, neither did he have Eggers' experience of doctors who assumed morticians were all failed medical students with macabre minds.

Eggers hurried out close behind the doctor, saying he would fetch a new load of ice, posthaste.

As Samuel came back into the embalming room he was struck again by the reek of the body. It amazed him how quickly the worst stench could stop troubling him, but as soon as he'd had some fresh air he had to acclimate himself all over again.

This body really was the worst so far.

The idea of having all his facilities in one building suddenly seemed like the greatest folly of all his many foolish decisions. He hadn't considered he would have such a ripe customer simply dropped at his doorstep. How would he receive another local patron in this situation?

Helen went to the office and drew a sign that read, "Temporarily Closed for Improvements."

Chapter 32—Duplicity

Samuel and Helen sat outside awaiting Eggers as they had no better idea. They had already sent for LaFevre, and there was nothing else to do but wait.

"He's going to try to find a way to make this man the city's problem," Samuel speculated. Helen nodded.

"Why didn't you go to mortuary school?" she asked him. She had wondered about this before a few times, and now she was reminded to ask.

"I've had enough of schools," he said, "by staying away, I have probably spared some poor mortuary school a terrible fate."

Helen looked at him, quizzically.

"The first time I went to school, they told my father that I was possibly an idiot." Helen sucked her teeth in sympathy. "Of course, that's not in doubt any longer." He chuckled at his own modesty.

Helen found this habit of his irritating. "What happened the second time you went to school?" she asked.

"The school burned down," he replied, and when she looked skeptical, he added, "Truly."

He explained, the man who cleaned up the school was smoking, or maybe drunk and smoking. "At any rate, he escaped the flames, but the building was destroyed and we didn't go to school for a year.

"That man was my personal angel," he continued. Helen laughed. "Unfortunately, my father thought that I should still have instruction and he tried to teach me.

"When I would mix up my letters he would give me a whack on my arm."

"Oh," said Helen, feeling a bit sorry for Little Samuel.

"It was well deserved and it worked eventually, I suppose," he said, "I don't know why, but I needed so much time to do my work." She knew this, having seen him concentrate mightily to write even short notes. She guessed working any figures on paper was probably just as much labor for him, if not more. He seemed to avoid writing implements in general.

"What about the third time you went to school?" she asked, smiling.

"Oh, if you mean the third school, by then I was interested in the theater," he said and seemed embarrassed to say so.

"What fun!" she said, "I never had the chance to do that; no bands or troupes for me."

"It was fun, great fun," he said more casually. "It's a wonderful place to shake off your cares. I thoroughly enjoyed it. Until the director told me I was rotten."

"Oh dear," Helen said, trying not to mock him with her tone. He couldn't know her ideas of a difficult school.

"He said that I was a dreadful liar, the worst he'd ever encountered, and that to be a genuine actor, one has to be capable of complete and confident falsehood."

"I don't support that," Helen said, "When I saw plays, I didn't *believe* any of it. It's like a puppet show with big puppets."

"No, no. A truly talented actor could be... this tree right here and you'd sit on him, unawares that he was not, in fact, a tree."

Helen stared back at him, her lips open, a smile dancing around their edges. After a moment, they both laughed companionably.

"I will help you," Helen said at last. "I will tell you lies and you shall tell me lies. We'll practice so that you can learn how to lie when you need it. Sooner or later you will need a good lie, if only to be social."

Samuel considered, "I appreciate the offer, but what do you mean? False compliments?"

"No no. Flattery makes mediocrity, I always say. And complete honesty can be a complete obstacle to kindness, of course," she said, pausing to pick an example. "Sometimes a lie can be more useful than the truth, particularly with the out-of-towners. When I was at the fruit wagon with Melvina, a stranger said to her, 'You must just love the watermelons,' assuming, because she's colored."

Samuel rolled his eyes, but stayed silent.

"Now this stranger was a dunderhead, of course, but she was a friendly dunderhead and Melvina had a chance to edify her. So even though she adores watermelon, and I know that is true, she answered that she only ate it to be polite."

"Excellent!" Samuel said and then sighed. "The trouble is, I do not want to lie," he said it as earnestly as he could.

"That's a lie," she said, firmly.

"This is going to take an eternity."

Helen nodded.

Chapter 33—Bargain

Eggers, who had no difficulty with lying in multiple languages, caught up the Professor Doctor before he reached the crossroads. He wanted to know how much a body was worth these days. Also, he inquired about the cash value of, say, a single adult leg or torso. Did they have particular needs as to the sex or race of the legs?

Cook maintained an odd, third-person way of discussing the details, but in the end, they came to a mutually satisfactory agreement. They would do a little trade that would benefit many eager students and harm not one living soul.

When Eggers returned with the cart of ice, Helen and Samuel were still milling around outdoors, exiled by the terrible smells.

Prior to the boom in their craft, funerals had been very speedy to avoid this very situation. The only thing worse than the presence of active rot would be the anguish of the beloved enduring it. This sort of reek was beyond description and indelible. Once smelled, no one would fail to recognize it when they smelled it again.

To Samuel's dismay, a flock of turkey vultures had detected the scent and were loitering. Most were beginning to roost on the roof while a few circled high in the sky, signaling to others that they found a target.

"This is terrible," he said for the fifteenth time.

They wrapped their unlikely pirate in a triple layer of oilcloth and put him on ice, still awaiting the policeman, LaFevre.

Even an entirely modern police force wouldn't do more than a series of measurements for identification, an examination and some photographs. LaFevre would use his resources to avoid doing any of this work. In consensus, the undertaking team believed the less he did the better; he was not qualified to operate a ruler, even when he was sober.

Patrick, the messenger, stopped by and Samuel asked him to give Sutton a message for the morgue. Sutton was to call the morgue and let them know the Port was in possession of a river body that was unclaimed and unknown.

They agreed that the fellow's own parents wouldn't know him in that state, but possibly when dried out he might become recognizable.

"He's not going to dry properly, all wrapped up," Helen commented.

Once more, Samuel said, "This is terrible."

LaFevre arrived a few hours later. He appeared to be sober, but he was in a dark mood. He complained he had a toothache and was half blind with the pain. This may have accounted for his apparent sobriety; the pain was cancelling out his efforts to dull it. After this, he was going directly to "the Chinaman," he said, referring to the most storied city dentist.

"Do you want to see the body?" Samuel asked, half-heartedly. He didn't think there was much point, and it would be an exhausting effort for the tired crew.

"No need," said LaFevre, "No one is missing around here in the vicinity, so we just need to photograph the body and plant it." He let out a low, gravelly groan as he rubbed his jaw. "No papers on him, I suppose…"

"Nothing at all; no tools, no money and no shoes," answered Eggers. "If the city coroner wants him, shall we let him go?"

"Absolutely," replied LaFevre. "I will nah object to that."

He was a pitiable figure on his best days, but today LaFevre was the embodiment of torment and dread. Samuel asked him about the Chinaman and where exactly his place of business was located.

"He has a dental parlor in a shoe store," said LaFevre. "They say the place is very clean, not private, and most important, he gives cocaine and gas."

He breathed as if the air itself was an irritation. "I don't care if he has to pull seven teeth if it stops this devilment."

Helen handed him an icy compress and his fleshy eyebrows drooped a bit further as he accepted it.

"We'll get their measurements of the body for you, but it won't be until tomorrow," she said.

LaFevre nodded, "I don't plan to die of this," he said, "but save me a pine box, just in case." He handed her a five-dollar silver certificate and was on his way.

"How pessimistic," Helen said, handing the bill to Samuel.

He smiled at his first pre-paid coffin fee. "And it's not enough to cover the grave. If we can't bury him, do you suppose we should keep him around for a specimen?"

"He might keep the vultures away," suggested Eggers.

As the light of the day faded, the morgue sent an ambulance carriage and collected their river man. Everyone was very relieved.

The morgue wasn't under official obligation to take him since he wasn't found in their jurisdiction, but they knew what a problem this body presented to the tiny operation.

In the previous months, Eggers, Helen and Samuel had taken half a dozen bodies off of their hands, so it seemed only fair to the coroner to claim an occasional stinker.

Eggers begged a ride with the ambulance, mumbling that he needed to see about a friend in the city.

They didn't see him again for two days.

Chapter 34—December

Helen stepped out of the house and stopped, listening. The sky rapidly filled with migrating birds. As their chattering amongst themselves grew louder, she waited and stared, their numbers so amazed her. She strained to identify them, but they were very high and were too small and indistinct. There had to be thousands of tiny birds in the flight. After several minutes, the cloud dwindled, but she remained transfixed, watching for the end of the flock.

She felt it was important to see the very last bird to completely witness them all.

There wasn't exactly one last bird at the rear, however. A group of four vied and struggled for position. None of the four were in the vulnerable last spot for more than a few seconds as they braided their way along.

Considering this, she made her way through the alley to the busy main street. She caught sight of Samuel talking to the man who owned the shooting gallery. He often did this while pretending not to wait for her in the mornings.

As she picked her steps carefully, she felt more than heard a sudden pop. Her vision swam and she staggered a few steps before collecting herself in an unsteady equilibrium. She felt warmth spreading down her neck and was only mildly surprised to see blood on her hand as she pulled it back away from her face.

Samuel rushed toward her; he caught her elbow and pressed a handkerchief to her bloodied lip.

"Murder!" shrieked Emma, the shooting gallery mistress.

"Do be quiet, will you," hissed Emma's lover sternly, as Samuel guided Helen toward the tavern.

Any swooning inclination Helen might have felt was obliterated by her annoyance with Samuel. She objected physically to his help, trying to twist away and mumbling through the cloth, "Ah cah wah."

"I know you can walk. Please. Just allow me to help," he replied.

The crowd parted to let them pass quickly into the tavern and he sat her down at a table in the middle of the dining room. Most of the tables had been pushed aside for cleaning the floor in the wee hours and hadn't been put back into position yet.

He looked at her injured face with a worried expression on his own. Her lower lip was split, not too deeply, but badly enough that the bleeding was very impressive. Her clothes were already gory and sticky.

"Well, you are not shot," he said, his voice filled with relief.

"Thcooth ee," she said and spat a piece of a tooth into her hand. She examined it and felt reassured to see that it was quite tiny. It had felt like half her tooth had been broken until she could see it.

The curious passers-by had pressed into the tavern with them and ringed her seat, asking what happened and who had seen it in a rising hubbub of cross discussions.

The barman provided a bowl of water and some cloths. She flinched away as Samuel tried to dab at her face and she took charge of her own nursing instead. It was obvious that the bleeding wasn't slowing very much yet, and she motioned to Samuel to pull a chair over so that she could lie back a bit and hold her lip until the bleeding slowed. She pulled off her hat and handed it to Samuel.

Black spots ringed her vision and she fainted as she put her head back. The blood was just a bit too much for comfort. The sound of her brother's voice roused her almost immediately.

"Helen, good God," he said, pressing into the room. "What have you done?" She raised her hand and eyed him sternly, a warning burning in her gaze. "What happened?" he asked Samuel instead.

Samuel told him that it was still unclear. The crowd could feel the angry pressure of her brother's gaze as an accusation was taking shape.

Just then, the crowd parted again and Kate appeared, pushing her younger son in front of her. His eyes were wide with fear as he regarded Helen in her bloodied state. Kate pressed him forward toward her, "Go on," she said sternly.

"I'm sorry, Miss Helen," he said, "I didn't mean to hit you with that rock." The conversations buzzed up again and subsided. "I was trying to hit my brother," he continued just a little bolder, "but I missed."

Since his older brother was the target of Richard's burning hatred, not Helen, what had started as an ordinary ambush had turned into public disaster.

"Huh fuh wuh huh?" asked Helen. The boy, Richard, and his mother blinked in confusion.

"How far was your brother from her?" asked Samuel, acting as translator. The boy spread his arms as far apart as he could and shrugged. "Well, that's embarrassing," said Samuel. "You have at least two reasons you should not throw rocks, then."

Helen looked at Samuel sharply and gestured, forming a large "C" with her left hand between her eyes and her bloody lip. "Indeed," he agreed. Turning to the boy, he continued, "How far from Miss Helen's eyes is her mouth where you hit her, then?"

The boy burst into hot tears and buried his face in his mother's middle. Unmoved, she pulled on his ear and shoulder to turn him back around to face his victim.

Helen was uncomfortable feeling admiration for Kate, but she was, for the first time ever, quite satisfied with the dressmaker's handling of a situation.

Helen mumbled again and Samuel passed on the message, "You can buy her a new bodice, she says. Or you can try to clean this one." The boy nodded vigorously and then wiped at his face. Kate nodded and led him away. Most of the people had already moved on, since there would be no more blood or excitement.

Helen's brother startled as someone said, "Of course, she works for the undertaker now." He closed in, questioning her and Helen groaned. She had hoped to delay this disapproving confrontation as long as possible.

"Daddy isn't going to like this," he said.

"Suh uh nuh ee-yoo kuh nuh duh muh wuh duh ma duh," Helen yelled through the compress.

"What did she say?" he asked Sam.

Samuel shook his head. "I have no idea," he replied diplomatically. He ushered her brother from the room. It wouldn't help matters if he told him what she was truly trying to say.

Outside, Samuel tried to reassure Wallace that their enterprise was a good position for her and that he treated her well. Samuel suggested that after her brother got her settled at her room at the Admiral's, he should come out to the shop and see the place for himself.

Wallace was horrified further to hear that she had not only changed employers but changed rooms and had said nothing of it in the interim. She had sat right next to him at Sunday dinners and said all sorts of things to compliment the yams, and yet she had not uttered those few important words about her own life.

Wallace didn't possess his father's diplomacy, but he did a good imitation of self-control when necessary. He escorted Helen, gently, to her new house and tried not to aggravate her with questions, striving to keep his tone casual.

She wasn't fooled. Thanks to this, Wallace was bound to inform her father about her shifting circumstances. After this difficult discussion, she could expect a near impossible talking-to from her father.

"You know, Helen," he said, as he turned to leave her room, "I envy you."

She was certain that Wallace had reached too far for the correct word and had tripped over a word that he could not possibly mean. "Eugh?" she asked.

He drew himself up, enjoying the realization that this could not become an argument; she would listen because she had to.

"I envy your freedom," he said, "You can come and go and keep secrets. You don't have responsibilities—not real responsibilities—to worry about."

She flinched a little in surprise. Wallace was so completely thoughtless. She knew that he was vain and selfish and fairly stupid, and that he liked to playact as the future head of the family.

Still, his ignorance of her difficulties was breath-taking. He had never considered the way she lived, wrangling with her options, few that they were. He didn't know what it was to press back hopelessness to reach for each possibility.

He was a man who could say what he wanted and have it accepted, almost as if it became a tangible thing to be placed in the center of the table. Her wants were merely a topic to be tampered with until they suited his vision.

She stood then, waved goodbye with mild exaggeration and shut the door firmly in his face.

She had only time to remove her bloody dress before a soft knock on the door interrupted her. Still feeling a tight ball of rage in her middle, she kicked at the heavy dress, as if it was to blame. Her foot tangled.

She hopped angrily. She knew that this was a tantrum best postponed, but she was strongly tempted to allow herself a free scream. Instead, she took a very deep breath, composed herself and answered the door in her underwear.

The fortune teller, Madame Grace, waited there with cotton cloths and warm water. Doubtless there was a flask in her pocket as well. Her eyes held a kindness that Helen had never seen there.

Helen cried then, holding her lips and muffling herself. The heat of her anger frightened her a little and the fright just made her cry harder.

Madame Grace pressed into the room and gently chastised, "You'll hurt yourself, dear. Try to be still. Reach out with your mind and find the still place inside yourself."

Still place? Helen thought and groaned internally at the phrase. She did immediately imagine a quiet, snowy clearing, however. She was calmed, just a little.

Ordinarily, the fortune teller irritated Helen. As a notion, she disapproved of mysticism and she disapproved of mystics, whether they purported to be genuine or were blatant shams. Helen had never consulted one professionally and she refused to be party to such nonsense. She could not deny her curiosity about the woman, however.

Madame Grace was a native of indecipherable age. She dressed in dark, billowy fabrics with bright, colorful embroidery. She didn't wear a head scarf, as the illustration on her sign would suggest. When she was outdoors she wore a top hat with bangles around the brim. Now, she was bareheaded, with her long, dark hair casually braided to keep it out of the way.

She had distain for the majority of her clientele, who were for the most part transient. She remarked from time to time that she was impressed by how few of them wouldn't know a Cherokee from a gypsy. They were satisfied with card readings and palm readings and the occasional hydromancy. They didn't require her to employ her real talents or even to be fully alert during most sessions.

Her local customers interested her much more than the Tarot tourists. Farmers and clerks and cooks all called on her for advice when they were desperate for encouragement.

Madame Grace didn't simply hand out hope; she offered reassurance at a very reasonable price. She listened with an intensity that many of them had never experienced. That in and of itself might make a despairing cook feel fortified to seek out a new situation. A woman like the shooting gallery mistress might decide in fact, to become finally, openly, a mistress. A mother might opt to give up a dependence on poison. A fireman might seek out the company of a freshly widowed woman, even though it wasn't proper—after all, they were not in a proper town, were they?

She didn't advise them as much as she steered them to listen to their own prattle. They knew what to do, and they usually knew the truth but were struggling to hide from it.

She appraised Helen's injury without any protest from Helen. It wasn't as bad as all the bleeding would suggest. She poured the water into the bowl on Helen's rickety washstand and began gently washing her neck without speaking for some time.

Finally, she said, "You are worried about your father and what he will think of your new situation."

Helen nodded, her eyes remained closed.

"You must not distress yourself. Truly, you weren't so very worried about your father before," Madame Grace commented.

Her tone was matter-of-fact, "if you were genuinely concerned, you wouldn't have taken up as undertaker in the first place."

Helen nodded again, more slowly. She liked that the fortune teller had said "as undertaker."

It seemed very simple the way Grace said it. Helen had done what she wanted to do, and she had nothing at all to be ashamed or worried about. Helen sighed then and smiled at her.

"Don't smile like that unless you want to start bleeding again." she scolded. "We should wash your hair, I think—"

Another knock on the door interrupted them.

Richard stood on the threshold looking back and forth between Helen and Grace with a fearful expression. In his little hands he held a small crock, wrapped in a rough, brown terry towel.

"Mother said to tell you that she didn't cook the soup," he said shyly, "It's from the hotel."

Helen sighed, amused by the disclaimer. Speaking carefully, for the sake of her lip, she asked, "Is that the soup she didn't cook?" She indicated the crock. She dropped the "p" from soup, the way a ventriloquist might.

Richard nodded solemnly.

"What sort is it?"

"Beans and vegetables," he replied. "Can I put it down now?"

Madame Grace took the crock from him and set it on the dresser. Helen rolled up her stained bodice and handed it to Richard and wished him luck.

"Your face isn't so bad," he said, becoming a bit more comfortable in the room.

"Do you want to study it?" she asked him.

"Yes, please." Richard moved closer to her and he started to reach forward as if he would touch it.

Helen pushed his hand down abruptly, "Germs!"

"Of course I know about germs," Richard replied, insulted, "I say, I know more about them than you! Mother says your people don't even get vaccinations."

Helen lowered her chin and then pointed to the round scar on her shoulder. Richard knew that meant she had had her small pox vaccination and his indignation deflated.

"Delightful child, run on home now," Grace said, "and don't forget to thank your mother for the soup."

Richard fled and he could hear their laughter all the way down the stairs.

Chapter 35—Grace

We are all in the gutter, but some of us are looking at the stars.
—Oscar Wilde

Wallace spent some time with Samuel and Eggers receiving a very educational tour of the undertaker shop and facilities. He took his time with his errands and hadn't returned home until late with the troubling news for Daddy Driscoll.

The next day, an early note arrived for Helen from Gertie saying simply, "The horse is out." Rather than wait for her father's ambush, Helen decided to pay him a visit.

Helen had spent the previous day with Madame Grace avoiding Wallace and everyone else. Grace had washed and tended Helen and she was gentle and sisterly. Helen found her feelings softening rapidly toward the fortune teller. She allowed Grace to rinse her hair and help her dress.

After all that, Helen felt much like herself again. They went downstairs together and ate the soup. They compared family stories and Helen learned that Grace was an orphan.

Grace had been told that her mother had been English and her father was a Cherokee. Her mother died in childbirth and she supposed that her father would not accept her, although she would never know the truth with certainty.

"I was lucky," Grace said. Helen wasn't sure *lucky* would have been her word choice. "The orphanage ladies doted on me, and they considered me an exotic specimen. Someone had said my father was a warrior chief, but I'm sure that's just something they say to embroider an orphan's story. I could never learn any more about my mother's family. I suppose they didn't want to keep such a colorful souvenir." Grace smiled to show that she felt it was their loss.

Later in the evening, they went outside to check on the chickens. The hens were in the hen house, but they were kicking up a commotion, which often meant a fox was near. Helen grabbed two tin cups to bang together to scare off the fox, while Grace reached instead for a shotgun that was resting by the back door.

Their presence may have been enough to startle the fox. Helen peered into the woods, but wasn't at all sure she saw anything. There might have been a momentary glint of wild eyes in the trees.

Grace pumped the shotgun and there was a faint scurrying in response. Satisfied, the women looked up at the clear night sky. Even though she was shivering, Helen was rapt with the sight of so many stars.

Grace asked her if she knew the story of the two dogs. Helen didn't know it. Grace had a vast knowledge of folklore, not from her kin, of course, but from being a voracious reader and a constant listener.

"The path to the land of souls is brightly lit in the sky so that it is easy to follow," Grace said. Her long hand traced the trail in the sky as she spoke. "What they call the Milky Way.

"The two dogs guard the path," she continued, "so, in order to pass the dogs, one has to bring food. If you feed the big dog, he will let you pass." She pointed to the constellation. "If you don't bring enough food to feed the small dog too, you will be trapped between them forever."

"And if you feed them both," Helen remarked, "they will both follow you forever."

Grace laughed as they turned back to the house.

"I'm not a very good friend, I'm afraid," Helen said.

Grace laughed again. "We can remedy that. I would like to have an evolving friend."

They retreated to the warmth of the fireside together.

Chapter 36—Daddy

In the morning, Helen was pleased to see that her face was barely swollen at all. She felt very well-rested and ready to meet her father's wrath.

It would not, in reality, be wrath from him, she knew. He would have statements to make, and then he would try reasoning with her after that. His reasoning wasn't always logical in her view, but it was always difficult to counter.

She knew that, when his reasoning failed to move her, he would continue to an emotional appeal designed to pluck at the female heart strings. If he was still going to persuade her after that, it would probably end with him expressing his disappointment in her.

That stung the few times he had used it. Even so, it hadn't been enough to make her move back to live at the farm before, and it wouldn't work the way he wanted it to now.

She walked to the farm, predicting and planning all the way. She congratulated herself on the steadiness of her resolve. The wind made her nose and cheeks tingle and she held fast to her collar to try to keep just a little warmer.

As she approached her old home, the place looked small to her. The fields were low and brown and only a few stray leaves flitted about in the humming wind. Only on the coldest days was the farm so quiet. She stepped onto the tidy porch and wiped her feet carefully, counting each swipe for an apostle as her mother had taught her, and then two extras for Mary and Mary as her Grandmother had taught her.

On the first Mary the door opened and Grandma Gertie smiled at her with approval. Her eyes were sparkling, but her voice was low and gruff as she said, "Come on in here, girl."

Helen went in and removed her hat and coat, looking around.

"He's riding the fence," said Gertie. "The winters are always much too long for him, even the short ones."

"Where are the twins?" asked Helen. She didn't ask about Wallace because she knew she didn't need to.

"They are having an adventure, even though they will claim they were reading with their little friend and working very studiously all day," said Gertie. "Wallace is at an auction."

Helen nodded and settled by the fire in the kitchen. She considered it a bad sign that Wallace was on his own at the auction; normally her father would supervise him while pretending to tag along. Her father was a man of very strong habits and this particular habit was never broken before to her knowledge.

"Here, I have just made coffee," Gertie said, handing her a half-filled cup.

Helen sipped it carefully. It was bitter and gritty and wonderful, but it hurt her lip to drink it. She wrapped her hands around the cup instead, drinking in the heat with her hands.

"It's good that you came so quickly," said Gertie. She stopped puttering at the stove and looked at Helen, as if to make sure she was listening. "For the most part, he's worried for your safety; and truly that is a worry." Gertie didn't add "for me" but Helen understood her meaning.

Helen sighed, "I'm as careful as I ever was."

Gertie clicked her teeth. "It's not your carefulness that's in question but the carelessness of others." Helen heard *of men*. She was sure that she knew as much about that subject as Gertie did.

The kitchen door opened slowly and a gust of wind swirled in strongly enough to rattle the drying herbs above the window.

Ephraim, Helen's father, entered without speaking.

She decided to approach this as directly as Gertie might and said simply, "Daddy, I'm keeping safe. Please try not to worry yourself."

"You are consorting with whores and whore keepers," he said. He began to remove his outer garments with what she saw was excessive gentleness and slowness.

"I am not a consort." She spoke evenly, although she was surprised that he had jumped to this stage of the discussion right alongside her. The word *disappointed* was going to make a premature appearance very shortly. She pulled in a very deep breath, suddenly aware that she had stopped breathing.

"You have squandered every chance for a good husband," he said, "and now this. This arrangement is a disgrace." He opened his hands as if inviting disgrace to appear there. "What people must think of us now— and of you."

Helen's heart was racing. "People will think whatever they like," she repeated these words, his own words, carefully. He looked at her then, his eyes shining with clear pain. She continued, "I must wonder what *you* think of me?"

"I think I have failed you," he said simply, avoiding her question. "What sort of homestead have I created that you would so desperately avoid it? That you would gladly run to ruin?"

"You would have me here, growing old and serving Wally rather than earning my own way in my own profession."

"Yes," he said it as if it were obvious. "Better to be here with your own that taking wages from a hypnotist and a depraved Swede."

"Norwegian," she said softly. *Hypnotist* was an odd characterization, she thought.

"What's the difference? They don't care about your reputation or your future as we do. That would be impossible."

There. There was something she could argue.

"Daddy," she said, reaching a hand to him but staying seated and small, "I'm not leaving until you understand."

He accepted her hand in his, tenderly. "Then I will never understand."

"Oh please!" exclaimed Gertie. "Sit down! The girl isn't a renegade to be hunted down, she's a visitor now. Sit down."

Helen intended to stay all day and overnight and then to go with the family to church. She would will the situation back to normalcy—she was convinced it was possible.

They talked and Gertie supervised for more than an hour.

"If you are so worried about what people will think of me, why not show them what to think? Show them that I have your support and that you believe I'm doing good works."

Ephraim shook his head at what sounded impossible to him.

"You belong with us. You owe a debt to your family," he said.

"And what does my family owe me?" she asked levelly. "I am not asking for anything but your loyalty and confidence in me. It would cost you nothing. I have income from the dress shop and the upholstery work, after all.

"Have I not been hardworking and honest?" She spoke quietly and her words came out in a low tumble. "Humbly and sincerely I ask you, please do not doubt my character now."

"You are resolute," he said. She nodded. "Have it your way," he shrugged, "but if I find that you are losing control of your conduct I will have you to the doctors to examine your mental condition."

Helen felt her innards tumble at the sound of his atrocious promise. She had never expected him to threaten to put her into the asylum, but that's what he was suggesting. It was not merely posture, he was earnest.

The threat confirmed a horrible new fact for her; he would prefer to see her declared insane rather than have her truly at liberty.

She kept her countenance placid and said simply, "I understand, Daddy."

Chapter 37—Called

Monday Morning, Helen and Samuel found Eggers in the office with his feet up. He was enjoying the newspaper much earlier than he usually was.

"I'm hiding out from my ladies," he said. Helen smiled in spite of herself that he would refer to them so. "I mustn't be in the midst of all of their menstruations. It's very dismal there with the bickering for hot water bottles and moaning for tonics—"

Samuel waved a hand at him as if to hush him.

"What? Oh. I beg your pardon, Miss Helen," He eyed her with mischief, "Do I make you blush? I can never be sure."

Samuel waved harder, but Helen was laughing, so he let it go.

"If men had to endure all that, they would award each other bravery medals," she said, a bit wearily.

"They would, just before they found a cure," replied Eggers.

Helen rejoined, "There's already the three-season cure, but it causes vastly more misery than the disease."

"Well," said Eggers, "I believe you have good reason to turn away from maternal feeling after one of the little monsters marred your face." He stopped himself, "Say, how is your broken tooth? Do we need to get you to LaFevre's magic dental man?"

"No no. I'm perfectly fine. It was just a tiny chip," Helen replied. "What's the news?"

"Philadelphia is at full stop with the strike. The city water supply is possibly causing all the typhoid fever. They are working to lift the ban on old Confederates enlisting again—England can well hear all their rattling spurs and sabers as it is. And we need to find an opportunity to bury a congressman."

Samuel only *tisked* at the mention of war, but then he perked up at the mention of burial, "They must be very expensive funerals."

"It says here that the Government has spent one hundred thousand dollars to bury Senators since we started having Senators, and the latest funeral cost twenty thousand dollars!"

"Oh my," said Samuel, "How on Earth?"

"And that one was a very, very rich man," Eggers continued, "so it's doubly shocking. The cheese budget alone would make you weep with frustration."

"Perhaps we only need get you to the Hill to use your powers of hypnosis," suggested Helen.

"I have powers of hypnosis?" inquired Samuel, uncertain of her meaning.

"There are rumors that I am here as your mesmerized captive with no will of my own," she informed him.

"Seems entirely plausible to me," Eggers chimed in, "he just hasn't mastered the obedience lot yet."

"Hmm. Hypnotist. That might explain the way people keep me at such a remove," said Samuel. "I thought it was just the somber nature of the calling."

"Oh no," said Helen, "it's not that. You are quite the suspect character."

Samuel was taken aback.

Eggers chuckled at him, "People assume you are a fugitive, I'm sure. No one just appears in this town and stays without some connection, or some introduction."

"Unless they're on the lam," added Helen helpfully.

Samuel had never been disreputable and it hadn't occurred to him that he could become so even in an imaginary way. After three months, no one had hinted at such a thing until now.

"Not to worry," said Eggers, "They will become accustomed to you, eventually. After all, Miss Helen and I are here to provide some familiarity. We'll start seeing a few shoppers perusing our wares here in the coming months, I'm sure."

Samuel groaned at Eggers' business forecast. How would they ever turn a profit?

Eggers cackled and got up to dress for departure, saying that he would be visiting his friend in the city, unless they had something for him to do today.

"When will we have an introduction to your friend?" asked Samuel.

Eggers only winked.

A knock on the door was followed immediately by the hurried entrance of Miss Emma.

Emma Chaney was always disheveled, but on this particular morning, she appeared like a cloud of chaos. Her hair was standing out from under her crooked bonnet and her hem was so muddied that they all instinctively moved to corral her.

She removed the glove from her right hand, dropped it and whirled around to try to catch it, exclaiming that she had already lost the left glove somewhere.

"Miss Emma," said Samuel kindly, "how can we assist you?" He took both her hands to steady her as he spoke.

"They sent me from next door," she said breathlessly, "Mr. McGuinness is dead!" Her round face quivered.

"Just now?" asked Eggers.

She nodded. "He drank poison!"

Squinty McGuiness was so called because he was extraordinarily near sighted. He rarely wore his eyeglasses, because he was also extraordinarily vain and felt that they did his face no favors. He was prone to both headaches and frequent accidents, but he was presumably happy with the way he looked in his misery.

"They found him slumped over the table with a bottle of poison in front of him," Emma continued breathlessly, "He may have thought it was the whiskey."

"Surely he could smell that it wasn't whiskey," said Eggers with skepticism. Accidental poisonings were made unlikely even for the nearsighted, by the nubby bottles that were usually employed. In his experience, people who drank poison knew what they were up to and had a predilection for death.

"I don't know anything about that," she snapped, "but he didn't seem very gloomy or mournful, either." She turned back to Samuel, "Oh, won't you come and fetch him?"

"Of course," said Samuel, "I'll escort you back and Mr. Eggers will see about the hearse."

Helen had been packing a bag with the bare essentials as they talked, and when she handed it to Samuel, Emma startled as if remembering something.

"Oh, we'd better not have Miss Helen come along. There's one of those old soldiers rooming there and he might be—oh, dear," she was becoming even more flustered with each word.

Samuel, very studiously not looking at Helen, answered, "Miss Helen is the undertaker. There is no way around it."

"But I thought," Emma stopped herself. She, like most people, had determined that he was the undertaker and that the others assisted.

Having multiple undertakers would be unusual, unless they intended to have services for both white and colored clientele. Neighboring towns had such an arrangement with back doors and downstairs entrances and separate accommodations.

"Simple mistake," replied Samuel, "but she is essential." He looked at Helen then, and she could do nothing more than enjoy his sincerity.

Chapter 38—Squinty

Outside the front of the house, they found a small crowd of people milling around, a few of whom nodded to one another when they caught sight of Helen and Samuel. The crowd shifted their attention from Eggers and the hearse to their approach.

Helen moved gracefully, expertly holding her skirts up enough to avoid the cold grime of the streets and walkways, while Emma was already too filthy and distracted to bother with the effort.

Emma had stopped a few times to catch her breath and was looking so gray that Helen had to wonder if they might not have another client a bit later in the morning.

She seemed to gain steam as they passed the shooting gallery, however, and was ready to face her audience with Victorian severity. "Scoot, everyone!" she commanded, "Mr. McGuiness has suffered a terrible accident and there's nothing more to report." The crowd only backed up enough to allow the four of them to enter the house. Emma whirled again, shouting at the bystanders, "Go on!"

As they entered, they could hear whispered bickering and shuffling noises emanating from the back of the house. The sound of a series of drawers opening and closing followed; Emma sprang into action as she understood what was happening. She gestured to Eggers to follow her and proceeded to storm into Squinty's room.

Three of the boarders froze as she entered, caught in the act of ransacking the room.

"Shame on you!" she yelled, "Mr. McGuinness isn't hardly cold yet!" She planted her fist on the dresser top and demanded that they empty their pockets.

"He didn't have anything to speak of," said one of the men quietly as he laid down an inexpensive, broken pocket watch.

Emma plucked a small bible off the bedside table and threw it backhand at the man and he whooped as it hit his chest.

"That's it for you! Now, get out of the house until we're done!"

Eggers stepped out of her way, smiling, "Good arm you have, Miss Emma."

"I had brothers," she replied, curtly.

They joined Helen and Samuel just as they began to examine the body of Mr. McGuinness.

He was in the large kitchen, exactly as Emma had described. One large, beefy hand was outstretched on the table and the opposite arm was bent, supporting his head, which was face down.

Samuel had sniffed at the bottle that presumably been drunk by McGuiness and held it for Helen to smell as well. She shook her head slightly, it was not a pungent poison. In fact, the bottle was stamped as "Zoa-Phora Woman's Friend."

His hand was still warm and flexible, surprising Samuel. Next, he gently pressed McGuiness's forehead backward while supporting his neck, which was also quite warm. His neck was supple.

"I don't believe this man is dead," he said to Helen.

Just then, McGuiness's eyes flew open, he sprang to his feet and roared. Everyone jumped backward as he staggered rapidly in a circle. He was every bit as tall as Samuel and twice as wide. His transformation from a corpse to a furious dervish stunned them all.

Pulling harsh, ragged breaths, he tore at the handle of the back door, succeeded in pulling it open. He crashed through the closed screen door with so much force he took most of the door with him as he tumbled down the back steps. He jumped up again immediately and then ran full-tilt into the side of the privy, roaring again as if he were trying to push a bear off a cliff. The privy won and he collapsed to the ground with a thud.

Eggers commented drily, "Well, that might've killed him properly."

Emma swore that he hadn't been breathing when she called for their services, but then she revised her story to admit that she had not verified that personally.

Helen told her that he may have suffered a spell and should see a doctor when he woke up again. Eggers said cheerily that they would return if he did not wake up again.

Emma shook her head ruefully at the sight of Squinty, prone in the mud. "I asked him one hundred times to take down that screen door for the winter. Now he has."

The team exited the front of the house and Samuel told the boarders that Emma would need some help with the temporarily revived McGuiness. The men were not enthused. One of them suddenly recalled that he needed to get to work and sprinted away.

The proprietor of the shooting gallery, Percy, waved to Samuel and they stopped at his entrance. "Is my Emma in a state?" he asked. Samuel affirmed that she was calmer now that the dead man was no longer dead.

Percy was an energetic and very talented man. He managed to keep a wife and ten children in the country and to have a happy mistress to help with his games here.

"I had better see to her," he said to Eggers. "Nothing puts her more in mind of some *rumpity-bumpity* than a brush with death," he leaned in with a large wink.

"Did you overlook my presence, somehow?" said Helen. She was smiling even as she rightly scolded him.

"I beg your pardon," said the proprietor, miming a tip of an invisible hat.

"Mr. Eggers, can you wait here and mind the store for a few minutes? Nobody has won the Winchester rifle yet." He mentioned that in a confidential tone, unable to resist adding a tiny sales pitch.

"Delighted," said Eggers, affably.

The man went on in search of his Emma.

"A Winchester?" commented Samuel in a shocked tone. "How does he stay in business with prizes that dear?"

Eggers chuckled. Samuel was always fussing about money these days. "You need a better appreciation of human frailty, my friend. People will always assume their aim is better than it is."

Samuel and Helen ambled back to their shop. She was still feeling worried and wistful after the weekend with her family and the horrible discussion with her father. She had no intention of talking about that, so instead she asked small questions.

"Did you see the sunrise?" she asked. Samuel shook his head in the negative.

"I did see the rosy light, but I didn't investigate further."

"It was one of the most glorious that I can recall since I was a girl," she said. "Any color you could imagine was vividly represented."

Samuel thought of Thoreau's words, "It's the beauty within us that makes it possible for us to recognize the beauty around us." He was too shy to say it aloud, so instead he asked, "What about brown?"

"Ah," she smiled, "there was brown if you count the tree branches that stood up to the sunrise. I wish I could paint it."

"Why don't you?" he asked.

She explained it as if he were a little bit dim, "First of all I am not a painter and second I have no paints!"

"Paint it with words?" he asked.

She tilted her head, accepting with a smile. "You know the way the clouds sometimes ripple, when they are the texture of an autumn sheep's wool?" He nodded, although he wasn't certain he knew what she meant. "Soft tufts that are becoming distinct; that's the shape they had," She explained, "They were lit with the fieriest pink and gold and the bluest sky peeped through. Looking only at the sky you would not be able to say which was shadow and which was lighted." She paused, discouraged. "I cannot do it justice."

"That's a fine description," he said. He had decided that her talkative mood presented an opportunity. "Can I ask you a question? It's about a point of curiosity I have."

"Questions usually are," she said.

"Ha, well, yes. I was wondering why you speak to the dead."

"It's absurd, of course," she said, "I'll stop."

"No! I only—"

"—I'm joking, of course," she answered. "I do it because I would rather do it. I don't pretend to have any certainty about where their souls are, but I think it's best to behave as if they are lingering, just in case they are."

"If they can hear you, you wouldn't want to be mute," he said. "That's what I thought you would say." It seemed very reasonable to him, although he wouldn't do it. "I'm not much for the idea of souls anymore," said Samuel ruefully. "To me the bodies are just husks. Or an overcoat that was left behind."

Helen was shocked. She knew that he wasn't a practicing Catholic, but she had no idea he was so faithless.

"What a lonely way to think of it," she commented. "To you they just vanish? Just wink out of being into not being?"

"Yes," he replied. "We honor who they were and respect the family they left behind. That's all." He paused for a long moment. "I am not afraid to accept the truth in front of me. If I'm wrong I won't fear judgment either."

Helen felt pity for him. At the same time, she wanted to understand how his thinking had landed there.

"When did you leave the church?" she asked. She didn't bother to apologize for prying. This was beginning to feel like the most personal conversation she had ever had.

"I cannot say there was one day," he replied, "Cracks began to appear. My questions were sometimes punished. Catholicism seemed to harm my mother more than it soothed her. My father was openly scornful of the sacraments." He sighed. "So many things. The word of God began to sound like the lies of men."

"No other church?" she asked. Helen was tempted to tell him all the reasons she loved her church, but she didn't want to appear to proselytize.

"I think I could be content as a Quaker," he said, "but I'm in no hurry about it."

"A Quaker!" she exclaimed.

"No," he said, "That was a lie."

"Well done!" She laughed. "You are improving by leaps and bounds!"

Chapter 39—Silent

In the days after her father's threat, Helen felt as though she was moving through a fog, particularly when she wasn't working. Talking with friends helped her turn away from her worries, but when she was alone again, the worries had waited their turn.

She considered confiding in Grace, and perhaps she should have. Instead, they had their usual friendly chats in the evenings, discussing anything other than Helen's thoughts. She could feel Grace studying her just a bit too long, but Grace never asked what the trouble was and if Grace had theories, she kept them to herself.

In considering remedies to her situation, Helen surprised herself to realize that she would flee, if only she had the means. The thought of leaving was terrifying and made her palms prickle with sweat. Where would she go?

She had a correspondence with a few of her school mates, but they were all so very far away. How could she collect the ticket money to get to San Francisco? Venezuela was in turmoil and Paris was completely out of the question. She could work a third job and save to get as far as New York, but then she would quite possibly end up in a work house.

The stories of young women cast to the wind were always awful. Without protection, she would easily be overpowered and robbed or worse. Here, at least she had the protection of her name.

Helen found sleeping difficult. These questions relentlessly swirled around at the edge of her consciousness and her fatigue built bit by bit during the following days.

On the third evening, she went to bed early and fell into a heavy sleep almost immediately. During the night, she had a vivid nightmare in which she shared a train compartment with a smiling man. His smile was livid and strange and she could feel her entire body straining to avoid him as she took her seat at the opposite corner of the compartment. The revulsion washed over her as she realized that his smile was painted on a leathery, reptilian face.

A long, snake-like tongue lashed out of his mouth, smelling her. She screamed herself awake and suddenly Grace was there, wrapping her in her warm arms and whispering comfort. Helen shuddered and felt the salty tears soaking her face.

"I'm sorry," she sobbed.

"You had a terror, no apology needed," Grace replied, stroking her hair gently.

Helen could feel her every muscle knotted. The pain in her burned so that she felt it might swallow her from the inside.

"Shhhhh," said Grace, "Come with me. Let's look at the snow."

Grace pulled her up and Helen's feet felt a shock as they touched the cold oak of the floor. Her throat was on fire and her thoughts were muddled with the reptile textures and erratic motion from her dream.

The snow had stopped falling, but the wind was still picking up flakes from the trees and setting them adrift in the air again. In the moonlight, the yard was glowing. Its twinkling blanket shrouded all the familiar shrubs and softened every sharp branch. The only sound Helen could hear was her own breath.

Grace put a blanket around her. "I think you have a fever," she said, sagely stating the obvious. Helen nodded minutely and agreed a fever was likely. Her eyes burned and her throat was tight with that strange sewed-up sensation it had when she was ill.

"I'll fetch us some tea," said Grace.

Helen saw black snow mingling with the drifting flakes, her senses reeled and she collapsed.

Chapter 40—Visitors

Helen awoke a day later. Gertie was sitting in her room clicking her knitting needles together fashioning the longest and ugliest scarf Helen had ever seen.

"Well, hello there, lazy bones," said Gertie, putting aside her knitting.

Helen tried to speak, but her voice was no more than a hiss. Gertie offered her a wet cloth to suck on. Her throat was raw and tiny; the drabs of cold water were everything she wanted in the world.

"Your funeral friends extracted a promise from me that I would send word when you woke up," said Gertie, "They don't want to be morbid by hanging about, I suppose."

Helen nodded weakly. Gertie was being jolly to cover her worry and Helen wished she wouldn't bother. The heavy bed-clothes clung to Helen's skin and she didn't feel the strength to wrestle enough to move them.

"I brought you some cake," said Gertie, "It was either that or leave it for the ducks, and I do not want to encourage the ducks too much."

Helen smiled then and Gertie took an impatient tone and said, "Get up."

So slowly that it was almost comical to her, Helen began to press back the covers and roll to raise herself to a seated position. Once there, Gertie shifted the pillows and pulled away the damp covers. Helen sank back against the pillows with gratitude and Gertie covered her with the extra quilt. Gertie didn't speak again but made tiny disappointed noises as she did so.

Helen felt that she had soaked up all of Gertie's age. How did her grandmother press back the weariness? Did all the practice at stubbornness do the job for her? Maybe all Helen needed was for her years to catch up to this dreadful fatigue.

As Gertie left the room, Grace entered. She was clearly pleased to see Helen upright. "You frightened me," she said. "Would you like tea now?" Helen nodded. She felt that she might cry but her eyes stayed dry.

Gertie came back, complaining, "That awful child has been hanging around so I sent him to your, uh, workshop."

Helen assumed she meant Richard. He had developed the habit of bothering Helen when he was bored. She didn't like most children, but he seemed to miss seeing her at home and his inquisitive nature was winning her over.

"Do you have your senses intact?" Gertie asked.

"Yes," Helen whispered.

"Good," said Gertie, "You will need them." Gertie made herself more comfortable. "You will need to be careful standing up to your father. He is never going to let you be truly independent."

"School," Helen whispered.

"Yes," Gertie said, "He let you go away to school, that's true. But he never gave you any more than pin money, did he now?" Gertie picked up her knitting as if the important portion of the conversation was over. "There are no prodigal-daughter stories, you know. That's because they never got the remittance to spend."

Richard returned from the shop with a note and a sort of tool kit. Helen opened the note first. "We are at the ready if there is any remedy we can provide. Your full recovery is our most earnest hope—your devoted friends, SK and OE." The kit contained a set of oil paints, ones of excellent quality. There were brushes and bottles of chemicals and a mahogany pallet tucked into the tin lid.

She replied with a sloppily penned note dictated to Richard that she was recovering and would expect to be back to work in a few days. She thanked them for the paints. Richard sighed heavily when she asked him to deliver her note.

She told him hoarsely that he could have some cake when he returned from the delivery and he nodded with a bit more enthusiasm.

Her strength returned, little by little. It wasn't lost on her that no notes or visits came from the rest of her family. Once Gertie was satisfied that Helen wasn't going to need another call from the doctor, she left too.

Why, Helen wondered, had she not heard a thing from her sister, Fannie? At the first notion, she had been worried that Fannie had experienced some mishap, but the more she mulled it over the more she believed that this was just another sign of banishment.

That evening, she joined the other boarders by the fire. The teachers cooed over her, exclaiming that they had several students who had fallen ill to fever. They had influenza according to the doctor.

Helen had been wondering and wanted to know what doctor they meant. She had been surprised that they had been able to fetch one for her so quickly.

"Your friend, Mr. Eggers, brought him around," Grace said, "He is very tall and Prussian. I don't recall the name now."

Now Helen was impressed. Eggers had managed to get her a doctor all the way from Baltimore, assuming this was the same fellow, that odd Dr. Cook they had met at their shop. It must have been him, she decided. The visit must have been expensive, indeed.

The teachers struck up a spirited game of Hearts against the Admiral and Thomas Jefferson in the dining room, while Helen and Grace stayed by the fire.

"Mr. Jefferson," chided the Admiral, "you must have the Black Lady."

"I always have the black ladies," replied Mr. Jefferson with a low chuckle. Their opponents giggled as if they hadn't heard this joke far too often.

Jefferson had a very distinctive laugh, Helen thought. There was a tiny whistling to it that was not at all unpleasant, and somehow it had the musical quality of a chime.

Helen was glad to be in proximity to their chummy competition. She had been teaching Richard to play Hearts while she recuperated and she teased the players that she would soon have a devastating challenger on her team.

"Excellent!" exclaimed the Admiral. "I welcome all comers as long as I can have Mr. Jefferson." Mr. Jefferson was never bested for long.

Helen and Grace talked quietly and Helen was enjoying the celebratory mood of the evening now that she was feeling much more like herself.

"I have not heard a peep from my sister," she confided. "I would not expect her to have such cold regard for me."

"There are many other reasons for a lack of correspondence," replied Grace. "Perhaps she has no knowledge of your illness." Helen hadn't considered this, and as it was the most comforting explanation, she seized on it.

"Of course!" she exclaimed.

"There again," continued Grace, "mayhap she is resentful that you are outside of your father's focus and she is feeling his concentration on her affairs, doubly so."

Helen just stared. "I prefer the first scenario."

"I'm certain that is the one, then," said Grace, affably. "I do not have direct experience with family troubles, of course."

"I know, I'm sorry to burden you," Helen said. She regretted tossing the subject out in the first place.

"Not at all!" Grace said. "It can be a tremendous blessing. When you are raised apart from your people you are always apart." She gestured, spreading her arms to draw an invisible shield in front of herself. "Then, you can live anywhere and be just as comfortable as you are anywhere else. With no homeland in the world, every place is the same."

"Or every place is just as uncomfortable as every other," said Helen with a sigh.

"Are you uncomfortable or just brooding again?" asked Grace with the mildest concern.

Helen chuckled, "Brooding comfortably, thank you."

"Try not to worry. Everything will be all right again in the end."

Helen didn't reply. She wondered why Grace would feel the need to lie so graciously.

Chapter 41—Painting

Helen returned to work once her stamina was good enough to make the walk. She had painted a view from her room on a small canvas and brought it with her to give it to Samuel and Eggers. As she walked, the paper wrapping swished against her sleeve.

She was elated to be outdoors. The teachers, Melvina and Lollie, walked with her, partly because they were concerned about her but mostly because they were going the same way. Normally they would have set out earlier, but they were both very tired from dealing with cooped-up children. They had dawdled their early morning away and needed to get to the school and were none too pleased about it.

Helen wasn't bothered by the grumpy companionship. She was fairly expert at diverting her attention from idle complaining. Her mind hopped around with agility, seeking another topic for them.

"Melvina," she said, "would you like me to show you how to re-work the sleeves on your green dress?"

Melvina's eyes widened as she turned toward Helen, delighted by the idea. "I would adore it. Mutton sleeves!"

The teachers were generally very conservative and old-fashioned in their dress. They only pretended to ignore fashion out of budgetary necessity, however.

"Lollie?" Helen invited.

Lollie said she would like to work on her spring dress too. The fashionably enormous sleeves were a confident statement for a young professional woman. "Here I am!" they declared, making the wearer's otherwise small shoulders an impressive presence.

"Good," said Helen, "Sunday afternoon?"

When the teachers left her, they were considerably more cheerful than they had been at the start of their little journey.

Helen pushed open the door to the shop and was surprised that it jingled now.

"Well-well-well!" Eggers exclaimed from another room.

Samuel set down his planer and hurried to the door. He grabbed her free right hand enthusiastically shaking it in greeting. His face colored as he realized how dusty he was and he produced a rag from his apron and began to try to remove the transferred dust from her hands.

"It's fine, it's fine!" she said, extracting her hands from the operation. "Please don't trouble yourself."

Eggers appeared, "We were terribly worried for you, you know," he noticed the wrapped canvas in her hand, "Ooo! Is that a present?"

She handed him the canvas. "It's my very first painting, for the both of you," she said.

Eggers pulled off the paper and held the canvas out. "I have never seen a finer example of a spider seen through a microscope!"

"Are you mad?" commented Samuel, "It's obviously a, uh, much more complicated subject."

Helen laughed, "It's the view from my window," she pointed at the black streaks, "these are the bare trees, these are shadows in the snow."

Both men nodded solemnly without actually absorbing her vision depicted there. What she identified as shadows were strange puddles of color which contrasted uncomfortably with the undeniably spidery trees.

"A remarkable first effort!" said Samuel.

"A remarkable job at lying!" replied Helen. "Let's hang it over your desk."

"I will build it a beautiful frame," he replied, beaming at her. It was so very good to have her back.

Eggers winked at Samuel in an exaggerated fashion and feigned innocence the instant Helen turned around.

The three of them slipped back into their patterns with relative ease throughout the week. At first, Helen was aware of a bit more intensity in Samuel's regard, as if he could not quite believe she was there. She strived to find the balance between being reassuring and not encouraging.

He seemed to withdraw a little whenever she was condescending, so she sprinkled a little haughtiness in her speech with him. It worked like a charm.

By the end of the week, Helen felt that she might run out of things to do if they didn't have another client soon. She could, reluctantly, stop by the dress shop and see what work there was to pick up, if need be.

Then, as if invoked, they had an order. Eggers had word from the Countess that she would like them to make her a casket for Myrtle.

Samuel was horrified. "I liked Myrtle! What terrible news! What on Earth has happened?"

Eggers laughed, "I'll be sure to tell her you were distraught about her death. It's not a real casket they're after," he explained. "What they want is more of a prop."

"Oh," said Samuel. After a pause he said, "Oh," again. If this was to be a prop in the brothel, evidently it was intended for faux necrophilia.

"Let's make it very fancy," Helen chimed in, unfazed, "All the best for your Myrtle!"

Samuel was brimful with embarrassment and wasted no time in getting busy again. He pushed any thought of the casket's utility away as he sketched the design.

He would not think of seeing Myrtle in that gauzy new dress. It had a strange, old-fashioned shape and yet was entirely transparent. He would further not think of the tufts of tulle that had almost certainly been tailored by Helen. He broke his pencil in the effort to focus.

After some deliberation, he decided on a walnut casket with ornate brass hardware. It would look exactly like a fine resting place for a dignitary, but he would add features for additional sturdiness and safety. This creation would have to accommodate horseplay.

In the end, they opted to leave the lid entirely separate to insure than it didn't slam on anyone. The Countess was not pleased with this arrangement at first, but they were able to persuade her by talking her through all the ways a lid could cause potential injury or dismemberment. After all, she was not inclined to take risks with her herd.

Chapter 42—Shunned

That next Sunday, when Helen arrived at church, her family was already there. The pews were only half full, but the Driscoll family pew in front was so thoroughly filled that there was not a space for her. The twins had invited two of their little friends to sit with them and everyone was staunchly taking up a full share of the space. There was no question that it was an oversight, which meant that she would have to seat herself somewhere else for the first time ever.

Her stomach flipped and fluttered painfully, as if she were some kind of cat that had swallowed a wild bird whole. She clenched her fist and pressed it against her middle, hard, trying to still the sensation.

Everyone in the church faced forward or politely pretended not to see her discomfort as she slowly took a seat near the rear.

Gertie stood up and moved to the aisle. She looked at Helen's father for a long moment before moving back to sit next to her. Helen reached over and clasped Gertie's hand with gratitude. Gertie in turn picked up that hand and patted it pointedly before placing it firming back on Helen's lap as if to say that no fuss was appreciated.

Helen maintained her composure through the service, but felt tears sting and form during the hymns. She willed them away with mixed success.

This ostracizing was shocking and agonizing. At least, she thought, her sister wasn't there.

She was comforted that Gertie stayed nearby, but during the greeting interval, Gertie gave her a quick hug and whispered to her to wait for her afterward. Gertie made her way back to the front with the others. It was then that Helen saw that she had been mistaken and that her sister, Fannie, was with them too. Her eyes burned again.

The unjustness of it was scouring and brightening her feelings into anger. She had done nothing to deserve this shunning. Who had she harmed? She may have been a bit duplicitous, but who had been injured? She had tried to spare them worry and in return they had discarded her. By the time the service concluded she was vibrating with fury.

She bolted out of the building and retreated to the graveyard, watching for Gertie and wishing she didn't feel obliged to wait for her. The cold air stung her nose and she turned away from the wind.

Gertie saw her and strode directly to her. As she drew closer, Helen saw that her expression wasn't grim and purposeful to match her gait. Instead, Gertie just looked tired and a little sad.

Helen was worried to see Gertie like this; just one more worry. She sighed heavily and unevenly, "Please don't tell me to come home again."

"He wants me to try to convince you. As long as he thinks I am he won't interfere with my talking to you," she paused, "He can't stop me, of course, but it's better for all of us while he is thinking he can."

Helen heard the words but only took them in as a collection of sounds and didn't reply.

Gertie continued, "You need to leave the Port if you are going to persist in this. The Port is full of nothing but whores."

Helen startled, "That's not true!"

"Yes it is."

Helen thought of the most unlikely person she could in defense of her home, "What about the Admiral?"

"He's a whore to his past, trying to make up for some terrible deeds by tending to other whores. Did you know that he is not an officer?"

Helen did not know. "What about Kate?" her grandmother couldn't equate her situation with prostitution, surely.

"She's a whore to her husband's memory and his property, like me," Gertie replied, unfazed. "And that Fabian's a whore to the whore trade, and so on."

Helen sighed again, "You're impossible."

"I may be impossible, but I'm not wrong," replied Gertie. "The peace here will not last, it never does." Gertie stooped and picked up a dry, fragile branch that had fallen on one of the graves. She snapped it absently into small lengths as she talked. "Sooner or later someone is going to challenge the proprietorship and when it falls apart, the Port will be dangerous again, possibly very dangerous."

"What 'proprietorship'?" Helen felt lost again.

Gertie smiled, "Have you never wondered who owns things? You might wonder about that. Are you certain in what you know?

"Consider it but don't linger; and start packing," she continued. "You must move on or move back. You cannot stay where you are."

Helen frowned. "You have always said that I am safer at home."

"Safety isn't everything," Gertie said.

***

While Helen was experiencing a terrible exclusion, Eggers was included in a situation he would rather have avoided.

That morning on his way to breakfast, Eggers approached the side door and was surprised to see the Countess standing in the partly open doorway.

She stopped him, placing her long hand on the center of his chest and then raising one finger to her lips for silence. He obediently closed his mouth, wondering if she was playing some kind of joke. She seemed very pleased about something, her smile was wide and winsome and her lips were as dark as pomegranates.

He peered past her into the room, and Eggers first saw Myrtle's hair. Her curls were bouncing with some ferocious activity. Her lovely breasts were contained only by a large pair of hands. Eggers's eyes widened in surprise, but he stayed quiet.

Eggers couldn't be certain of the identity of Myrtle's client. The man was leaning back in an armless chair, facing away into the room. His linen shirt was disheveled, and it concealed the shape of his shoulders. Only the back of his head was in clear view. Myrtle was not wearing her gloves, and had her fingers tangled in the man's hair as she rode him.

Someone was having a very special breakfast.

Eggers was utterly taken in by Myrtle's performance, and only realized it for what it was when she glanced surreptitiously at the man's face and then looked calmly at the Countess. As she gazed at her madam, Myrtle breathlessly exclaimed, "You dirty, dirty boy!"

The Countess gestured in a negative waving motion. After a few more thrusts, Myrtle moaned, "Marvelous boy." Eggers saw the Countess make another signal, also somehow negative and not at all clear to him in its meaning.

Myrtle groaned far back in her throat, still pounding the man in the chair. Her motions slowed but lost no intensity. She said, softly, "My strong, strong man." The Countess finally approved and made a tiny, silent clapping gesture.

Eggers whispered into her ear, "Is it the piano tuner?"

She smiled and mouthed the words, "Look again."

The man shuddered and Eggers heard a meek, broken groan escape from the man. It was Samuel.

He raised his eyebrows at the Countess and she silently closed the door and pulled him away for everyone's privacy. She was very pleased that Samuel had finally made a choice.

"It will do him a world of good," she said, chuckling.

"I daresay," Eggers replied.

Eggers was feeling equal parts aroused and annoyed by the situation. And the Countess only smiled at him with perfect understanding. She handed him an apple and led him away toward the back door.

He had a new secret to add to the collection of things he could discuss only with her. He would not even let Samuel know what he'd seen.

Chapter 43—Angry

Helen held onto her anger all day Sunday. Even with its bright, sharp edges it was more comforting than any of her other feelings about her family.

She had bright, hard smiles for the teachers that afternoon as they cut the fabric and pinned pieces into place. Her posture was strong and her movements steely and assured.

Her mind was kept clear and focused; she allowed only room for the few things immediately in front of her. She enjoyed the company of the teachers quite completely.

They were both possessed of such sweet and straightforward natures that they only suspected that Helen may have had a bit too much tea. Perhaps she was always this quick and clever at her work, they thought.

The following day, she had no such success getting her anger past Eggers.

He walked into the shop already talking, announcing to Samuel that he had seen the piano tuner at the Countess's place again that morning. Eggers found the almost daily piano tuning visits quite comical. Gustav, the tuner, was not-so-secretly in love with at least one of the artistes.

"Gustav was skulking about again this morning—" he began, but then he interrupted himself looking at Helen, "—but what happened to you?" Eggers feared that she had learned somehow about Samuel's tryst and had taken it badly. He wouldn't want to be to blame for that, particularly not as a mistake he had not made.

The genuine concern on his round face caused Helen a start. She could feel a crack develop in the shiny, hard armor she had constructed. "I am just tired," she lied.

He looked sharply at Samuel, who only shrugged helplessly. Whatever new-found confidence Eggers expected to see there was missing. Samuel had been oblivious that anything was amiss. If he had noticed, he would have no idea how to inquire.

"If by 'tired' you meant to say 'devastated' I think I understand," Eggers said to Helen. "Say, you are not distraught that Utah has entered the Union? That can't be it. I would never have guessed you had such bad feelings toward Utah."

"Utah didn't shun me at the church service," she said slowly, "so I have nothing against her at the moment."

"Bastards!" exclaimed Eggers, a bit too loudly. He pulled himself back, quite out of character, but it was the briefest hesitation. "I do apologize, that is your family, after all," he corrected himself, "but what dirty bastards!" he re-corrected.

"Thank you," said Helen simply. Her eyes brimmed with tears. She realized that she had never enjoyed hearing an insult as much as that.

She sat with Eggers in their tiny waiting area and Samuel stood in the doorway imagining that he lent silent support as she talked.

Each time she interrupted herself to say that some part of her story was inconsequential or unimportant, Eggers would encourage her to continue. Confiding in them felt natural and yet unseemly, just the sort of "bad behavior" that her family was expecting.

Even so, she told them all about her dilemma, with the exception of the threat of insanity treatments. That part was still too horrible and vivid to speak aloud.

"I have something to tell you both," said Samuel shyly.

Eggers held his breath.

"Perhaps it will help you with your worries," Samuel said to Helen. "I have decided to share the business with you both as partners, officially and properly."

Helen took in a little gasp of air. "Are you certain?" Eggers only grinned.

"Yes," he answered, "of course, there's nothing much to share yet, but there will be."

"I would be proud to share your nothings, Mr. Keegan!" exclaimed Eggers. "It nearly puts lie to all the times my sainted mother used to say, 'Eggers, yer worthless!'"

"She did not!" said Helen.

"Quite right," he admitted. "My mother never called me Eggers."

Samuel let them know, a bit shyly, that he had already asked the lawyer to prepare the papers and they only needed to go back into town and sign things to complete the arrangement.

***

The lawyer's office was next door to the bank, presumably because Mayflower Joe could be trusted not to burrow into the bank building in his spare time. The Rottweiler that slept in the bank was a litter mate to Joe's guard dog, although visitors were often confused to see it, at first believing that the same dog had appeared in two places as a canine magic trick. Like her sister, Jenny would spend the day sleeping on her side, ignoring visitors unless she sensed some ill intent. In those instances, she would roll up just far enough to swivel her gigantic head toward the newcomer and fix them with a toothy but bored expression as if to say, "Really?" Ordinarily, that was sufficient to dissuade any trouble making.

Jenny's sister, Hecuba, maimed a would-be robber or three during their years on the job. She had a talent for chomping down on the gun hands of impulsive fellows before they could draw their weapons. Jenny didn't begrudge Hecuba the more exciting duty. They could switch at any time and no one would be the wiser.

Joe's office was permeated by evidence of his weakness for the pipe. His preferred a pungent cherry-licorice concoction of his own making. It was so distinct, on the street one could retrace his steps minutes after he had passed, even on a windy day. The plaster in his office was yellowed with the stuff, as were the sticky piles of papers that threatened to bury him.

Helen imagined, one day when Joe was buried in the ground, a tobacco cloud would form over his grave. She managed to mask her revulsion at stepping into the chimney he called an office. Helen stooped down to pet Jenny and each pass of her hand over the dog's silky black coat lifted another tiny cloud of fur. Helen hesitated and the dog nuzzled her hand, insisting she continue to pay homage.

Joe sat at his desk and yawned broadly in greeting. A shelf full of pipes stood behind him and Eggers wondered why he would collect so many and only use the one in his hand. He was never seen carrying the mermaid meerschaum or any of the more peculiar pipes.

The lawyer was not expecting them and so had not seen their contract since he had completed it himself. He scanned the piles and it seemed likely that he had command of the paper chaos. He muttered as he looked; remembering, reminding, and collating as he went.

At last, he lifted a stack of long pages to reveal a wooden box underneath. "Here we are," he said speaking to the papers affectionately.

While they read over the short contract, he lit his pipe, striking a match broadly on an oversized match box. Samuel released a tiny reflexive whelp as he did so; the place seemed to beg for fire in every way. Joe leaned back in his creaky chair and regarded the three of them. His sharp face revealed nothing and his dark eyes moved quickly from one target to the next.

Joe was not curious about their business or their arrangement. He had been in the Port for a long time and kept a dry and jaded perspective on all of its business. If anyone had asked, he would have characterized their modest ambitions as "quaint."

"Remember, having a partner is the same as having a master," he said, as they handed him the signed pages.

Helen pulled her chin back in surprise, but quickly decided that she would not be mastered in this partnership. She would make it work. There was none of the language she had expected to read, she was not less a partner than either of the men, and not merely a tie-breaker in decisions.

As they left, Jenny followed Helen, and Joe could be heard complaining, "Go on then. See if I care. It'll save me a fortune in kibble."

Out in the street, Eggers said, "Now, we must have a toast!"

Helen immediately started to pull away from the notion. She did not need to be seen drinking in the tavern in the afternoon.

Eggers knew her worry. "It is not an option to decline," he cajoled, "Norwegian tradition demands it!"

She rolled her eyes, "It demands flaming burial boats too, but we are not doing that sort of funeral either. Are we?"

"I'm afraid you must come along," said Samuel. "Besides, no one from the congregation can admit to seeing you in the tavern."

Helen considered. "All right, but we'll have to be quick as the quickest Norwegian."

Eggers cocked his head, "Should I be offended?"

"No!" said Samuel. "Let's go."

Chapter 44—Toast

The tavern was busier than Helen would have expected at such an early hour, but then, she was rarely about town during midday. She was not surprised by the rowdy collection of patrons as much as she was interested to see what went on. She had theories, of course.

Helen had observed previously that the pursuit of vice seemed to pull people away, even as they congregated. Whether they were alienated by shame or walled off by the roar of their needs, it didn't matter; they would not sober long enough to see how alone they had become. The tavern wrapped their loneliness up together and disguised it.

These were not people who were infected, she thought, not pitiable monsters as the temperance types proclaimed, but rather people who had forgotten how to find the strength to care for anything but their primary need.

She was still a bit fearful, despite her compassionate ideas, at any encounter with large drunken men. She was well aware of the hazard they presented.

Her entrance didn't entirely stop conversation, but there was a distinct lull. A few of the patrons nodded in their direction. Squinty McGuiness barked a greeting and waived his large hand with great animation.

"McGuiness!" replied Eggers, "Nice to see you are still not dead!" McGuiness laughed and resumed his merriment with the butcher and two other men at his table.

The butcher had a fondness for rum and he could indulge in it utterly in mid-winter. No one was buying meat when they could slaughter their own animals and spare their winter feedings. He held court there in the tavern for all of December, and without his apron was likely to leave his disheveled shirt open, exposing his enormous hairy chest. No one dared complain.

Eggers looked sidelong at the remaining tables, deliberating on which one suited them best. He made a selection and pulled out a chair for Helen. She took her seat gracefully, reminded that she was among friends.

Samuel sat next to her as they watched Eggers approach Gannon, the barman. "Gannon, dear soul, be so kind as to bring us a horn filled with mead."

Gannon didn't look up from polishing a glass, "No mead, no horn." His tone was bored, with the usual bit of irritation.

"Then ale in your finest ceremonial stein!" suggested Eggers with greater enthusiasm.

"No stein neither," replied Gannon, finally allowing himself to be interrupted. He drew a large portion of ale into a hefty loving cup and placed it on the bar.

The butcher said to Gannon, "Is that the cup wit' the—"

"Shut your gob," growled Gannon.

Eggers raised his eyebrows to wordlessly ask if it was the cup with the ceramic frog cemented to the bottom. Gannon winked unhandsomely in answer.

This certainly is a special occasion, Eggers thought as he paid the barman with a flourish and presented the cup to his new partners as if he had won it.

"My friends, my partners," he began, "Let us mark this occasion with celebration and tribute in turns."

He continued to stand and paused to collect his thoughts before he continued. "May Odin the Furious, patron of the outcast, smile upon our efforts!" He drank from the cup and then held it out to Helen.

Helen stood, as did Samuel. She held the cup with the fingers of both hands curled under its handles and raised it. She was not entirely certain what to do next and decided to carry on in the spirit that Eggers had initiated. "May Jesus be well pleased with our work in the world, his lesser kingdom, as we hope to deserve his love." She paused, decided that was enough of a toast, and sipped from the cup. The tangy fluid tickled her throat.

She pretended not to notice the other patrons looking her way with curiosity. She knew that they were listening with one ear while still carrying on their own conversations but she was determined not to let them distract her from hers.

Most people find it difficult to gauge how blunt to be with those they do not know well. Eggers had no such difficulty. "Mind your own ceremonies!" he commanded the others.

The butcher's nearest pal, who was overfond of his mustache, only petted it and chuckled toward his cloud of unruly friends. Another man in the group laughed too, like a chipmunk with a cold.

Helen remained standing with Eggers as Samuel followed suit. He thought that a nautical toast would not alarm anyone and so he said, rather loudly, "May the unknowable force of the universe cause the winds to blow in our favor! Praise Odin, Jesus, Zeus, *et cetera*." Eggers chuckled.

"That's the spirit!" said Eggers, "And now, a toast to our heroes! First, my hero, Ivarr the Boneless, cursed and born with no bones at all. He prevailed to become wisest and craftiest of his eleven brothers. He made them unstoppable in conquest of the great cities!"

"No bones," commented McGuiness drawing his own chin back skeptically, "that's daft."

"All the more reason he's a hero," replied Eggers, "Only the truest hero could conquer in such an impossible condition. How far do you think you'd get with no bones?"

Helen smiled broadly as she started her turn, "To my hero, Lizzy Borden, master criminal and free woman!" She giggled at the abrupt silence. "Just joking," she said. There was a ripple of relieved laughter. The butcher laughed longer than everyone else; he thought nothing was funnier than a woman making jokes about axe murders.

The one-armed man next to the Butcher took a long gulp from his mug, set it down and rubbed that same hand slowly down his beard. His wooden arm was cast casually in the center of the table.

Helen started again, earnestly, with no regard to the broader company. "To Marianne North, the 'wild bird,' who traveled all of the world on her own to capture and paint the beauty she found in every corner." She drank.

Samuel paused, feeling a rush of sincerity that he could not ignore, "To Edward Jenner and his extraordinary perseverance in the face of terrible ridicule. He would not hear a word of deterrence and he would not stop until he conquered smallpox and spared countless lives."

"Well, that is a very generous toast from an undertaker," said the butcher, belching robustly as he spoke his little declaration.

"Perhaps. All profits in consideration, I would always rather bury the very aged and most satisfied people," replied Samuel warmly.

"And now," Eggers took the cup and looked down, as if to collect his next words carefully, "My friends, you are dearer to me than the siblings I never knew I had," a bit of a hush descended on the establishment again. Eggers voice took on a slightly higher tone than normal, "To Miss Helen, my sister, skillful in *nearly* every art and right thinking on every subject, and Mr. Keegan, my brother, who leaves his heart open to the world and still shines a searchlight of optimism all around." The joke that everyone was waiting for did not come and his siblings melted a little at the unusual candor.

Helen took her turn with a bit of reluctance. She could feel the sensation of her decision, as if a tiny door closed in her heart. To be frank was impossible, so she would retreat to humor. "To my dear Mr. Eggers, your words never fail to surprise me, and I do mean never. You have caught me quite unprepared to praise you both properly! And to you, Mr. Keegan, I... I hope you will be the one to bury me when I die of embarrassment!"

A loud whistle of approval was sounded by one of Squinty's companions and Samuel beamed at her as she took another dainty sip from the cup and handed it to him. He knew by now that she was never at a loss for words, but she was deliberately keeping them quiet.

"Eggers, I drink to your sense of adventure and constant state of motion. I must say, I never knew I could love a man so well without getting arrested!" Everyone in the place erupted into laughter and jeers. Samuel leaned toward Helen conspiratorially and said very softly, "I would rather die than bury you, you know." He hurriedly took a swig from the cup and moved to set it down on the table, wishing to conclude their very public toast as privately as possible.

As he put the cup down, Samuel's eyes locked with the gaze of the shiny frog peering up at him from the bottom of the cup. He shrieked and hopped backward an impressive distance before he had the intelligence to realize it was only a ceramic frog, expressly put there for the purpose of pranks.

Gannon was tremendously gratified that Samuel was the frog finder. It was everything he's hoped for when he selected the cup for them. By the time he told the story a few times, he had Samuel doing a terrified double shuffle dance and bowling down four other patrons.

Samuel's only defense was to say he could not dance, even in a panic. His partners would chime in to agree with the truth of that.

Now that their partnership was formally established, they wouldn't have long to wait for a funeral. It was only a matter of weeks before there was a death in the Port.

Chapter 45—January

Helen woke one January morning to find an ice storm had crept into town overnight. As she rose and swung her feet to the floor, the cold of the floorboards filtered through to her feet with ease. Her little fireplace had gone completely cold and dark in the night and she shuddered as she regarded it.

She moved to pull back the curtain and looked out her window as she always did; she found a landscape that had never been waiting there for her before.

A hush coated everything, along with the coating of ice. Helen stood very still and listened.

She felt a hint of dread taking hold, imagining that she had lost her hearing overnight. As if in answer to the thought, a branch gave way under the weight of the ice and tumbled and crashed, crackling to the earth while pulling more of its companions down with it. A raven called to its mate and received an answering scream. Then, the hush took hold again.

The woods looked shiny and indistinct. She wished that the sun could pour over on all the tiny branches encased in ice.

The pine trees suffered most from the burden and were wilted looking. The small ones bent to the ground under the weight, pulled into painful positions.

In the pre-dawn light, everything was silver and black and unclear, like a poorly made photograph. Trying to rid herself of the ominous sensations, Helen shifted into her routine and pulled on her dressing gown and quietly made her way toward the kitchen.

Normally, she wasn't the first awake; most mornings she was second after Mr. Jefferson. He liked tea in the morning, as she did, and since there was no scent of tea in the air yet, she expected to find him in the kitchen.

But on this morning, the kitchen was dark and cold. She stoked the stove and was relieved to find some water was still in the pitcher. No one would relish crunching through the ice to get to the well on this kind of morning.

She waited for the water to boil, standing close to the stove to keep warmer, even though it had little effect.

She prepared two cups and carried them through the dim house and up the stairs. She left one cup on the hallway table by Jefferson's room.

Once back in her room and shivering a little, she proceeded to pull on her outdoor clothes. The gray dawn light crept into her room more and more.

Her ashes of roses dress replaced her dressing gown. She intended to put on her sturdiest boots when she got back down to the entry. Those young trees needed a reprieve from the heavy ice and she would do what she could.

As she stepped back into the hallway, Helen was surprised to find the cup she had left for Mr. Jefferson was still there and had grown cold. She tapped on his door and got no response. She peeked inside and saw that he wasn't there and may not have been there all night.

He might have wandered up to the hotel or any number of other places to sleep overnight. She retrieved the cup, thinking he must have let the icy conditions keep him from coming home late.

Once she was bundled for the cold, she went outside, taking tiny skidding steps to reach the outhouse. Helen often thought that the lack of indoor plumbing was the only disadvantage of the Admiral's house. It had so much charm in every other aspect. Lack of charm aside, nothing would awaken one quite as thoroughly as a visit to a frozen privy.

Feeling very alert now, Helen slipped and stepped across the yard, her boots crunching through the icy glaze only a few times until she reached the bent trees. The first tree crackled at her touch as some of the ice fell away, but it was only raised a little and stayed stubbornly bowed toward the ground. She shook it vigorously to release the ice and it sprang up until it was only tilted. Its green spiny leaves were mostly revealed, providing a splash of color in the gray dawn.

She moved to free the second little tree, and with a few shakes it relaxed with its companion. Helen felt like she was repairing and painting the trees with her hands and smiled contentedly at the notion.

The fourth tree sprang up to reveal something crouched underneath. Helen jumped back and fell to the ground. She scrambled briefly on the ice and turned to look again.

The face of Thomas Jefferson stared at her. The icicles in his eyelashes told her everything. He was certainly dead.

She pulled herself up and stared at him for a long, long moment. His normally brown eyes were a dark, icy silver. His body was twisted as if he had been curled up and then tried to roll onto his back with his legs still pinned in place. His mouth was open, but not suggesting pain. Altogether, his expression was one of surprise.

Why would he be here? She wondered. His clothing was inadequate for the weather, as usual. The members of the household were always coaxing him into warmer clothes. Somehow his mind was stuck in springtime and he wouldn't remember the winter right in front of him.

Had he been looking for something out here? He misplaced his things routinely and was often on an expedition to locate his watch or his pocket knife. The Admiral had replaced them and Jefferson's favorite book of poems at least a dozen times.

She stayed there, looking at him for so long that a raven became bold and hopped over to investigate. When she turned, the huge bird screeched and she let out a little squawk of alarm in reply.

Startled from her reverie she turned back to Mr. Jefferson. "I'm sorry," she said simply. "I'll be back with help." She didn't realize that there were soft tears on her face as she covered him with her coat.

Helen hurried toward Samuel's boarding house and nearly fell in the street. By the time the door opened she was rubbing her hands together trying to revive her fingers in the cold.

As Samuel opened the door, he was met by a wave of cold air and the scent of rose water and clean sweat, announcing Helen as always.

"I need your help," she said simply.

"Anything," he replied.

Chapter 46—Fetching

Samuel pulled Helen into the foyer and wrapped her in his coat. She whispered to him to explain the problem. Her shoulders pulled up to her ears and she shivered as she spoke.

"I think we can manage with a stretcher," he said. "Are you alright?" His concern was both genuine and fleeting, as his mind raced on.

"I will be. We have to do this without delay," she replied.

They agreed that getting him into the Admiral's house was the best course. Samuel stopped Hops, who was just leaving, and asked him to alert Eggers or anyone likely to encounter Eggers that he was needed at the big house.

"Don't let on that it's important, just say that I need to talk to him, or, uh," Samuel hesitated, wishing he had a code phrase, "Just use your discretion." Hops frowned and nodded minutely, understanding and not understanding.

Helen and Samuel crossed back with a blanket and stretcher, moving as quickly as they safely could. Helen let her borrowed coat drag along the ice using most of her attention to avoid a fall along the way.

As they rounded the house, Helen saw that Grace had found Mr. Jefferson. She stood back some distance from the body, her head tilted as she studied him in her odd, detached way.

"Surprised to find you awake this early," said Helen in greeting.

"Oh, the world sounded wrong and woke me," replied Grace. "This is wrong too," she said. She sighed, regarding the body. "I'll take care of the Admiral. He will be inconsolable, I think, but I will try."

"I would like to tell him," said Samuel.

Grace only nodded, but Helen thought she looked skeptical. She rested a hand on Helen's shoulder for a moment before gliding back toward the still, dark house.

To their relief, Jefferson wasn't frozen firmly to the ground, but his icy clothes made alarming crackling noises as he was moved to allow the stretcher to be slid under him. He was in rigor mortis, so the shape of his body would not properly fit on the frame. They centered him as best they could and began the treacherous process of transporting him safely to the parlor. Samuel walked backward using tiny steps, while Helen steered and directed him. She tried without much success to conceal her breathlessness. It was very hard work, and tricky.

As they progressed, Helen's shoes lost traction and she slid sideways on the ice, keeping her balance but taking the end of the stretcher with her. Samuel pivoted, which kept the stretcher flat, but allowed her slide to continue much longer than she liked.

At last, she stopped and took a huge breath. "Let's avoid the skating," she said. She shuffled forward and began to skid in the opposite arc. Samuel thought it would have been a very entertaining game under any other circumstances.

Eggers arrived, pulling a long window shutter behind him, as an improvised combination stretcher and sled. "What's this folderol?"

He skidded over to Helen's end and took it from her. He gestured for her to slide the shutter under the stretcher and she did. "Now put him down," he directed Samuel. They pulled the stretcher the rest of the way, using the ice instead of fighting it.

"You got here very quickly. How did you know to bring the, um, shutter?" asked Samuel.

"What in thunder would make you send for me this early if nobody's dead?" replied Eggers.

Helen cast about in her mind to recall the furniture in the parlor. Most of it was small and spindly; there was no sturdy table that would do. They would have to put him on the parlor piano, at least temporarily.

The house was very quiet as they struggled in through the back door and carried the body the remaining distance. Grace hovered and helped them into the parlor. Helen asked her about the Admiral and she whispered back that he was still sleeping.

Helen carefully lowered the top of the piano and covered it with a blanket. They lifted Jefferson up and placed him on top of the instrument, with his head closest to the keys. The way he was curled up, it almost seemed like he could have died right there.

Helen checked his fingers again to determine how long they might have to wait to reposition him.

Her best guess was that it would be a full day before he could be re-positioned. She shook her head ruefully. In the meantime, he would have to remain as he was, crouched like a clumsy cat.

"We'll go get the kit and some boards so that we can place him better," said Samuel. He looked around for Eggers, but he was already gone. Helen nodded, still thinking.

Grace said that she would go see the Admiral, but Samuel raised a hand, surprising even himself.

"I will do it before I leave," he said.

Samuel slipped out and Helen fidgeted around the room, pushing the chairs to the walls and making space where they could work. When she was satisfied that she could do no more than wait, she sat on the piano bench and looked up at the shape under the blanket there and said in a quiet and conspiratorial manner, "We are going to give you first-rate service, Mr. Jefferson."

Chapter 47—Finest

Samuel thought he heard the Admiral stirring, and waited in the hallway, perched uncomfortably in one of the low-backed Windsor chairs. He stood and knocked on the door tentatively, and the Admiral's low voice commanded him to enter.

The Admiral was dressing, and Samuel hesitated. That hesitation was all the invitation the Admiral required to launch into a detailed account of his terrible night's sleep. He was never particular about his audience for such lectures and he seemed to have no curiosity whatsoever that an undertaker would pay him an early visit.

"I woke myself up shouting, 'Mind the roll!' and when I checked the clock it was 1500," the Admiral shook his head. He finished fastening the last of his buttons and opened the door before crossing back to collect his pocket watch. "When I awoke each time, fancied the sea was too rough—the clock said 1500 every time, ticking away an endless night."

"I'm sorry," Samuel said, "It's a dreadful thing." Samuel burst into tears.

He was choked with emotion and could not wipe the hot tears away fast enough before they were replaced by even more tears. He inhabited what he imagined the Admiral's grief might be, if only he could tell him that his dearest companion lived no more.

The Admiral, perplexed, leaned toward him and patted his shoulder awkwardly, "Now, now. What's the matter? It's not like the clock is broken, you understand."

Samuel cried harder, failing in every way to make himself understood. He cried with the borrowed grief and his own terrible embarrassment too.

Grace came in and looked from one to the other of them. Samuel had made an impressive job of botching the delivery of news. She closed the door again and insisted the Admiral sit down. Helen listened at the door, anxiously, as Grace started by saying that she had "the most distressing word."

The Admiral questioned her, but Grace refused to say more until he sat down and readied himself. She prepared him just as she might have prepared him to receive a punch.

The Admiral listened to Grace, murmuring, "…that so," and, "I see," as if the news were not at all remarkable. Samuel gradually stopped sobbing and absorbed the calm of the conversation, only hiccupping with all sorts of regret.

They went very quiet and Helen held her breath, expecting an explosive reaction. Instead, the Admiral began giving orders to Samuel. He wanted them to have the viewing in his parlor; he wanted a huge wake, and a parade to the cemetery. He would say yes to every single question of the proceeding.

When recounting the details, Samuel told Eggers that he was concerned that they might be taking advantage. The Admiral was in such extreme distress, perhaps they should wait to confirm when he was less stricken. Eggers hushed him and reminded him that they were in the business of giving people what they wanted. "If it pleases him to present a massive tribute, we have a duty to oblige."

The Admiral had insisted on seeing Jefferson right away. They arranged the body to obscure its contortions and placed pennies on Jefferson's eyes.

Viewing a body should help the grieving to confirm the terrible news and begin to move toward acceptance. This is always the hope of the exercise, but acceptance of such a loss may not come quietly.

The Admiral has used up all his quiet. He wailed. His guttural cries caused the hairs at the nape of Helen's neck to stand in warning. Grace was steady, and kept her long arms on him all the time. She softly reminded him of the things he needed to remember.

At last, he fell to weeping in near silence. His whiskers were flooded with tears. He gently stroked the cold hand of his friend. "I'm sorry, Jefferson," he said, finally, "So sorry."

Eggers whispered to Helen, "Not entirely wholesome, eh?" She scolded him with her eyes.

The news spread widely and they had to keep working in order to be ready for a visit from everyone in town and beyond.

Most of Helen's fabric handiwork was brought over and she spent the much of the first day draping the black bunting at the front of the house, covering all the mirrors, and shrouding the parlor.

Eggers kept busy arranging food and refreshments. He spoke to Reverend Price about a service and placing the body in the winter crypt. They wouldn't be able to have a burial until the thaw, since the ground was even more frozen than usual.

The Reverend asked Eggers to what faith did Jefferson ascribe? Eggers told him blithely that the man had been a Baptist but that "any flavor of Jesus" would do. The Reverend clucked in response, but Eggers slipped him a gold coin and a wink and made a hasty exit to avoid any further discussion on the subject.

The second day, as Helen had predicted, they were able to proceed with the preparation of the body. Samuel had brought the equipment and the portable work table supports. They had kept him cold until the chemistry of his muscles relaxed.

As they bathed Jefferson, they were appalled by what they found. His back and legs were ruined with scars. His narrow back bore a dense web of raised flesh that had replaced nearly half of his skin there. Helen gasped at the sight and Eggers gave a low whistle from across the room.

"He might have died from such a beating," said Samuel.

Helen felt her tears sting. Her fingers traced the livid scars as if reading some hidden meaning there. She spoke softly to Jefferson, her voice slightly choked, "You are free from even this now. You can go wherever you like and truly forget the story of this body."

She looked at Samuel plainly. "I feel the need for a moment away," she said. He started to follow her out of the room, but she halted him with a hand and let him know that his company wasn't welcome.

When she returned, they could see that she was still disturbed but prepared to get back to work. A conversation hovered in the room, but they would not have that until they were done.

Chapter 48—Freedom

Fabian offered to keep watch over the body while they all went to supper. He poked at the piano experimentally until he settled on a soft tune, his wide fingers finding the ivory from their own memory. He was as unperturbed that Jefferson's body had so recently lain on the piano, and he would fit a funeral into his routine with no more effort than using an umbrella when it rained.

Helen was anxious to get out of the house. She was proud of all her needle work, but she found it difficult to stop repositioning things in the home and had to leave the premises in order to truly be still. She had dithered in circles to find herself polishing the same table corner one too many times.

The ice had thawed and the road was slushy mud. The walkways were little better and it didn't bode well for the procession that the Admiral had in mind for the next day.

They settled in to a corner of the tavern and accepted the meal that was the only choice for the evening. The chowder was a little too salty, but it was warm and filling.

"Do you suppose he remembered being a slave?" asked Samuel.

"I'd say not," answered Eggers, even though the question had been directed to Helen. She nodded.

"He remembered how to play cards," Helen said, "but I could never get a word from him about his family or his past. It's possible he remembered in some way that he couldn't put into words, but I don't think so. He was a happy man.

"People who remember those days don't like to talk about it, but when they do talk about it, I listen," she said. "Did you know that there's a former owner in the Port? Well, someone from a family of owners, that is."

"Who?" asked Samuel, who had no guesses at hand.

She shook her head. "They want to forget, and really what good would it do to tell you who she is? She said that her people didn't like the idea of slavery but fought to keep it because they were so terribly afraid of what would come after it was abolished."

"Understandable," mumbled Eggers, frowning.

Helen ignored his presumed joke, "They were afraid they would lose everything—everything that was built on the backs of their slaves."

They finished eating for a bit in silence. Each of them, but Eggers in particular, seemed lost in thought.

"Families were separated because the owners believed that family is power," Helen continued. "They would interfere with any strong attachments, because they thought that was their right, even their obligation." She stopped for a moment, her voice clogged with emotion. "How they didn't see that they were just like pharaohs." She stopped again and sighed. "Pharaohs with crops instead of monuments to misery," she finished.

"Who said that?" asked Eggers. "Alexander Crummell?"

"I just did," said Helen.

Eggers chuckled appreciatively and she went on, undeterred. "Some people killed themselves in their despair," she said. "I can't imagine how anyone could stand to profit from that kind of pain."

After another long, thoughtful silence, Eggers spoke again. "I believe that people are born with a sense of freedom," he said.

Samuel smiled, "That's very American of you, my friend, but I am not so sure."

Helen shook her head, "You haven't spent much time with babies," she was smiling at him as she went on. "They come into the world expecting things and understanding fairness and freedom."

"Fairness, eh? You think so?" said Eggers.

"They know when they aren't getting their fair share of things. And they hate shoes. They just know shoes are wrong."

Eggers released another small laugh.

"I think," she continued, "that we learn how to live without freedom, bit by bit." She nodded with great seriousness at him as she went on speaking, "And it all begins with the shoes."

She stared at him until Eggers laughed more heartily.

Abruptly, an indignant voice rose from behind one of the panels in the tavern. The sound of further shouting and scuffling drew all attention to that direction.

Eggers eyes were wide as he looked from one to the other as he recognized the voice, "It's the Admiral!"

As others backed away the three of them moved into the private room that had erupted into a brawl.

They found the Admiral, restrained by the burly butcher, his clothing askew and tearing as the larger man grappled for a better grip. A large knife lay on the ground amongst broken shards and tableware.

"He's berserk. Said he's earnest to end his life," said the butcher. He arrived at a confident hold of the Admiral and then continued, "We thought he was foolin' and after all, he was buyin' all the drinks…"

The other men in the room spoke all at once to declare their beliefs on the seriousness of the Admiral's intentions. The din made it impossible to distinguish who said what about all that. It was clear all of them had enjoyed many rounds of his farewell generosity.

"I'm done for!" shouted the Admiral, although he seemed to lack conviction and his words were muffled.

Samuel stood protectively ahead of Helen, but she pushed forward to talk to the Admiral, his face was pressed to exactly her level. "How did you slip away from Grace? She'll be worried about you," she said calmly.

The Admiral melted a little. His breath was hot and vile with whiskey as he whimpered in response. "Turn me loose. I'm settled now," he said to the butcher.

The butcher released him and the Admiral straightened his coat, took a deep breath and smoothed the front of his garment over his belly as he did so.

Helen felt a powerful jerk of her arm and was suddenly behind a pile of men as the Admiral lunged for the knife once more. He succeeded only in being bested by the butcher again as the knife clattered to the wooden floor.

The expression of satisfaction that had come over his face was replaced again with the indignant grimace and more keening.

"Listen, you," said the butcher, irritated now and speaking with uncharacteristic clarity, "I don't care what sort of abomination you are, you are not going to gut yourself in this place tonight. You understand me?"

Eggers tried this time, "Sir, if we have to get the police to take charge of you, you may miss the funeral. You don't want to miss that, after all."

"No," said the Admiral, deflated and weeping again with renewed intensity.

The butcher began to speak, but Eggers made a gesture to silence him. And moved to take hold of the Admiral. "Come on, friend, let's get you back home safe for a good long sleep you can wake from."

In that way, they steered him home again and had no difficulty keeping Eggers out of the whiskey for another day.

Chapter 49—Funeral

The visitation at the Admiral's house was indeed the finest the people of the Port had ever seen.

Visitors began filing in mid-day to find Jefferson in repose in the parlor. Black clouds of drapery lined the room, and the gold stars that were dotted across them flickered and moved in the lamp light. The piano was played in turn by several visitors who were able to recall favorite pieces that Jefferson had asked for at one time or another.

Thomas Jefferson was laid in a walnut coffin, which was beautifully lined in green satin and equipped with the fanciest extension handles available. His face had been arranged in a gentle smile that was familiar to everyone. He wore a fine dress suit and patent leather shoes that had never touched the ground.

Most of the visitors remarked at how very fine he looked as they moved on into the dining room to judge the refreshments to be very fine as well. Samuel surveyed the scene with a great deal of pride.

This, Samuel thought, was precisely what he had in mind from the very beginning. Shaping a gathering to honor a life and soothe the hearts of a community in the process; that was all he had wanted. Certainly, he had underestimated the difficulty, but he believed in that moment—still incorrectly—that he had mastered his craft.

Samuel's satisfied thoughts were on display, and many people noted the way he rocked on his heels and smiled a bit too much. More than one mourner could be heard later to say, "I'll be blest if that undertaker fellow wasn't enjoying it all too much."

The Admiral seemed calm after his stormy evening, and greeted everyone in his usual hearty, low voice. "Good of you to come," he said to some and, "Thank you, friend," to others. "A sad day to be sure," he said in response to any personal condolences, but he was emotionally remote and odd.

Before the influx of people, the Admiral had leaned toward Samuel and confided, "I am of the belief that I am cursed." When Samuel protested, the Admiral went on to say that everyone in his acquaintance met with calamity—every single person. Samuel decided not to argue, but nodded without saying that calamity is natural and inevitable, of course.

Later, Samuel would always wonder if he had made an error in judgment. He accepted that the man had moved on from the worst shock of his grief, and it seemed obvious that he was much changed from the night before. It was a stark contrast, however. The Admiral's cheerfulness might have been a signal. If it was, it was a signal that Samuel simply did not read.

Chapter 50—Confession

The procession to the cemetery was made very difficult by the mud, but they persevered and delivered Mr. Jefferson to his intermediate resting place in the winter crypt. Reverend Price did his best to eulogize a man he was only familiar with in reputation, and he left the amusing stories for others to tell afterward, indoors.

Helen slogged back to the house with both partners beside her. Her black skirts were filthy with mud and the men tried not to make her aware that they were ready to catch her if she stumbled. She disliked gentlemanly protectiveness and would suck her teeth in disapproval if she sensed it. She was still annoyed by the way they had pulled her back from the knife scuffle the night before.

"I have a confession," said Eggers when they were clear of the other mourners' hearing.

"You wish you were a female so that you could have my wonderful laundry?" guessed Helen with her greatest dose of sarcasm.

"No. I think I need to include you two in some other business," said Eggers seriously. They stopped at the front of the Admiral's house and Samuel and Helen turned to him to listen, curious now.

"My visits to the city," began Eggers, "I know it has been assumed that I was on some romantic missions," they nodded. "And make no mistake, they could have been trysts, and you might have deduced that was my purpose—"

"You told us that!" interrupted Samuel, "No deduction was required!"

"But my purpose was generally otherwise," concluded Eggers, inconclusively. He let the words hang there for a moment. Helen grimaced and gestured impatiently; she was cold and had yards of muddy fabric to wrestle with.

"Remember Dr. Cook's request? Well, I found a solution for him at the asylum. They send for me any time they have a body and I make the arrangements to ship them quickly and discretely to him." He smiled broadly and proudly, "It is quite perfect, in fact. The facility gets much-needed funds and I—now we—get the fee. And Dr. Cook's school gets the body parts, of course."

Samuel rubbed his jaw, "I'm not so certain it's perfect."

"How can you just take them?" asked Helen. "These people cannot want to be used for study—or do they?"

"There are papers," Eggers replied. "When the inmates are put in, the family or the authorities relinquish all rights to their possessions including their persons. Most of them are old soldiers."

Helen imagined wards of older men, confused and ruined by cannon shots, their bodies the only testimony they could give any longer, their families dispersed or unwilling to care for them in senility. She winced and pressed a fist to her chest.

"That doesn't sound legal," said Samuel, doubtfully.

"Ha!" replied Eggers. "It is as legal as anything the lawyers concoct over there. The place has a duty to bury the bodies, and they consider the donations a public service. I suppose if anyone gets affronted, we will see what the court has to say, but until then…" Eggers handed Helen a small stack of coins and then one to Samuel.

"We can't continue this," said Helen in an anguished tone.

"Well, uh," Samuel was muted by the money.

"I know you don't like the idea of utilizing people," he said to Helen in particular, "but you must see the value of having Dr. Cook obliged to us."

She nodded solemnly. If not for Cook, they had no fully experienced medical help and certainly none at all were willing to put them on an irregular route. This was better for the people of the Port, to be sure.

"Let's make certain the papers show that they agree to the donation," she said, "But you are correct; I don't like this one bit." She didn't have to remind them that all of them could get charged with mutilation or criminal desecration. It had happened in other places and the law was murky. There might not be laws against shipping a body disguised as a grandfather clock cabinet, but they would be tempting disaster to continue doing such things.

"We need the money," said Eggers simply.

Samuel nodded. They had only half a year left to turn a profit.

"I know," she replied, "for now. The instant there are clouds of trouble forming, it's over."

Chapter 51—Circuit

They had no summons from the asylum for all of that month. Helen planned to talk to Mayflower Joe about it, in a general way, to see if he might be able to clarify points on the rights of the dead. She thought she could craft it as a few questions of professional curiosity. She would say that a customer had inquired. That wouldn't be too terribly suspicious.

In February, Eggers kept them updated on the murder of the month. Helen didn't like reading the accounts in the papers and said that she thought the reporting was ugly; she disliked the way a gory court case could pull the eye to read all the lurid details. Eggers had no such qualms; despite his delicate reaction to in-person violence, he was fascinated by far off stories of gore.

This particular murder was a very nasty one. Still, Eggers was able to find comedy in the notably knuckleheaded way that the murderers were caught.

Not at all hilarious in their conduct of the murder itself, the killers had enticed one man's sweetheart to travel with them both. They drugged the woman by tampering with her beverage. The drugging was thoroughly witnessed by a great many patrons in the tavern where they did it.

After taking a long, peculiar carriage ride into the country, they eventually murdered her. Not satisfied with terrifying and killing her, they also decapitated her. The men had used her own valise to carry her head away. Their plan was to destroy it in a furnace. They were apparently confident that removing her head would make her body utterly anonymous.

They had not considered that the young lady would have her name clearly printed in her shoes. The newspaper had quoted one of the killers, "Damn those shoes!" he said.

Eggers chortled, "It has been proven that they *planned* this and still were utterly daft and feckless. I would be a much, much better murderer," he opined. "Now, if they had burned the valise and the shoes it might never have been solved at all."

Samuel scoffed, "You still would have had a missing pregnant girl and the fifty-eight people who saw them drug her sarsaparilla."

"True," admitted Eggers. "A perfect crime must be perfect in every way."

"You cannot plan enough for stupidity," commented Helen, "it always shines through."

It was plain enough in the details that the woman wasn't the main target of the murder, although she did reportedly expend a lot of breath screaming at the men about her delicate situation.

The pregnancy could have killed her, after all, but they weren't interested in waiting, and had decided to kill her rather than let her ruin their reputations. They had continued with their misbegotten plan even after all the cats were out of the bag.

"Even we don't take surgical tools to supper," commented Helen. "Murderous dunces," she shook her head.

"And what would you do?" inquired Eggers with a challenge in his tone.

"I would not get a girl pregnant, of course," she replied. The men snorted. "You know," she continued in a more confidential tone, "people assume I know how to procure abortions. I finally had to find a place to send them because it happens so often."

"Perhaps it is your trustworthy demeanor?" suggested Samuel. She turned to snipe back at him before realizing that he was sincere. She let his comment sit alone too long.

"Couldn't you perform them?" asked Eggers. "Help one of these gals rid herself of a baneful bairn?"

Helen scoffed. "It's not a simple matter, and furthermore, even if I had the skill and had the tools, I can't abide the blood."

"You are curdling my breakfast," said Eggers, "Let's get out of here and see how it goes with the judge! The Wiltz business should be enough to get him ruffled."

The judge's circuit brought him to the Port at irregular intervals, but when he arrived, the tavern was re-arranged to form a court room for the day. He preferred to sit behind the bar, since it afforded him a superior position, as long as he had a tall stool brought there on which he could perch.

His stenographer sat on the other side of the bar below him and operated her machine while maintaining a bird-like attention to all the bits of testimony. The custodian of a modern marvel, she did not speak or make any sound at all, except to tear the paper from the back of her machine at the end of each case.

Most of the matters were minor disputes or routine agreements that required his hearing and seal of approval. In some situations, he would inform the plaintiffs that they would have to travel to the orphan's court, but he handled all manner of small situations. The disputes were what drew crowds.

The entertainment value of his proceedings kept him in his job as much as his general reputation. When he became aggravated, his eyes would bulge, and he would begin to scrape his teeth on his fleshy lips; a signal to the assembled that a great carnivore was about to feast.

It was impossible to discern whether or not the judge was fair-minded in all things. He understood the basic disadvantage that the poorer and uneducated of his constituents faced, but he also had a tendency to interject with such commentary as, "Of course you are familiar with the precedent of Stonesifer versus the Commonwealth of Virginia…" when no one in attendance had any idea what that suggested.

By the time the funeral crew had arrived, the judge had already dispensed with the most mundane of his matters and had moved on to hear a complaint from a laundress named Sallie Wiltz.

Sallie stepped up stiffly and began to tell her story. Helen was riveted and dismayed to hear the details as Sallie explained. Her husband had come home drunk and had broken some of their furniture and then had beaten her about the face and shoulders.

Sallie was small, but not as small as Helen. She was calm despite the circumstances and only showed a hint of nervousness in the way she repeatedly smoothed her skirts as she spoke.

Benjamin, her husband, sat near the front of the improvised courtroom. He held his head in his hands and seemed properly ashamed of himself and certainly hungover.

The judge asked him if what she said was true, and Benjamin nodded. He half-stood and said, "I suppose I did, but I'm not entirely persuaded it was me."

Sallie's face showed a faint bruise at her jaw and another under her eye that was darker. That was liable to swell more the next day in Helen's estimation.

The judge then asked if anyone else could corroborate Sallie's story.

Samuel leaned over to Eggers and asked why he would ask for a witness when the man confessed. Eggers shrugged theatrically and indicated that he should be quiet and listen.

The fireman, George King, stepped forward and took an oath to tell the truth. He related his version of the incident in the unhurried way of an Englishman who enjoyed the opportunity to speak. "Your honor, I was attending a gathering in the house next door…" George pronounced it *gavering*. Helen knew that the "gathering" was most likely a tryst with Kate, the widow.

"A terrible rumpus could be heard," George continued, "and I heard Missus Wiltz scream and so I departed to investigate what was the matter. I was sure to find a row, and I did. The living room was mightily disturbed and I found Mr. Wiltz thrashing his wife with his hands and fists." George paused for emphasis and looked about the courtroom. "I pulled him away to allow the lady to escape and subdued him until the police arrived."

Kate applauded energetically.

"Stop that nonsense," admonished the judge. He turned back to George, "So in your professional opinion as a fireman, Mister— uh—Wiltz was the aggressor?"

"Indubitably," replied George.

The sentence for such an offense, which was still only considered a drunk and disorderly infraction, could be meted out in days in jail or dollars fined.

"I hereby order the defendant, Benjamin Wiltz, to pay a fine of five dollars," said the judge. An approving murmur spread through the room until the judge scowled them back to silence.

Sallie Wiltz stood again and raised her hand, "Excuse me, sir," she said, "I have a question."

Sallie had endured many years of mistreatment from Mr. Wiltz, who often remarked that she was a dullard. She was not. In fact, she was quietly imaginative, scrupulous with figures, and careful with her spending.

"What's your question, then?" asked the judge impatiently.

Sallie lowered her hand uncertainly and waived her little fingers as she asked, "Sir, for five dollars—how many days is that?"

The assembled witnesses erupted in laughter at the notion that Sallie would rather have a vacation from her husband than have him fined. There was general approval that she would say so in front of everyone and anyone, too.

The judge banged a gavel on the bar for a full minute before their laughter subsided. His eyes bulged and his own mirth had been completely subjugated to the rowdy crowds' disrespectful enjoyment.

These Port people were the very worst sort of citizenry; with no respect and no ambition to be respectable. He would press hard to get all the business concluded so that he could escape this rabble and get back to the better parts of the county.

Chapter 52—Admiral

After the court day was concluded, Helen went back to the house and found the Admiral sitting alone on the front porch in the fading sun. He smiled vaguely at her as she took a seat in the rocking chair next to his.

She and the other boarders had noticed a change in him since the death of Mr. Jefferson. He was aloof, although friendly as ever. He had lost interest in many of his pastimes and didn't tell his stories as readily as before.

Gertie had told Helen that he was not who he pretended to be. When pressed on her assertion, she had said that he may have been in the Navy, but he was positively not an Admiral.

Gertie said that one signal trait of old Navy men of rank was their affinity for other old Navy men of rank. The fact that he never paraded in a uniform or received guests who were freshly returned from parading in their uniforms was very telling, she said.

Like Helen's grandfather, who had made his money in guano trade, the Admiral may have been on the water, but if so, he was doing something that was lucrative and distinctly non-Naval.

Helen wanted to draw him out. "You might have enjoyed the court today," she offered. "It was diverting at the very least."

"Ack," he said, "I don't like rubbing up against all those lubbers. I would rather be enjoying the fresh air right here."

"It's cold," she pointed out. He made only a non-committal noise in reply. She rocked for a moment and then launched very directly although quietly to ask, "You knew that Mr. Jefferson had been a slave?"

The Admiral stopped rocking and turned his head toward her. "Of course," he said, regarding her with icy eyes. His lips slowly pulled into a small, misshapen snarl. Helen might have been afraid of the angry change in him then, but his gaze went somewhere past her and she knew that his feelings were not for her.

She waited, perfectly still.

When, at last, the Admiral exhaled, he drew a hand up to his brow and sobbed violently. His huge shoulders fell and shuddered as he wept.

Helen watched as he made ugly, strangled noises. She started to reach for his shoulder, but he seemed to sense it and jerked away from her. As the outburst passed, he wiped his beard with his sleeve, and did not turn back to face her at all.

"It is a terrible thing to live with," he said, speaking very slowly. "You survive it, but you also perish from it. You do not truly return from that place. No matter how long afterward you are in safety and peace, quiet cannot be restored to your health. Some people manufacture a veneer of their old selves, but underneath, they are still shaken and wounded."

Helen wasn't so certain that he was speaking of Jefferson now.

"Your father was in the war?" he asked.

She shook her head, "Club foot."

The Admiral nearly chuckled, "Ah, yes, I had forgotten he's a cripple."

Helen let it go although this irked her. Her father was able-bodied enough, but his problem was inconvenient for uniformed service, and so he had been passed over.

"Men from the war understand," he said. "You cannot witness that monstrosity and be unmoved, unless you are a monster yourself, of course." His voice trembled just a little as he went on, "And the ones that are compelled to mangle and destroy... even if they are convinced that they are dealing with inferiors, they cannot ever, ever forget stacking up bones or hauling bodies like so much garbage."

Helen pulled back, feeling his words painfully pressing into her middle. She realized that she didn't want to know, nearly as much as she did want to know what he had done. Had he been a soldier too? Was he talking about the Navy after all?

"You didn't have that sort of combat at sea, did you?" she asked.

"At sea? Combat? Not like you mean," he replied, "What we had at sea was combat for our souls. We lost, I suppose." He wagged his head back and forth for a moment.

Helen didn't understand and she started to think he had decided not to tell her more, but then he continued in that same strange rusty tone, "My people never understood why I went to sea. They didn't understand when I gave it up to be a hull inspector and they never would have understood my going to war."

"Union?" she asked quietly.

"Of course not!" he said bitterly. He glared at her like a stranger.

She recoiled. Who was this man? What was wrong with him? Why had she ever accepted space under his roof?

The Admiral went on, quite oblivious to her distress, "They didn't want my sort, but they lacked the numbers and pretended to ignore my unsuitability. They started off so proud and righteous, but by the end they only understood the language of fear."

He rocked and nodded, having become detached from his own words now. Helen felt as if his previous upset had been transmitted to her heart. She felt hot tears forming, but still she was transfixed and had to listen to his terrible tale.

He hunched, and as he murmured his atrocities, he ran both hands over his thin hair, trying to push the thoughts back. His words were full of dark judgment for himself and his unit. So many boys, so many beautiful boys, he said.

Finally, he stopped talking. He could spit no more poison.

She asked softly, "And you never deserted?"

"Oh no," he replied. "Guns before you, guns behind. There was nowhere to go."

Chapter 53—Difficult

Helen had a very difficult night. She didn't want to sleep and pestered Grace to stay awake with her, insisting that she wanted to finish a minor needlework project.

Grace knew that there was some other bother at work, but didn't press Helen to explain anything. Instead, she stayed near and read aloud while Helen stitched.

Grace stopped to yawn with great exaggeration three or four times before Helen agreed it was very late and they should get some sleep. They put out all the lamps in turn as they made their way up to their bedrooms; Helen dragged her fingers along the polished banister thinking of all the ways she was fond of the house and its other inhabitants.

In the morning, Helen told Samuel and Eggers that she had heard far too much dark history from the Admiral and was very pleased she didn't have nightmares afterward.

"Do tell," asked Eggers, "Did he run on endlessly about exploding cotton gins?"

"A bit worse," she replied, "It turns out that the old seaman is a repentant Confederate faker." She told them that 'Admiral' was his nickname from the war, because they found him haughty and nautical. He might have been infamous for grisly tactics.

Samuel gave a low whistle of surprise. "He seems so harmless," he said and then stopped, having no other words offer themselves for the occasion.

"I'm pained to think of him spending so much time with Mr. Jefferson. He could have been very cruel, after all, and we'd have no idea," Helen said.

"Oh, no," said Eggers, "I think treating Jefferson well was his form of penitence. He's lost that too."

Helen had no inclination to sympathize with the Admiral's losses, but she wanted to understand her friend's thinking. "Do you think they were lovers?" she asked Eggers, "Is that why he's so undone?"

"Oh, no," replied Eggers again, shaking his head and frowning with pursed lips. "Jefferson may have forgotten a great many things, but he never forgot that he preferred a stroll on the mossy lane. I'm quite sure."

Helen felt reassured by the total certainty in his tone, but she only shook her head at her disagreeable situation.

"If you want to make a change," said Eggers. "You could do better with a room at the Countess's place. You wouldn't though, would you?"

"So you think that the only decent landlord in town is running an indecent house?" She exhaled with an unfocused exasperation. "I don't want to dwell on old evil things, but they do keep turning up."

"We could trade," suggested Samuel, "but my housemates are loud and unsavory much of the time. I'm not sure that would improve conditions for you."

"You can avoid him," said Eggers cheerfully, "until we find you a suitable perch elsewhere."

Helen nodded, "I suppose. I would miss the others very much." She thought how strange it felt, as if she had been tripping over an old branch every day and then realized it was actually a crocodile. It was very unnerving.

"No. I won't give up my room," she said finally. "He may be a monster–a partly reformed monster–but he's still a good-enough landlord."

Eggers grinned at her, "So Methodical."

"No one wants to fight the war all over again," Samuel said, surprised to hear his own voice. And that ended the conversation the way such conversations always ended in the era, closing the past in a drawer that didn't quite fit.

***

Next, they went over some plans. Eggers suggested that Samuel visit a few of the city morticians, and inquire about formally offering support services. The city might have a flood or fire or contagion that was too large for any one operation; it had happened before and with some regularity. It wouldn't hurt to make sure they might come to mind for any of the parties who could be overwhelmed by a calamity.

Eggers and Helen would make some gentle suggestions to some of the penny-conscious residents about pre-paying funeral services. It was a popular option for those who either wanted to spare their survivors, or wanted to make sure those survivors didn't simply pocket the funds intended for a nice, complete funeral package.

Helen suggested that they have a tasteful little advertisement placed in the paper, something reassuring about knowing who would see to your final wishes.

They were beginning to make some money at last and they were more and more hopeful that their venture might survive.

To that end, they navigated the delicate balance of advertising their business without appearing to wish ill fortune on the superstitious populace.

Eggers had little cards printed up that were adorned with a printed black ribbon at the edges. Their address was published under two lines that read:

Keegan Family Funeral Services
Kind Attention – Finest Furnishings – Very Reasonable

They rarely needed to produce the cards, but they were handy whenever they encountered anyone who didn't know them yet. Eggers jokingly distributed them a few at a time, saying things like, "*You* won't need to call on us, but be sure to tell the family."

Chapter 54—Methodical

Helen didn't object whenever Eggers teased her for being a "Methodical." She was comforted by her study and practice and she felt that even a sideways mention of her methodical approach was a perfectly comfortable compliment.

She still attended services, despite her family troubles. Stubbornly, she would sit near them, never speaking or attempting to speak to them; neither seeking nor avoiding their eyes. If a ghost went to church it would be much the same, she thought.

The pain she felt at first was only a bit diminished over the course of weeks. She prayed hard for guidance and understanding and found that a dull kind of healing was taking hold as her ghost-self developed. She held a slim hope that she could endure this for just a bit longer. Her anger was helpful and it made her feel strong, but it must be shed too.

Reverend Price always skirted her carefully until her family was out of sight. She felt a little sorry for him. He could not afford to offend anyone and so he was gently offending everyone.

He commented that he hoped she was well and he seemed earnest enough. She told him that she was, but that she was struggling with some animosity for particular persons. He nodded and suggested that she didn't need to ask him for guidance; she knew what to do.

She did, and once she was convinced there was no other way, she began another prayer practice. She began to pray for the Admiral and her father during her daily meditation. Helen found that, just like adopting her ghost self, praying for their souls became easier over time.

She worried that she might become more ghostly, not just in church, but everywhere she went and in every way she was. What if, she wondered, stifling her anger stifled her entire being in some way? Just the same, given time, her anger eased by tiny measures.

Eventually, she found that she no longer needed to clench her hands tightly when the Admiral was near. Her wariness had eased but it had transferred to Grace, who would watch him quite pointedly, knuckles livid.

She was so grateful for Grace, and still she ached for her sister too.

Helen had expected that of all her family, Fannie would be the one to break with the others to contact her. Because of that, it came as a surprise when, one afternoon, she found Bonnie waiting near the chicken coop instead of Fannie.

It was unusual to see one of the twins without the other, but they were reaching an age when they found one another disagreeable. Adolescence was so itchy and anxious for the girls in her family; if they hadn't been having disagreements it would have been remarkable.

Bonnie stood with her feet pressed together, hands clasped behind her back. She rocked forward slowly, studying her sturdy pegged shoes as she did so. She didn't look up to acknowledge Helen, but Bonnie was sly and knew that she approached. Still without looking, she spoke to Helen petulantly.

"I hate these shoes," she said, instead of a greeting.

Helen reached into her apron and pulled back a handful of feed for the birds and began to scatter it. She asked, "Are they pinching?" referring to the shoes.

"No," replied Bonnie, "but they are so manly." They were not, in Helen's estimation, manly at all. "Some of the girls at school have kangaroo calf leather with the pearly buttons." She sighed at her ugly man shoes. "Daddy says I should be grateful that I have feet."

Helen smiled, knowing just how such a conversation would go. Daddy would disapprove of her pining for fancier shoes. He might say that ducklings don't quack around about wanting better feet. To Bonnie she asked, "Is that why you came to see me?"

Bonnie looked up at her then. Her brown eyes were shining out from under her bonnet in the afternoon light. Helen thought she could see a quiver in her pretty lips as she said plainly, "I missed you."

Helen strode for her and wrapped her arms around her little sister, hushing her and folding her close. "I know," was all she said.

"Daddy's been disagreeable all the time, and everyone has been so awful to you," she blurted, "It's just not right."

Helen pulled back, holding Bonnie by the shoulders and speaking with authority, "I won't discuss Daddy with you. Do you understand? Anything else at all, but not him."

Bonnie nodded, although she didn't really understand. Her sisters, who had always seemed so steady and permanent were slipping away and becoming strangers. Bonnie only knew that it felt terrible and the situation must be wrong to feel so wrong.

"You are welcome to come and see me any time," Helen hesitated, "Are you supposed to be at a piano lesson?"

Bonnie nodded again, "Yes, but her house is smelly. Besides, I have a tradition of missing lessons when the weather is fine and I don't want to go."

"A tradition? I'm impressed."

Bonnie stayed for a little while to visit, petting the chickens that would allow her to pet them. The big orange hen clambered over some of the others and tried to get into Bonnie's lap, but Bonnie declared that was too much chicken familiarity and shooed her away.

Tired of the chickens, Bonnie purposefully startled the doves and they flapped away into the nearest tree with their particular fluttering coos. Helen told her not to bother the doves and explained that she considered them her charges, just like the hens.

"Why aren't your hens smelly like at home?" Bonnie asked.

Helen frowned. "I wouldn't say they smell of roses. Maybe you should clean out the coop?"

Bonnie rolled her eyes and rejected that idea. She complained that Wally made her clean one of the barns all by herself. She groaned as she spoke like an old woman might protest foul weather and joint pain.

Helen tried not to laugh at her misery and reminded her that they all had to do it at some time; that's just life on the farm.

"Ah, I know," said Bonnie with exasperation, "Be grateful you have a barn!"

Chapter 55—Bakery

The following week, a woman half-fainted at the baker's. The tiny shop was crowded and warm. As the woman began to swoon, it was easy enough to keep her from falling, since there wasn't much room for her to reach the floor.

The baker's boy, penny loaf in hand, started to go to the hotel to look for a nurse, but Patrick stopped him.

"I know who she needs," Patrick said and headed in the opposite direction to fetch Helen. He sprinted to the undertakers' and arrived without winding himself in the least.

Helen looked around the room distractedly as he explained things, and then she quickly fastened her coat and arranged her hat as she walked briskly to the southern edge of town.

She entered the shop and was ushered into the rising room where Gertie sat among the racks of sticky buns and knotted rolls. The room was balmy and filled with the cloying sugary smell of the sweets.

"This would revive anyone," Gertie said, waving a hand as if introducing Helen to the room.

"What happened?" Helen asked, moving closer to inspect her grandmother.

"I might have had a dizzy spell," she said. Helen could hear the quaver in her voice, even as Gertie tried mightily to smooth it. The baker had brought her a cup of water, which she had been sipping and a slice of raisin bread which she had left untouched.

Her pulse was normal and her skin was not clammy. Helen rested her fingers on her grandmother's papery cheek a moment too long.

"Why are you still here?" Gertie asked, irritably.

"Show me your tongue," said Helen. She peered into the old woman's perfectly healthy mouth. She tilted her head, thinking, until Gertie began to protest the prolonged oral evaluation.

"Ack," said Gertie.

Helen then had an idea. "Your corset? Is it, yes, it's far too tight. I'm surprised you didn't faint on the walk into town!"

"Bah," said Gertie, "I'm turning to fat. If I don't keep it cinched I won't get in my dresses."

Helen frowned. "Well, then, new dresses would be better than suffocating yourself, wouldn't you say?" She considered, "I can rework your bodices at the dress shop and you don't have to say anything about seeing me."

Gertie was back in possession of herself fully and still grouchy. "I can spend time with my grand-daughter if like," she said.

Helen beamed at her.

"Stop that," Gertie snapped, "You smile too much. It makes you look simple-minded."

Helen smiled even more, but not to be spiteful.

As they made their way to the dress shop, she told Gertie that she'd had a visit from Bonnie, too.

Gertie huffed a little and opined that the child was full of mischief. Now that the twins were often going in separate directions, they had become nearly impossible to supervise. She wouldn't admit that their supervision was her foremost pastime, but she didn't have to. Ephraim and Wallace weren't interested in the mundane minding of the girls; they preferred to simply direct them as minions.

Helen knew that Gertie would always find the gaps in the family and would mend them any way she could. Gertie loved to tell long complicated stories that illustrated the perils of family quarrels. One petty jealousy could lead to murderous rage, given enough time and kindling, she said. When she urged Helen to leave, Helen suspected that Gertie believed she was the kindling.

"Be careful, my girl," Gertie said in her most serious tone. "A family can only fracture so many times before it is forever altered. It is not like rending and sewing. A family will stay torn. No one has the skill to mend it after that."

***

They stepped into the deserted dress shop and moved back from the cluttered front room into a spacious area used for fittings and measurements. Helen hung her bonnet on a shapely dress form and pulled forward a comfortable chair for Gertie.

Helen unbuttoned the bodice and released Gertie's corset for her under minor protest from the old woman. Gertie's knuckles were knotty and stiff, and detailed work took her more time every year. She could not stifle a very contented sigh as her torso flowed into its natural pose.

"We'll just make a little more room," said Helen, although her intention was to expand the bodice some inches. "You'll be very stylish with the contrast."

"Nothing fancy for me," grumbled Gertie, "Stick to the black." After a moment she added, "Please."

Helen smiled as she leant over a bit to pull the seams.

Kate wafted into the room to check on them and Helen explained that this was a bit of a rescue. Kate wondered aloud if Helen would mind the shop while she went to the bakery herself. Even as Helen felt the "no" surface to her lips she agreed to do it anyway.

Their working relationship had improved over the months, primarily because they didn't work together more than half of the time. While neither of them would have claimed the other for a friend, they had formed a mild mutual appreciation and kept up their cool collaboration.

Helen was happy to have Gertie to herself for a little while and took her time to get the work done. They talked about small things and gossiped a little. Gertie rubbed her swollen knuckles in small methodical circles and stopped the instant she perceived that Helen saw what she did.

Feathers and sequins and gaudy buttons were scattered about the room, notions that didn't appeal to all of the clientele, only to most. Gertie asked her why did she suppose that whores liked to wrap themselves up like presents?

"I have no idea," Helen replied, "I've never given it such a thought. Maybe the ribbons and baubles are just a bit of fun. I would imagine they need to have some fun of their own."

"Pfft," was all Gertie would say.

Helen knew from observation that the harlots enjoyed showmanship. The girls she had dressed chattered about photographs they had done or were planning to make. Visuals were important to them. If they didn't enjoy spectacle, they were in the wrong line of work in the wrong town.

The Countess encouraged them to circulate their photographs. If any of them achieved fame, she reasoned, it was all to the good. She wouldn't allow them to pose as lesbians, however, even the girls who considered themselves chiefly of a lesbian bent. She had an unshakeable prejudice that clients attracted by such ads wouldn't pay well enough to be worth the trouble.

When Helen was finished her work and Gertie was back in her "armor," Helen asked if she was going home.

"Nonsense! I still need to get the bread," said Gertie. She sounded like she was accusing Helen of wasting her time, but even as she said it, she reached over and nipped Helen's chin between her thumb and forefinger.

As a child, little Helen had learned to see Gertie's playfulness through all her stern words, and in the same way, she accepted her peculiar affection. Only now, as an adult, she returned it with a feather-light kiss on the cheek that her grandmother was too slow to duck.

Chapter 56—Spring

Spring arrived with a flurry of small disasters. The undertakers had been exceptionally busy. Even though they had no outside calls, the locals were dropping dead at an alarming rate. No one had been taken to the pest house, but there was a superstitious flood of worry in town as unconnected funerals became a weekly occurrence.

William Alcock, a tinsmith, had died of pneumonia. He had no family to speak of, which everyone agreed was quite sad. The larger tragedy, Eggers joked quietly, was that they had no vessel that would fit him. Alcock was a large, hunchbacked fellow and he required a custom coffin.

His brothers in the trade arranged for a marvelous tin coffin, and they made a bit of additional ceremony in soldering the lid of it.

Samuel, who was very relieved to have their assistance, told them that Napoleon Bonaparte had been interred in a tin coffin that was not nearly as fine as theirs. The men beamed proudly.

It was the sort of detail that they would all fondly carry with them in their memories permanently.

Helen mostly approved of Samuel's way with the mourners. She appreciated the way he did not go on to include mention of all the extras that Bonaparte would have had. Samuel didn't push people to extravagance, and it set them apart from their competitors. The other shops didn't pass up opportunities to pile on extras and charge for surprises. "You only die once," Doeger famously said.

The most professionally upsetting incident they experienced that spring, was in regard to the handling of the body of Nannie Briggs. She had lived alone with her husband George, who was an insurance man, a claim agent with a large territory. He had been out and about traveling when Nannie died.

Nannie and George lived in a somewhat remote, street-level room and had poor relations with the neighbors. Because of this, in his absence, no one had realized that Nannie had passed away. George returned home one evening and found her, sitting bolt-upright in a chair, days dead from a sudden heart failure.

Despite the fright and distress of finding his wife in such a state, he had very exacting ideas and had the wherewithal to be very particular about his funeral preferences.

George was an extremely traditional man, and even though the practice of casting death masks had been almost entirely replaced by photography, he was adamant that he wanted a mask made of his beloved Nannie's face.

Helen was as tactful as she was able, but she wondered about this insistence on a mask. Nannie could not be the subject of an oil painting that was both realistic and pleasant. Her face was almost a nice one, but it was also a face that could be much improved by kind memory.

Samuel tried to persuade George that a mask was ill-advised on a body that was not entirely, ahem, fresh, but George wouldn't hear it. Samuel then said that if they did make the death mask, they would not be able to present her afterward. George agreed, brusquely, and handed a voluminous white gown to Helen without looking at her.

It was a catastrophe, but ultimately, George got what he wanted. George received a lifelike mask mold, detailed down to the eyelashes, and Nannie was buried in her white gown, with a wax copy of her face over her face.

In addition to those funerals, there was an infant, an old man with phthisis, and a messenger boy who died miserably of tonsillitis.

Helen declined to go along to fetch the body of the boy because she was so agitated about the case. His mother had only treated his condition with hot lemonade and had not taken him to a doctor or consulted anyone. She had delayed facing the truth of the situation and deluded herself until his condition worsened into quinsy. He was horribly dehydrated from fever and beyond saving before the first medical person had seen him.

This sort of incident had bothered Helen when nursing. Some people mulishly refused to be helped, and the frustration of facing them was intolerable to her. Had there been any religious nattering, she might have said that it was His will to have hospitals, too. Her partners cheerfully left her to other work during such calls.

Eggers remarked that for all their idle time before, it was good fortune that there were three of them when such a flurry of individual disasters hit. Aside from the small aggravations, they were jolly to be busy and working together, no matter the exceedingly grim work.

***

The girls at the Countess's place had been busy, too. The season had energized their clientele and the traffic all around the place had taken on a hectic, festive air.

As the first blossoms of spring appeared, the house's landscape was the gaudiest example of the season. The house itself was ringed with bright yellow forsythia and frothy white spirea. Flowering azaleas swirled under the trees in nearly overpowering shades of red and purple and the most garish pinks. Hyacinths perfumed the walkways until the lilacs could take over.

One morning after Samuel had visited for breakfast, the Countess asked him to help carry chairs into the yard. In an uncharacteristically casual manner, she draped herself on the front steps to supervise as the men arranged a sort of outdoor parlor.

They were hosting a novel type of garden party, she said. There had been a story on the social page about a group of young people enjoying a hat trimming and tie making party. The women made ties and the men fashioned hat decorations for the ladies. The Countess had the idea to entice some of their young customers for a garter-making party.

"What will the girls make?" asked Samuel.

The Countess laughed her throaty laugh, the most genuine laugh she bestowed. "Larger garters!" she said.

That would make for some distinctive souvenirs, he supposed.

"You should stay for the day," she cooed, "I'm expecting a gift of orchids from the Coroner and some other illustrious fellows will be stopping by."

He was happy to see her so near giddy, but he was also happy to make his escape. He apologized and asked her to take pity on him and make certain that everyone survived the party; then he hurried off.

Instead of walking along the street, he struck out in the general direction of his shop. He followed the rough road past the Countess's house and then he turned to follow a track that paralleled an old fence.

Years of sparse foot traffic kept the path visible, but there were no other footprints on the packed earth. Once the vegetation asserted itself, it might be more difficult to find this particular short cut, he thought. For now, it provided a shady and pleasant route.

A few offended squirrels raced away as he approached and the frantic bird song only diminished slightly nearer to him. The dappled trees swayed in the breeze without any regard for him. He wished he could tell Helen what birds he saw and heard, but his memory for them was very poor. He might report that there were some "gray-ish, loud-ish" creatures and she would then make gentle fun of him in the usual way.

Catching sight of the school, he knew that he was on the right path and was tremendously pleased with himself. He had discovered a new short cut and it was—

Suddenly, his left foot sank into a hole and he staggered perilously, nearly wrenching his ankle with his own momentum. He stepped back and freed the foot from what was likely the tunnel of a whistle-pig. After that, he kept his eyes firmly on the ground for the rest of the little journey.

When he reached the shop, Samuel got directly to cleaning his muddied shoe. He wasn't finished before the door opened. He set the shoe aside as Helen came in.

She seemed dejected or possibly just pre-occupied with something. Her eyes were downcast and her distress was only evident to someone who had studied her many entrances into many rooms.

"What's the matter?" he asked in greeting.

"It's silly, really," she replied. She put up her bonnet and started to move past him.

Samuel was not accustomed to evasion from her, and he realized that he didn't like it. He reached toward her arm without touching her, stopping her in the gentlest way and asked again, "What's the matter?"

"It's the doves," she said. "There was only one of them milling around with the chickens again today." He blinked a little and she could see that he didn't understand. "They are a mated pair; each of them is the only mate the other will ever have." She sighed a little. "I don't like to see one without the other. That's all."

"I'm sure it'll be alright," he said. "It's not like there's a fox around."

She winced and he understood that there had been fox. "There's always a fox around," she said.

"What's the matter with your shoe?" she asked, firmly changing the subject.

"There was a bear," he said solemnly and leaned toward her with a conspiratorial tone. "It charged at me and somehow I muddied my shoe in the scuffle. It was a very small bear," he continued, "and when I roared at it, it scampered off."

She regarded him critically for a few seconds before replying, "You should not start out with, 'There was a bear.' Tell it in order and draw the listener in a bit, then swing out the details—just not too many details." She smiled then. "Your stony face is much improved, though."

"Thank you!" he replied beaming.

Because she was already studying him, she regarded him in a frank way that she ordinarily tried to avoid. His eyes twinkled and he seemed to be brighter than his surroundings. If he were in a painting, he would represent the sort of creature whose motives had been deemed pure and right. She thought she saw rather than felt something flare brighter still and looked down and stepped back in dismay.

Feeling foolish and reprimanding herself, she looked up again, but the odd shining aspect to Samuel had gone out and he was himself again.

"You will need a better brush," was all she said as she hurried out to pretend to look for one.

Chapter 57—Forbidden

There had been moments when Helen considered her affectionate feelings for Samuel and thought that they might deepen into something more passionate.

That was not something she was willing to allow, however. Such experiments had ruined friendships and now her livelihood might depend on the strength of this partnership. Even though she judged him to be a good sort of man, who would not hurt her, it didn't matter. An entanglement was too much of a risk.

Before, Helen approached such decisions with great care because of her mother's warnings of her terrible heart condition. Any pastime or relation that was likely to include exhilaration was forbidden to her especially. No amount of fun had killed her, but she had to approach pleasure with that grim certainty that it might.

A medical student beau had taken a keen interest in her rumored heart condition. He wanted to know, was it a valve defect? What was it called? What were her symptoms? Did she turn blue and faint?

She had nothing to illuminate him. Her memory of childhood scoldings was blurry and no help. She had no symptoms, she said. She admitted that she had secretly tested herself with the most strenuous activities she could think of and found no fainting—just the usual fatigue that anyone might experience.

After her mother had died, Helen asked her father what to call her heart condition. He had looked confused and said, "Hysteria?" Neither he nor her grandmother seemed to know anything of the story she had been told.

Her beau listened to all this and then he listened to her heart intently, his warm ear pressed firmly to her breast as she lay in the grass, gazing at the far off clouds.

He rolled toward her, a shiny smile playing on his face, "I have an exercise we can try."

His experiment did not kill her either, but she felt that it had been more successful for him, just the same.

Each time she had surrendered to that sort of passion, she had been disappointed. The boys transformed from creatures of gentle enticement into greedy domineering tyrants. If she granted them a second encounter, they would only disappoint her more. Her infatuations fell away like petals from a dying flower.

No, she would not explore such territory with Samuel, she decided again. Their business partnership was on the cusp of succeeding and she needed to protect that as if her future depended on it, because it did.

Her heart could take it. She knew by now that her heart could take anything. It was her mind that refused.

Chapter 58—Sensible

For his part, Samuel was continually considering a romance with Helen. He was torn with circular mental arguments that swirled in two directions. First that he should not make any unwelcome proclamation of his affections. She might feel ensnared by their business arrangement and forcing his advantage would be wrong. His worthy reasons to remain patient were countered only by a wordless drive to pursue her anyway. The drive was strong and confident that there could be nothing but beneficial consequences. He was weary of himself on the subject.

Samuel had acquired an additional sense that focused on her, and it followed Helen without his direction. He knew precisely where she was at any time when she was near, and he knew where she was placing her attention. He knew these things and more without ever looking directly at her or having any audible clues.

He believed that he could not be faulted for this sympathetic awareness. And he hoped that his observations of her were remote enough to remain undetected.

When they conversed or looked at one another, he masked his true sentiments with what he imagined was a neutral, friendly expression. This exercise was quite exhausting, but he believed it was superb lying practice for a worthy protective purpose.

He kept up his disguise, hoping he could maintain it; she must not know his feeling until he had some glimmer of greater affection from her.

Even though Samuel had not confided in him, Eggers teased him regularly about his "affliction." Despite the teasing, Eggers was also sympathetic, and told him that it was a shame that he wasn't merely horny; at least he knew there was a simple cure for that.

Simple as it might be for other men, Samuel still felt terrible guilt about his one adventure with Myrtle.

Indeed, there was no cure for his problem, and any measure that satisfied his longing to be near Helen made the struggle more difficult. At its worst, his ears hummed and his concentration was so disrupted that he would have to murmur some excuse to get away and collect himself.

Fortunately, he was well in control of himself the morning that the Admiral appeared. The Admiral stormed in and grabbed Samuel's hand jovially and shook it a bit too long, saying that it was time to see about his wares.

They toured the place and the Admiral smiled broadly and seemed to be listening carefully to all the details as Samuel explained the improvements he had made to the building.

"Still," the Admiral said, "It's not a place where you can lay someone out properly. You'll have to think about a genuine home, something much more hospitable than an old mill. Besides, out of the way like this, you could have people wandering around looking for a funeral." This conjured an image of a meandering, lost funeral procession and Samuel had to smile. "No, eventually you will need someplace larger and more central."

Samuel agreed. He was uncertain of precisely how he would go about it, but the idea of having a large gracious funeral home appealed to him, of course.

Many of the people in town had stopped in as the Admiral was doing, to window shop and satisfy their curiosity about the enterprise. None of them had done what he was doing presently, however; selecting a casket type and making all sorts of advance arrangements.

He joked that he was getting a bargain by buying at today's prices so that he wouldn't have to pay the higher prices of tomorrow.

Samuel had assumed the Admiral meant "tomorrow" in a broad future sense, but the next day, they learned that when he said "tomorrow" he meant quite literally tomorrow.

Chapter 59—Discovery

Friday morning, Eggers, Helen and Sam arrived to work together, discussing the need to pay a visit to the asylum. They had been too occupied to work out the legal problems, but Helen had received some suggestions from Joe.

Mayflower Joe stopped in at least once a week now, looking for his dog, Jenny. Jenny was usually there and would lift her big head as he entered the shop. As he rounded the corner to Helen's office, Jenny would gaze at him blandly and then let her head fall to the rug at Helen's feet again.

He pretended that this did not offend him, but Joe was a bit wounded to have to share Jenny's affections this way. She wasn't entirely his dog anymore.

While Jenny ignored him, Helen asked him about the asylum problem. She wanted to know how they could be sure that any bodies donated from the asylum were legal.

The first step, he said, would be to get a sample of their admission papers to review. Joe said that it should be as simple as asking for a set of papers; if the clerks were dismissive they should say that he sent them. People tended to cooperate with Mayflower Joe.

Now, the next day, Helen told Samuel about the conversation and offered to make the trip to request the papers. Samuel hesitated, uncertain that she would get cooperation on her own. She bristled a little, but before she could speak, they were interrupted by a scream from Eggers.

It was more of a screech than a scream, really. It was the sort of noise that Helen had never heard from him, and Samuel had only heard it once before. That memory led him to expect that they would find that poor Eggers had stumbled upon a snake in the embalming room.

A snake was not the problem, however. Eggers had found the entirely dead body of the Admiral on the floor of the shop. Their large work table was overturned beside him.

Eggers was quite shocked by the discovery, and he had only recovered enough to utter a bunch of babbling near-obscenities as he backed toward the door. They tried to enter, but he prevented them in his panic and it took some frantic effort to push the door open to join him.

They gasped at the sight and looked to one another in confusion. The Admiral was contorted on the floor, wearing nothing but a light-weight undergarment. His back was arched and his head thrown back as if he had been twisting to escape some force pulling against him. His face was stretched in agony. He presented an uncommon spectacle in every way.

His clothes lay neatly folded on a side table, his shoes placed on top of the pile of fabric. Two small glass bottles, which had not been there previously, stood by his things. One was labeled "Whisky" and the other had a hand-written label that read simply, "Strychnine."

Eggers delicately picked up the second nubby glass bottle and turned it over in his hands. "You're a terrible bartender, friend," commented Eggers. He was regaining his composure.

The police and the county coroner were summoned and the coroner arrived very promptly, having already been in town for some unstated business. He stepped with delicacy around the scene, pausing to polish his spectacles. He scratched a few notes and then paused again, rubbing his hip as though it pained him.

He reached the obvious conclusion.

The Admiral had poisoned himself, and having poor information on the process of death by strychnine, had used an inadequate amount of alcohol to sedate himself. Even the coroner, who had been an Army doctor, was uncertain if any dosage would allow a peaceful death.

"He was probably in a great deal of pain from the spasms until his breathing stopped," he said.

Samuel imagined that the Admiral had taken the poison, maybe mixing it into the whiskey, and then had lain on the table in a last thoughtful gesture, to make their work a bit easier.

"He didn't want the teachers to find him at home, I would guess," said Helen. "Nice of him."

Eggers noticed that she didn't address the body directly and he smiled ruefully at her. He didn't believe the Admiral had actually cut throats to steal supplies as she did.

She caught his look and said, "No one feels that guilty without having really done many wrongs."

Under his shoes, Samuel found a letter. The handwriting was clear and confident and the signature was that of the Admiral.

My friends,

Do not fret. I resolved to die some time ago. Each morning I wake to more disappointment and more regret. Bit by bit, it is wearing me away.

I cannot bear to live in the world any more. This is not a passing sadness. It will go on and on. My only hope is that it stops when I do.

My only request of you is that you accept the gift of my house, as it is clearly suited to funerals. I hope you will care for it and welcome any freed men who may visit.

My other instructions are with the lawyer, but I ask you privately, please bury my heart with Mr. Jefferson.

"That's peculiar," said Eggers, "His only request is three or four different requests."

Samuel studied the note, then the body. He said, "Do you suppose at his age everything is a misery?"

"Of course not," replied Eggers. "Don't be morbid."

"I will take his heart out," offered Helen cheerfully.

Chapter 60—Imposter

The body of the Admiral was prepared in proper style and according to his wishes and the turn-out for his funeral would not have surprised him. Samuel, however, was more than a little surprised to see the Countess there. She generally did not appear in public for any reason. He recalled that he had never heard her refer to the man other than "that old seaman." Perhaps she held some affection for the aged faker.

He was dressed in an old-fashioned white suit, which was far and away the best in his wardrobe. His head lay on a handsome pillow of spring flowers. Their delicate pinks and yellows were giving reflected color to his pale face, despite all the powder.

Helen had never seen such a huge invoice from a florist. It was all paid by his estate, but she had never heard of anyone purchasing their own tribute floral displays. Irksome as it might be in concept, she had to admit the Irish heather was delightful.

Discrete inquiries were made with the Navy and it was confirmed that their faux Admiral was not entitled to any sort of burial benefit. The grateful nation reserved its honors for actual service men.

In the documents that Joe received, the old seaman had specified that he wanted to be buried at sea after the other "accommodations" were made.

Samuel expressed to the Countess that he wasn't certain that he would be able to arrange the sea burial.

"Nonsense," she said, "You are a very resourceful fellow. If funds are what you require, I would oblige to see the thing done as he wanted."

Samuel gratefully and awkwardly declined her assistance and he found that no one else who had turned out was any more seafaring than she was. They were a lot of lubbers, the Admiral would have said.

Eggers urged him to ride with him to the bay and to trust fortune to give them a solution. "At worst, we'll have to spend a little time haunting the piers to locate a crew that's willing to take the man."

Samuel nodded and continued turning the problem over in his mind. As he and Eggers walked off discussing their plan to take the Admiral on one last adventure, the Countess approached Helen.

Helen was wary of the Countess and fascinated by her at the same time. She had watched her all the while. The Countess moved through the house as if she were alone. She didn't interact with the others during the viewing, as far as Helen had observed, anyway. People moved out of her way to maintain a layer of separation, but otherwise provided no acknowledgment of her person.

Perhaps that was why Helen was alarmed when the Countess headed directly toward her; would she confront her about her staring? She looked around for her partners and discovered that they were absent.

The Countess smiled, alleviating Helen's anxiety a little. She stretched out her hand and said coolly, "I must at last introduce myself, Miss Driscoll."

Helen accepted her hand and felt her face smile unbidden in response, "You require no introduction."

A low, musical chuckle emanated from the throat of the Countess. It was the sort of sound the doves might make if they were swathed in velvet. "Enchanted," she said.

Helen felt genuinely enchanted in return. She didn't mind the sensation. She didn't mind that the Countess' eyes seemed to barely resist playing up and down her person. She felt frankly flattered that she would be an object of study for someone so independent and so elegant.

At the same time, her reaction was tinged with embarrassment at her own easy gullibility. She knew that while she was falling into this thrall, this was only the Countess plying her trade of seduction and deduction.

"Doesn't it seem odd," said the Countess, "that our meeting would be so long delayed?"

Helen gazed at her quizzically, uncertain of her meaning.

"After all, we are nearly in the same trade," the Countess smiled, "just different branches of service."

Helen laughed, "Service to bodies, you mean?"

The Countess laughed too and took her arm to stroll through the room companionably. "I supposed I had to call on you since you were never going to call on me."

"Indeed," replied Helen, "I have often thought I would like to have been at liberty," she hesitated, uncharacteristically. "I'm afraid that convention rests heavily on me at present."

She gently extracted the Countess' grip on her arm and held her hands between them instead as she spoke.

"You believe you would be at some risk to visit my home?" The Countess softened to realize that Helen held none of the routine judgement she had come to expect from other women. "I can assure you, there is no safer place for you in all the county."

"Thank you," said Helen. She still had no intention of accepting the invitation.

"There is no need to trouble yourself with convention when we live in such an unconventional place at a time when so much convention is struck down and reformed."

"I'm sure you are right," said Helen. She was feeling discouraged. She would not and could not explain her own difficulty with conventional-thinking people.

To her, there was no point in being a traditionalist if you did not fully understand the traditions. It was possible to be jeopardized by traditions that one rejected, just the same. One did not have to be a believer to suffer the tyranny of outside opinions.

As they arrived at the front of the house and prepared to part company, the Countess asked her abruptly, "Do you suppose there are bicycles for armies?" She said it as if she were inspired to invent them if not.

"I have no idea," said Helen. "They are the most wonderful, peaceful machines; it seems like a very strange notion."

"Ah," said the Countess, smiling again at her own cleverness. "Can you think of any wonderful, peaceful conveyance that men have not fashioned into a weapon?"

Helen thought of war horses and any number of military contraptions before shaking her head.

The Countess nodded sagely, "You see? Perhaps women should be in charge of all of the lovely new inventions instead!"

Helen returned her smile and accepted her flickering kisses as they parted. "Perhaps," Helen said, "but even if men are the ones that make the war machines, it is still the women who make the warriors."

***

Helen dreamed that night. In her dream, she walked barefoot toward the Countess' house. The flowers glowed in moonlight and they seemed to turn toward her as she passed them. Fireflies blinked all around and some twinkled high in the tree tops.

She raised her hand to knock on the heavy door, but it opened before she touched it. The Countess was there, holding the door wide. She was dressed in a man's tailored evening clothes. Helen had the impression of pearled buttons and shiny black fabric.

The Countess looked at her sadly and Helen felt dreamlike confusion. She looked down at her own small, exposed feet and saw that they were bloodied and torn. She heard the Countess say, "You are too late."

Chapter 61—Departures

Rather than leave after the viewing, Eggers and Samuel prepared to leave the next morning to avoid night travel on the long country road to the bay. While Eggers fetched the hearse, Samuel went looking for Helen.

Samuel had, in the course of just a few days, taken over the Admiral's quarters in the house. He offered the rooms to Helen, but she was adamant that she did not want to move her things or have more space than she already had. Besides, she liked her window on the garden and that was that.

He found the housemates were most welcoming and the ladies made comments to say they were pleased to have a man on the premises. Old Fabian would have been offended to hear that since he had always described himself as the "man of the house," even when he was one of three.

Grace asked if she could stay on or if she should find new lodgings. Samuel was as earnestly reassuring as he could manage and told her that she was only to consider leaving if the hosting of funerals was a bother to her. Samuel joked that at least she would have advance notice, being a fortune teller. Grace, who would not be bothered to explain that she was merely forward-thinking, didn't laugh.

The mood in the house was not somber; in fact, it was lighter and more a reflection of the gracious outdoor weather than it had been before the Admiral's death. A peace was taking over the place.

Samuel moved through the lower rooms, finding only the casket in the parlor and then the deserted dining room followed by an empty sitting room. As he reached the rear of the house, he saw Helen standing out in the garden. His breath caught in the way it always did now when he saw her.

He walked toward her. She faced away from him and because she had forgotten her bonnet, as he drew near, he could see the curls of her dark hair resting on the narrow nape of her neck.

He wanted to sweep his arms around her and put his lips there. Instead he waited a moment, watching her as she watched her birds.

"We are heading to Annapolis shortly," he said. His voice was low and sounded strange to her.

She turned to look at him, ready to say that it was fine, everything was fine. Instead, she saw his eyes, unguarded and filled with the regret of leaving her.

Her shoulders fell and Samuel felt his longing reflected in her gaze at last. He closed the small distance between them and stopped, swaying slightly as he studied her face. She did not look away.

She did not want him to leave just as strongly as he did not want to go. With a tiny sigh she reached up to him on tiptoe and met his lips with hers.

Later he wondered if she only meant to kiss him goodbye, but he did not believe it. Their pent up passion was finally freed and they embraced, pressing close and breathless.

After many moments, he had no sense of how many, she lowered her heels and slipped away. "You should go," she said, "We'll speak when you return."

"I love you," he said simply.

She didn't look at him again.

Chapter 62—Journey

Samuel was terrible company for their journey and Eggers told him so often. Samuel sighed rather than putting forward the effort to speak, and when he did speak it was only to complain that he felt as if his stomach would leave him.

Eggers sang and surveyed the countryside as they went along to stave off boredom. Had they been in town, they would have kept a somber demeanor while driving the hearse. Here, out between farms, there was no requirement to keep up appearances. With their relative privacy, Eggers felt free to sing some of his bawdiest sea shanties.

He was pleased with everything except Samuel. He had to watch for ruts in the swampy areas, but it was an easy ride. The horses were well-trained, and Eggers knew that they would not balk unless it was called for. The rig was in fine condition and he felt as if he could comfortably cover twice the distance they planned and if they got lost, so be it.

Samuel sat with a long pistol in the seat beside him. His gaze was unfocussed and Eggers suspected that even if very large and obvious wild dogs presented a problem, he would have to prod Samuel to shoot.

Eggers had a fondness for dogs, and he routinely refused to be part of any pack hunting party, but it was sensible to be wary of the motley dog packs that formed near the city. If only one of the animals became rabid, total havoc would follow.

The hearse proceeded at a stately pace, so as not to jostle their cargo. This allowed them ample time to take in the surroundings as the road took them past large furrowed fields, some of which were clouded by the scent of manure. Eggers preferred the wooded stretches and he gawked upward for long intervals at the pale blue of the sky peeping through the leaves. So doing, he recklessly let the leads rest slack in his relaxed hands.

Occasionally, the road turned abruptly, when they happened on some property whose owners had denied the roadway access to continue through. These compounds were of great interest to Eggers, but one could never see more than bordering orchards or other spacious obstructions. They were likely hiding nothing more than some prize goat-breeding facility, but he was tempted to investigate anyway.

His curiosity was a terrible weakness, his long-lost mother used to say. He disagreed with her, convinced more and more over time that his curiosity was one of his best attributes. Why, he had much in common with the first person to travel this path, he thought. They would have wondered what they would find at the end of the long slow decline and would have been rewarded with the magnificent bay.

As the carriage passed into the open meadows again, Eggers's reverie was stopped by the sight of an animal moving alongside the road ahead. It was a very large, tawny fox, prancing at a calm pace. When it turned toward them, it registered no alarm. Its panting tongue curled up and its face held a friendly expression.

Eggers hissed at it and nudged Samuel to pay attention. Samuel jumped. By the time he brandished the pistol, the fox laid down in the grass and let them take the lead, still smiling its crafty smile.

"It's strange to see one in the daylight," Samuel said. It was the first sentence he had uttered in ten miles.

"Oh, they will hunt any time if they are hungry, I do believe. He probably missed whatever he was chasing after a good long pursuit," replied Eggers. When Samuel made no comment he said, "What is the matter? You are not at all yourself today." Samuel stayed silent. "Surely you're not so ill from the ride? I've been going so slowly people are likely to think we are courting."

"I have declared my feelings for her and had no answer," Samuel admitted, miserably.

"Oh, that," replied Eggers. He looked back to confirm that the fox was not following. "Rejection is just part of the game. You know better." His words were light, but his tone was kind.

Samuel was annoyed that Eggers seemed to have a misunderstanding, and he was further annoyed with himself that he would try to explain, much as he did not want to discuss it. "She has not made any reply at all. How many rejections can one man endure?" his voice rose with unintended drama.

"There, there," said Eggers. "Thus far, you have only had the one rejection." He considered for moment before continuing. "She is a thoughtful lass," commented Eggers, "and she may need a bit of contemplation to collect her thoughts, since she has so many. How you could have surprised her with such an obvious testimony of your affections is the true mystery."

Samuel only sighed in reply.

Chapter 63—Returning

The return ride the next day was a festive affair by comparison. They had delivered the Admiral successfully and had avoided staying in a temperance hotel for the night. Instead, they found lively and mildly dangerous accommodations, rooming with traders and tinkers and men selling dubious medicinal wares.

The overnight stay was needed since it had taken most of the day to locate a ship that would load the casket. When they did find a vessel, the captain was reluctant to accept the cargo. Samuel slid him the pile of coins and told the Captain that for this substantial fee he had two options. He could deliver the "Ambassador" to his home island of Lessos, or he could choose to provide a sea burial if he deemed it necessary.

The Captain did not want to admit that he wasn't familiar with the island, and he accepted the money and the casket rather hastily. Many more significant decisions needed his attention, and the dispatch of this body to the ocean seemed like an easy choice.

Had he troubled himself to learn more, he would have found that the island they named was entirely fictional. Samuel had learned that giving a choice, even a false choice, was a remarkably efficient method of getting strangers to cooperate.

Eggers was congratulatory on the ride home. His friend had bloomed into a magnificent liar after all the months of practice. Eggers said he could not be more proud of him.

"The old dog will get his wish and you have crafted a speedier solution than I could have imagined," he crowed. "I thought we might be knocking on doors for two days at least."

Samuel smiled broadly. He was anticipating telling Helen about it and enjoyed it all the more. He drove the horses faster and they returned in half the time.

On the way to the livery, Samuel leapt from the hearse and told Eggers he would go directly to the house instead. He rushed toward the front door, hoping to find Helen. He was met by the two teachers instead.

Melvina's eyes were red and Lollie looked stricken and pale. "Thank goodness you're back," said Melvina, "she's gone missing and we don't know what to do."

Samuel refused to understand her meaning at first. He had just begun to convince himself that they were referring to Madame Grace, when Grace strode in from the back of the house. His budding theory crumbled and he knew that they meant Helen. Helen was gone and no one knew where.

Chapter 64—Sinister

Of the chief characteristics of the Port, the spread of information was its most ordinary small-town attribute. Over the next few days, the ranging conversations revealed that everyone knew that Helen was missing. They also revealed that no one knew what had become of her.

It seemed terribly sinister to Grace. As she spoke to everyone she encountered, she had an uncanny sense that one of them was lying, though she could not say who it was. When she confided this feeling to Samuel and Eggers that night, they understood precisely what she meant.

They found that one of the bicycles was missing, but no one recalled having seen Helen riding it that day. Her traveling case was still stored, empty. Her good shoes were missing as was one of her best dresses, which contradicted the bicycle theory. Why would she dress up to ride? Why wear a corset? Why not just wear a riding costume?

She and Grace had taken to bicycle riding without all the structural undergarments and they had agreed that it would be unconscionable to ride laced up and weighed down. Grace doubted that Helen had ridden off on the missing cycle.

There was no sign of her that day, and Samuel slipped quickly into a very melancholy state. He became convinced that she fled on a kind of impulse to escape him and his unwanted affection. Eggers squeezed his shoulder firmly and told him not to give in to dark fantasies.

"Be reasonable," Eggers said, "Have you ever known a woman less likely to flee? When she ran away from home, she went one little mile. Besides, if she had decided to leave, you would have had difficulty in stopping her from telling you precisely what she thought first."

Samuel agreed and a horrified look spread across his features. If she certainly didn't run away…

The only method for fighting the worry was to search.

While a large contingent joined them, fanning out across the fields and into the woods, each horrible possibility was eliminated. She had not been struck by a train, not drowned in the river nor mauled by a wild animal. At least, there was no evidence of any of those things.

Her grandmother joined the search and after a day her father and little sisters did too. Wally struck out on his own and was very distracted and upset. The twins behaved as if it was a game, even though they were old enough to know better.

Ephraim, Helen's father, was angry most of the time. He seemed to become only more angry as time passed. He knew something like this was going to happen. He knew it, and now he could not enjoy being right for even one minute.

On the second morning, Patrick appeared at the farm house with a message for him. Ephraim frowned at the paper.

"Has anyone ever seen such a long telegram?" he commented tiredly as he passed it to Gertie.

Patrick stayed put to hear the message, and they didn't fuss at him for hanging around in the doorway. He said, "It's a message from the telephone. He had to print it for me to bring it over."

Gertie read it, pausing to try to untangle the poor transcription:

> *Philadelphia, Please do not fret Miss Driscoll is safe but is set to be Missus Reverend Price today. We help you will celebrate our joy from afar and accept this news with aloft it is sent with. We did not want to dribble the divided family with the problem of a wedding cat home and there is the Reverend's ancestry problem too. No obstacles can keep us from our love for each other camphor all of you.*

Gertie sat down hard, "No obstacles, except they ran away from obstacles!"

"I cannot believe Helen would run off with that silly man!" Ephraim was even more shocked, if that was possible.

Gertie started, "Not Helen—it's Fannie that's eloped!"

Ephraim stared. He turned to Patrick and Patrick shrugged as if to say it wasn't his idea.

"Two daughters gone missing in one week!" Ephraim said. "Where's the little ones?"

The twins giggled from behind the wingback chairs and Bonnie yelled, "We're going to 'lope with Patrick!"

Patrick ran away at that.

Chapter 65—Theories

Grace searched each place she visited for any kind of clue, quietly convinced that something was being overlooked. Helen would not have meant to create such chaos and agony.

The policeman, LaFevre, was unmoved and said that until there was a sign of a crime, it was not his purview. When Daddy Driscoll got word about that, he stormed around town looking for the man to let him know that this unacceptable shiftlessness would not be tolerated.

LaFevre was drunk when he found him, lolling beside a table at the tavern. The butcher, who lounged with him, was equally relaxed. LaFevre blinked slowly as Ephraim Driscoll lectured him through clenched teeth. LaFevre seemed to be attempting to focus on Ephraim's chin on the way to his words.

"Praps," suggested LaFevre, "—does your little gal have any acrobatic talents?" His voice was slurred and lilting. Ephraim only stared in reply. "Dere's word of a circus passin' through. Maybe as her sister, she married herself some kinda wolfman—"

Ephraim punched him quite suddenly then, and the assembled patrons abruptly hushed and then cheered as LaFevre fell senseless to the dusty floor.

"Useless," said Ephraim, as he strode out to re-join the search party, far down the river.

Chapter 66—Persistent

By the third day, all of the searchers were exhausted and listless. They kept on, but the persistent false rumors and lack of any actual news created a prickly discord. Everyone gave Ephraim a wide berth, since his usual equilibrium was dangerously disturbed. He had punched two men, in addition to LaFevre, and no one was keen on becoming his next target for fury.

Eggers, who had barely avoided punching a few men himself, checked in with the Countess again at breakfast, but just as before there was no update for either of them on the missing woman.

Grace fed the birds and wept with frustration. Her sleep had been fitful and she felt a blank fatigue in the morning sunshine. She took no notice when the second dove returned.

She had dreamed of Helen. They were having a picnic beside a creek while their bicycles were dropped carelessly in the ferns nearby. The water burbled so that she couldn't make out what Helen was saying, but she had shucked her shoes and stockings and began to wade into the water, laughing and splashing and merrily making her indecipherable comments. When Grace awoke, she was bereft all over again. The dream was so much like a lovely day they had spent together, her heart ached all the more.

Samuel was weary and chaffed from riding out to interview people all along the thoroughfare. He had had a surge of hopefulness as one woman reported that she had seen someone like Helen.

She went on to say that she had seen her in an opium den. His hope shrank toward doubt, but pressed her for more details.

"It would be about a month back," she said, looking up as if a book of days hung in the air next to his head. "Maybe more, I cain't be positive. Dressed real fine, though, like you said. And she were very small, and she were definitely not a tart."

He would continue to ride out and stop at each business or gathering and ask his ever-growing list of questions; have you seen this small, well-dressed woman? This woman who is definitely not a criminal? This woman who I am not set to harm?

People hesitated until they could see that his distress was genuine and that his intention was to be a rescuer. His method was effective in getting the news spread beyond the newspaper readers, as strangers enjoyed speculating about the mysterious disappearance of the young lady undertaker. It aligned with a certain morbidity of imagination that was the height of fashion, too.

He had a photograph that her grandmother had given him. It was very small and he would keep an anxious eye on its progress as it was handed around in a crowd. Exclamations about her loveliness and tisks of sympathy were the typical reaction, time after time. People would say, "Haven't seen 'er," or, "I pray you find her," and he would move on.

He remained focused, but at times, unwelcome images of her surged into his consciousness. They were dark images of her trapped in quick mud, or images of her bleeding like the man who had been shot in the road. At those times he was nearly overcome with the sickness of worry.

When he returned to the house that night, Eggers and Grace were waiting. Grace sprang toward him as he hung his hat.

"I know where she is," she said, "and we must organize very quickly."

Chapter 67—Waking

Helen woke shivering. The room was warm and damp. Although her cotton garment was dry, the shivering continued.

She had never been so angry. As the hopelessness of her situation settled on her again, her fury surged and there was even more shivering.

She could hear moaning, low and rhythmic. Another voice sighed and yet another muttered unintelligibly until she heard, "Why, why, why?" Then the gibberish resumed.

The large room they slept in was clean, but it was in a state of disrepair. She stared up at the high plastered ceiling. It had water damage and mildew stains as its only features. Some light leaked in through the windows, as there was nothing to prevent it. The iron grates covering the tall windows would throw irritating shadows a little later in the day, as usual.

Much of the furniture, the iron beds and tables, were fastened to the tile floor. She had seen wooden chairs and small side tables scattered in other rooms. A few of the tables were covered with lace and topped with yellowing ferns in a misguided attempt to evoke a homelike atmosphere.

She knew that from the outside, the building looked like a hospital, it may even have functioned as a regular hospital before, but now it was populated by mental patients and keepers. She did not know that she was in the hard-case wing, due to a space problem. Nor did she realize that the old soldiers enjoyed a much less prison-like accommodation, sleeping on the porches and walking the grounds if they could, whenever they liked.

During her stay, she had been unconscious for at least half the time. Elixirs were gently but insistently administered with no set pattern or method that she could discern. Some of the concoctions only made her dizzy and she retreated into a sort of twilight consciousness while the effect lasted.

She found that if she pretended to be in that state, the keepers and inmates would generally leave her alone, but only generally. The previous day, while she was sitting in a chair and mimicking that vacant state, one of the keepers, a man, had approached her and put his hands on her shoulders.

He slid his hands up her neck and began to stroke downward in a familiar fashion, groping in the direction of her breasts. She whipped her head to the side and bit down on his arm. She could have done it much harder, but she meant it as a warning.

He yelped and jumped back. He was fortunately too timid to overcome the embarrassment of his failed attempt at fondling a semi-conscious woman and he left her alone.

His name was Mr. Jones, she learned, and she made another mental note; Mr. Jones tasted terrible.

She watched as one of the women begged for a pen and paper to write a note. Her voice rose as the rush of words continued, "Please, please, please, please. A mistake here, please." Because of her pleading, the woman was subdued and medicated. Evidently no note writing would be permitted. Helen wondered what the woman might write besides "please."

The attendant said, "It's for your own good," as they often did while administering the curatives, like hot and cold baths that were really cold and colder baths. The Please Woman slumped into a relaxed attitude as the drugs took effect, and she was gently positioned so that she wouldn't fall from the chair they had placed under her.

Any attempt at conversation, even after dark, was met with the same procedures. Because of that, Helen didn't speak or acknowledge any signals from the others. She kept reciting all the details in her mind; it helped with the growing fretfulness she felt.

Helen reckoned that she had been there for three or four days, but she could not be entirely certain. She remembered being dragged into an examination room and waking from the first dose to find her clothes had been substituted with the odd night dress she now wore. The very same one still hung on her body. Or did it? Uncertain, she pulled out part of the hem stitching to distinguish it from another like it.

She recalled, or maybe she dreamed of, talking to a man who resembled a doctor. She remembered—or dreamed of—laughing and struggling to form words. The doctor had asked one of the keepers if she had been medicated and the keeper said no. The keeper was mistaken, of course. Hysteria, the man had said. Helen had only leered and drooled in response, helpless to defend her sanity to this alienist.

The clerks were uncertain how to classify Helen, so they put her with the colored patients. Her brother, who delivered her to the place, looked colored to them, and he had a witless way about him, which made them fearless to offend him.

More than a dozen women were corralled in the room where she had spent the subsequent days. There were no compartments in the room, only the bolted-down beds and tables and chairs. Some of the women would only lie in bed.

No one showed any enthusiasm for the meals, and some did not even turn their heads when a cart appeared near them.

Their drinking water was clouded with quinine. She heard the keepers muttering nervously about fevers caused by the river mists. They drank the preventative too.

They weren't given any utensils for their meals, Helen was disappointed to discover. There were chunks of hard bread, pieces of slippery cheese and the soup-like substances were to be drunk directly from the rough bowls. She had hoped to get her hands on a fork, at least, but no tools were ever in reach.

The events that led up to her incarceration were perfectly clear in her mind. She turned them over and over, even though it flared her anger so severely that she imagined her anger would burn right through her and ignite her surroundings.

Her brother Wallace had done this to her.

Helen had not noticed that he was following her in the city, but he must have done just that.

Throngs of people had been converging for an equestrian statue's dedication. Somewhere in that sea of people in their warm-weather finery, Wallace must have spotted her heading for the asylum.

She asked the sleepy clerk for a set of forms to arrange the delivery of a patient. The clerk had squinted at her skeptically, since he was not accustomed to women making such requests.

"I'm the undertaker," she said, "and I need to be sure that the papers are complete—"

"That's very amusing," said Wallace behind her.

Helen jumped, "Wally! What are you doing here?"

Wallace ignored her and nodded to the clerk, "She's very far along into her delusions, you see." The clerk pulled his lips back and nodded in swift understanding. Wallace went on in a very convincing paternal tone, "I was worried that she was going to take charge of the parade outside, too, when she got away from me."

"Stop it, Wally! What are you doing?" Helen felt more than a tinge of fear.

The clerk was scratching some notes as Wallace continued. "She is an admirer of Lizzie Borden." He seemed to be casting around in his memory for the worst details he could find, "And she lives with three men, you know." Helen hissed his name again but he didn't stop. "She keeps company with whores and maniacs instead of staying home with her family. We just don't know what to do any longer." Wallace's feigned concern horrified her more than his words.

Sensing her hostility, the clerk kept his eyes firmly on Helen as he reached over and lifted a brass bell from his desk. It only rang out for a moment before two large men appeared on either side of Wallace. The clerk pointed at Helen to correct them and they closed on her and quickly pulled her through a doorway into another room.

Helen had no chance to resist as the men lifted her completely off the ground and controlled her arms in the process. Her legs were hampered by her skirts and none of her attempts to regain the ground were beneficial. She heard Wallace protest, "Hold on! What's happening here?"

The clerk eyed him impatiently, "She'll be examined," he said. When Wallace started to protest and explained that he wasn't serious the clerk interrupted and went on, "If this is some kind of prank, you will find yourself in a great deal of difficulty too. We have space for you if you like." Wallace backed down and the clerk continued again, "There are hearings if you have more to say."

"When?" asked Wallace.

"How should I know?" the clerk replied sharply.

That was the last thing Helen had heard from the outside world before she was encased in this damp room.

She wondered if there really would be a hearing. Who would hear her? Would they be able to see that she was no sort of lunatic? Would she be a lunatic by then? Would no one ever give her a fresh gown? She checked the seam again and started over, recounting the steps that brought her to this pale, hellish room.

Chapter 68—Answered

Grace described the visit she had had from Helen's brother. Samuel listened with growing agitation.

Wallace had appeared at her shop, which was quite uncommon. He was a bit drunk and very distraught. Mrs. Wiltz had been sitting with her, but when Wallace barged into the little salon, Mrs. Wiltz shied away and slipped out before Grace could halt her frightened and mumbling exit.

He sat across from Grace and sighed heavily, filling the room with a whisky cloud. "I've done a terrible thing," he said simply. He stared at her with red-rimmed eyes, but he said no more, as if he expected that she knew everything he could say already.

Grace did not. She felt ill with apprehension at his statement. Had he done something to Helen? It seemed certain that whatever he had done it was very bad for her friend.

Wallace sobbed. Grace sprang to his side, feigning concern for him while mightily concentrating on getting him to tell her what had happened. She wasn't good at pretending, but it hardly mattered. In his condition he didn't notice that she was defensive and studying him intently.

His hands were dirty and his clothes were dusty and ill-kempt and he had apparently misplaced his hat.

"All is not lost," she cooed, trying to comfort him, "We'll find a way to mend it."

"I've tried," he said in a mournful tone, "but they won't tell me anything. My father is going to blame me for whatever happens now."

"Who won't tell you?" she asked trying to sound calmer than she felt.

"I wanted teach her a little lesson and I thought my father would approve, but it's all gone wrong." He sobbed again, sorry for the thing itself or only for himself, it was hard to say.

"Where is she?" Grace tried again, fighting a rising panic.

"She was at the city asylum," he said. "I didn't mean for them to keep her." He groaned and shook off Grace's gentle touch on his shoulder. "I've been back every day to try to get someone to listen—someone to understand it was all a mistake."

"I'll take care of it," she said sternly, standing behind him. "For now, just get some rest. You can stay right here if you like."

Wallace dropped wearily to the divan and was snoring before she had pulled the door closed behind her.

When she finished the story, Samuel was shaking his head, trying to ensure that he understood. "He didn't tell anyone before you? He let this go on for *days*!"

"Here now," said Eggers briskly, "I'll get to the Countess. You go see the lawyer. Wake him up if you need to. We'll have this sorted by morning."

Chapter 69—Hearing

In the morning, the meeting room of the lunatic asylum was packed with curious people, most of whom had never been there before. Those who were familiar with it found the building unchanged for decades, except for the dilapidation that was taking hold. Many of the windows no longer functioned and the whitewash on the high arches was neglected. Tiles missing from the floor created a secondary, unintentional pattern.

The judge entered from a side door and was noticeably surprised by the throng in the room. He was not pleased to recognize so many faces from the Port, and he scowled as he arranged himself on a large chair at the broad wood desk. It was his only protection from the riffraff.

Chairs had been brought in and were lined up to leave a central aisle, but people stood all along the walls and spilled out into the main hall too. The warmth of their bodies was already creating unwelcome balminess.

The crowd was relatively calm and quiet as they shuffled themselves about in the high-ceilinged space. It was as if they were expecting to attend a lecture by an important orator who would elucidate for them some new discovery of the times. They were ready to argue, however, and therefore not as well-behaved as a crowd attending church.

The Countess sat in front, off to one side. She nodded imperceptibly to the judge, but he only squinted back in answer. She had been instrumental in assuring that the hearing took place at this time. It could scarcely have been sooner, unless they had the city fire brigade round everyone up the night before.

The judge behaved as if that sort of rough summons was the level of ruckus he was dealing with, and he was very displeased to be abroad in the early daylight. His recorder was sympathetic and impatiently asked the clerk to have someone fetch coffee for the judge. "And a sugar bowl," she added.

The recorder also asked the clerk to remove the large dog that was stubbornly sitting in the entry. The clerk pretended not to hear, uncomfortable with wrangling with Jenny. The dog had been hanging around for days and made him very superstitiously anxious.

Grace and Samuel and Eggers sat in front, flanked by the teachers and Old Fabian. Helen's brother was there, looking very bleary and ill. Her father and all her sisters sat together, but apart from Wally.

Ephraim was furious with Wally. He told him that he had briefly considered sending Helen to a treatment refuge, naturally, but he would never have had her committed to a madhouse for the poor. It was all too much to bear.

The baker had left an apprentice in charge of his shop, as had the grocers and the tavern men. The messengers, the mailman and the telegraph operator were all there, not from a desire to report information, but from a personal interest in the situation. Everyone who had searched for Helen was there too, hoping for the satisfaction of a mystery solved.

The Countess's artistes were there as well, but they had lost the chance at good seats by arriving too late. Samuel could occasionally hear Cherry's distinctive giggle from the hall, and he was amazed that she could find anything funny.

The crowd's anticipation was heightened by several false starts. Everyone quieted with attention as a small woman made her way down the central aisle. Gertie had tried to negotiate with the clerk to avoid all this and finally gave up to enter the hearing room. The crowd parted and Fabian offered Gertie his seat in front. Her son shifted uncomfortably but otherwise stayed composed.

The judge's coffee arrived and everyone hushed as they watched him dole a disturbing portion of sugar into it.

"All right," he said at last, adjusting some unseen undergarment; the adjustment did not seem to make him any more comfortable. "Bring in Miss Driscoll," he instructed the clerk. To the assembled onlookers, "I trust you reprobates will keep yourselves under control. There's more than one paddy wagon at the street and I'm predisposed to fill them." He scowled for emphasis.

"Sir," said Wallace, "May I say something?"

"No," replied the judge, without looking at him. "I will tolerate no nonsense from you, boy. Sit down."

Wallace looked confused. He was already sitting.

The other side door opened and a small woman was escorted into the room. Her hair was as white as the gown she wore and the crowd gasped.

"Miss Driscoll?" asked the judge, unperturbed.

"I am Louise Bristol, sir," said the small, white-haired woman.

"What? What do you mean?" he looked at the Countess then, and she made a tiny shake of her head. "Would it be too much to ask for you people to fetch me the correct madwoman?" asked the judge bitterly.

After a re-shuffling and a shushing of the crowd, the correct madwoman was brought in. The confused Miss Bristol did not struggle but looked around intently, perhaps hoping to catch sight of someone she knew.

Miss Bristol was replaced at the front by Helen.

She stood straight and kept her eyes on the judge; she was afraid that if she looked at anyone else she might lose hold of her emotions. It was essential that she make her best case if she was to save her freedom. She could not let her tears of her anger get ahead of her.

She was so intent that she wasn't aware of the large number of people behind her. She sensed rather than saw her friends and loved ones nearby. Only the judge could see how raw and vulnerable her eyes were, but he wasn't looking.

The Judge took his time, reading over the papers. The room grew even quieter until only the sounds were furniture squeaking, the pages turning and Jenny's panting. "It says here that you were not in control of your locomotion and not capable of right speech—and they determined that you are an idiot," he said finally. "You are walking on your own today, I see. So, are you an idiot?"

"No sir, your honor," she replied. Her voice was strong but a bit rough from disuse. "I was drugged."

The judge nodded, "So you were drugged and just happened into the facility?"

"No sir, I was here on business and there was a—" she paused for the best word, "misunderstanding."

Ephraim stood and Helen flinched just a hair at the sound of his voice, "Her brother—"

"—I'm not interested in her brother," said the judge sharply. "And I'm not interested in your opinion of her mental condition.

"You're the father?" the judge squinted at the two of them in turn as if forming his own opinion of the likelihood.

Ephraim nodded.

"And you can afford to send her to a proper asylum?"

Ephraim nodded again, uncertain now what was happening. "Yes," he replied, "I suppose; you see, we are very concerned about her unconventional ways."

At least four hands gently reached for and restrained Gertie. She kept her seat, but she was coiled like a spring.

"You are free to be concerned, but you are not free to take up space that could be used charitably for a genuine madwoman. Sit down.

"I am thinking, Miss Driscoll," the judge continued, "that it will be better for everyone if you are found to be cured."

Helen drew in her breath sharply to say, "Thank you, your honor." She stepped a tiny stop forward and continued, "I would ask you to disregard the findings from my admission. It was not my fault that I was not able to comport myself in a normal manner."

The judge studied her and replied, "Your father is concerned, and it seems to me rightly so."

She tilted her head, not agreeing with what he said, but trying to maintain a cooperative demeanor. "I believe it is his right as a father to be concerned about all his children. But just as a parent may be frightened for the child who dares to swim a channel or scale a mountaintop, should that parent stop the endeavor for the sake of his fear? How can a person discover anything if they are swaddled in caution?"

The Judge nodded.

"I am not attempting a daring feat, I am merely working at a profession near my home. There is no depravity in that, is there?"

The judge pursed his lips to conceal that he was enjoying himself a little, "Your brother made some statements about gambling, and other vices."

"Sir, I have never made the first wager, but I have played parlor card games to pass the time as any person might. It may be that my brother, like my father, has let his protectiveness color his understanding of circumstances."

The judge raised an eyebrow. "You have a cunning way of speech, Miss Driscoll."

"I'm sorry, your honor," she said, although she would not have taken back a word of it. "I am striving to be as clear as possible. I am hoping that you will see that this incarceration is not only unnecessary, but unfair.

"My independence may be an affront to some people, but it is my life to direct, even if it is only a woman's life. I mean no harm to anyone or to myself. I mean to conduct my business honorably and to serve and console my neighbors in peace."

The judge motioned to the recorder, "Put down that the finding is that the inmate is cured." To Helen he said, "You are free to go. It seems that all this wonderful rabble would like you to get back to burying them."

The judge stood and waved his large arm outward, "I hope you stay very, very busy," he said loudly, concluding the hearing.

The crowd laughed and cheered at the news. Everyone began to chatter and move out of the overly warm room at a leisurely pace.

Helen's father took her elbow. She didn't turn more than her head toward him. "We'll take you home now," he said, gently.

"No," she said, "My home is not with you.

"People in my home don't tell me who I am and what my purpose is."

He stared at her, mute as she continued, "I will never be the person you imagined you could control. Not ever." Her tone was matter-of-fact. "You cannot prevent my mistakes. You can't."

Ephraim was stunned and released her elbow. He retreated to a polite stance, "I hope that you can forgive me," he said.

"I have," she said simply.

"What about Wallace?" he pressed her.

"Wally can't help it. He can't grapple with a real problem. He never could." The words stung him visibly. He knew that she was correct. And somewhere remotely, he knew that he had been cruel to them both by denying it.

"You taught him that he deserves all good things," she said, "and now he will have some bitter desserts. What will you teach him now?"

She turned away from her father toward Samuel, but her father was not ready to let her have the last word and he growled one more comment. As sometimes happens in very crowded rooms, the room fell still for a beat, just long enough for everyone to hear. "And you will have funerals for whores!"

"Somebody has to," commented Wallace, making an effort to sound jolly. Ephraim whirled on him and Wallace took a step back, "I mean," he stammered, "At least we have some whores…"

Ephraim clenched his fist, but left it low, poised like a gunslinger for an instant. Then he stopped himself. He shuddered as he dropped his arm and sighed. "Shut up, Wally. And go find my hat if you're able."

Helen finished turning to Samuel at last, leaving her back toward the bickering men.

Samuel reached for her, the relief of finding her and knowing that she would be home with him again was a thrill like nothing he had ever felt. He had believed he would never see her again and that this impossible moment would never come. His hands trembled as he reached for her face, intent on covering it with kisses.

"Wait," she said, "I may have bugs."

"Surely a lie!" He laughed and embraced her anyway.

Chapter 70—Home

Grace wrapped Helen in a summer walking coat and let her know how relieved she was without saying a word. As they all moved to exit the building, the clerk approached and handed Helen a thin sheaf of papers—the papers she had asked for all those long days ago.

"I am glad to know that you are cured," he said awkwardly.

"Praise the Lord," replied Helen dryly without breaking her stride.

As soon as she was out of the building she knelt down to Jenny and let the dog bathe her face in kisses. Jenny liked tears, especially drying tears, and she liked Helen.

Eggers opened the carriage door for her, but Helen preferred to ride in front with Samuel. He offered her the reins and she shook her head, too tired, but pleased at the gesture.

Grace climbed inside the carriage and insisted they allow Jenny aboard too.

They passed through the city until the wide avenue became a narrower, shady lane approaching the river. The Port was laid out before them, the stone mill and the old bake house still stood like they had for as long as anyone could remember.

The ramshackle buildings between them, some of which might not survive a strong summer storm, were a welcome sight indeed. She didn't know that the people who had stayed behind in town were ready to greet her and congratulate her on her sanity as she rode past, but they did. They always had the ability to generate a peculiar parade, and her return provided an excellent excuse for one.

Just as they approached the bridge that crossed into the Port, Helen heard a call and looked back to see her sister, Bonnie, pedaling a bicycle with some intensity to catch up.

They stopped the carriage to let Bonnie meet them.

"Where are you going?" Helen asked.

"I'm coming with you," said Bonnie.

Helen shook her head, smiling. "Are you ready for another battle so soon?" Her father would be fit to be tied over the flight of one of the twins.

Bonnie pointed her little chin up at her sister with a familiar defiance, "I'm ready if you are."

***

When they finally arrived at her boarding house, Samuel asked Eggers to take the carriage so that he could have a moment with Helen. The others went inside, leaving them at the steps. Helen seemed much like herself but weary and a little resigned to having one more conversation.

"I don't mean to press my suit," said Samuel softly, although he was doing just that. He hesitated, but he knew he had no power to be sensible and wait. "Am I to believe that you have not rejected me after all? When you were gone, I was afraid, it seemed—" Words were tangling in his mind. "It's very unfair of me to expect any encouragement."

Helen looked downward and sighed. She looked up at him and spoke carefully, "I am torn. I must speak to you as your friend before I speak as your lover."

His heart leapt at the word *lover*, but Samuel was able to force his mind back to listen as intently as he was ever able, his eyes searching her face for clues as she spoke further. He barely breathed.

"It is entirely unsuitable for you to court me, and it is wildly ill-advised for you to court your business partner," she said. "As your friend, I must remind you of the terrible possibilities that this brings forth. Eggers will be horribly disappointed in us, I'm sure. All my father's predictions of my downfall might be made manifest. If our courtship is successful, the business might suffer, and if our courtship is a failure, the business will certainly suffer."

"So as my friend, you reject the notion?"

"Yes."

"And as my lover?" he felt a swoon of fear at his own question.

"We have to try, don't we?" Helen flung her arms around his neck to deliver the most reckless of kisses.

###

Thanks for reading!! If you enjoyed this story, please take a moment to leave a review. Your feedback is very important and it helps other people find my work.

If you have questions, you must have been paying attention!! The next novel in the series is underway. I did not expect this to be more than one novel, but it has developed a life of its own and it is not leaving me alone.

Having an empty nest strategy is important, after all. I will need to get this done before my kids start moving back in.

May most of your undertakings be joyful!!
Mege Gardner

Let's tweet!! @MegeGardner
Or Face!! facebook.com/MegeWrites
Maybe even subscribe!! blog.askyermom.com
Subscribers receive a bonus scene in email.

A little bit about the author

Mege Gardner is called "mom" by most of her six kids, who are all very inquisitive and intelligent. She has been writing and blogging to educate and irritate them and others for more than twenty years. The emptying nest and eerie quiet of a large square house in the country has inspired her to create the first of a series of novels about people who do not want to have kids in the first place. "Undertakers, Harlots and Other Odd Bodies" is set near her ancestral home, which is far less fancy than it sounds.

Undertakers, Harlots, and Other Odd Bodies

Lightning Source UK Ltd.
Milton Keynes UK
UKHW012026191119
353854UK00001B/50/P